ANYTHING **COULD** HAPPEN

B.G. THOMAS

Dreamspinner Press

Published by

Dreamspinner Press
5032 Capital Circle SW
Ste 2, PMB# 279
Tallahassee, FL 32305-7886
USA
http://www.dreamspinnerpress.com/

Cover Art by Aaron Anderson
aaronbydesign55@gmail.com

Cover content is being used for illustrative purposes only
and any person depicted on the cover is a model.

ISBN: 978-1-62798-026-5
Digital ISBN: 978-1-62798-027-2

Printed in the United States of America
First Edition
September 2013

Passages from the play *Tearoom Tango* © Douglas Holtz, 2008. All rights reserved.
Used with permission of Douglas Holtz.

The quote from *Torch Song Trilogy* © 1998.
Used by permission of Harvey Fierstein. Thank you, Harvey!

Lyrics to *Superphallicrealisticdoubleendeddildo* © Amos Joseph Bullock, 1996. All rights reserved.
Used with permission of Amos Joseph Bullock.

This is for

Joanne "Jo" Papin
Jan 27, 1958 – July 10, 2013

She was one of the first people I ever told I was gay
She loved me
She was proud of my success
She always took my calls, no matter how late
And she was a voice in the dark....

Jo, I will miss you forever

ACKNOWLEDGMENTS

Special thanks to Cynthia Levin, Producing Artistic Director of the Unicorn Theatre, for the tour and a hundred and one answered questions. What a delightful woman. Any mistakes about the stage and theater made herein are mine and not hers.

Also, thanks to my dear actor friends Curtis Smith and Paul Burns, as well as a host of actors, directors, producers, and more who were there every step of the way.

And of course to my selfless editors Sal Davis, Chris Miles, Rowan Speedwell, Kat Weller, and of course Andi Byassee—I don't know what I would do without you!

"If life is just a stage, then we are all running around ad-libbing, with absolutely no clue what the plot is. Maybe that's why we don't know whether it's a comedy or tragedy."

~ Bill Watterson

"Where were you, Katmandu or something?"

~ Sam Shepard—Fool for Love

ACT *ONE*

AUSTIN SHELBOURNE knew the minute he walked through his great-uncle Boden's door that the old man was gay. There was no mistaking it—the most naïve person in the world would have figured it out. A mannequin would have seen it. It wasn't so much the man. Uncle Boden was a rather nondescript older gentleman: probably in his late seventies/early eighties, balding, slim, blue-gray eyes, slightly stooped, and wearing gray slacks and a frayed brown sweater. Nothing obvious; no gay pride T-shirt.

No. It was the apartment that said it all. With the three-foot-tall, gold spray-painted statue of David just inside the doorway, the print of a nude young man on the beach on one wall, the fringe on the lampshades, and the scarlet Chinese pillows—not to mention the yapping red Pomeranian—the old man might as well have screamed, "I'm a homosexual!"

Gay? Uncle Boden, gay? Austin found all his anxiety and worries about his 200-plus-mile move to Kansas City were submerged under a wave of complete surprise.

"It is so good to see you, my boy," cried Uncle Boden over the equally exuberant greetings of his little dog. "Lucille! Stop that! You've done your job. Be a good girl now and hush." The dog stopped—mostly—and sat at her master's feet, looking up with adoring brown eyes and only one or two barks.

"Ah…. Good to see you too, Uncle Boden."

Leading Austin to a threadbare couch, Uncle Boden said, "Sit. Please. You must be exhausted."

"Not too bad," Austin replied, but took the offer of the couch. A small sculpture of two men wrestling, one actually clutching the cock and balls of the other, sat on the coffee table. He tried not to react.

Uncle Boden smiled and sat down next to him, and Lucille jumped up between them. "I am so honored you agreed to come stay with me for a while, my boy. My God, you've grown. Has it been… ten years?"

Austin thought about it a moment. Ten years might be right. He hadn't seen his uncle since at least fourth grade. "It was the big family reunion," he answered. He remembered a sad man, and yes, he remembered the dog.

"Yes. Yes, it was ten years. I was still driving then. They won't let me now, the bastards. I miss driving. Now I have to depend on the kindness of a couple of the tenants when I need to get around. Shopping. Groceries."

"Well, you have me now," Austin said.

"For a while at least, yes?" Uncle Boden petted his little dog, who immediately climbed into his lap for more intimacy. "I am sure living with an old man will soon cramp your style. You're on your own for the first time. You'll want to sow your wild oats. You won't want to worry about me. Or try to explain me."

"Explain?"

His uncle rolled his eyes. Spread his arms and waved to indicate the room. The painting of The Blue Boy on one wall, the small statue of a nude young man examining the bottom of his foot on the end table next to the couch.

Austin blushed. Uncle Boden was addressing the elephant in the room. Austin shook his head. It was all so weird. The last thing he'd expected was to arrive at his uncle Boden's and find out the old man was gay.

Like me.

Austin turned to his uncle, a hundred questions in his mind. Gay. His great-uncle Boden was gay. He didn't know what to say. "You're gay!" he blurted and clamped a hand over this mouth.

His uncle's eyebrows popped up. "You're surprised? I figured everyone in Buckman talked about 'bachelor' Bodie."

"No," Austin said. "I mean, Gram and Gramps call you a bachelor, but—"

"My dear boy." His uncle chuckled. "That's old-people speak for 'queer.'"

"Oh," Austin said. *It was?*

"What gave me away? Was it perhaps Hercules and Diomedes there?" He pointed at the wrestling statue. "They've got quite a grip on each other, heh?"

Austin felt his cheeks heat up even more but didn't say anything. What was there *to* say?

"Can you imagine something like that in today's wrestling? I would be addicted to such television antics. I might even go back to college and see if they'd let an old man join the team."

Austin burst into laughter, then slapped a hand over his mouth once again.

"What? Am I embarrassing you?"

"I-I don't know... I wasn't expecting.... This is all such a surprise. And you're so, ah—"

"Old?" Uncle Boden asked. "You didn't think homosexuality was anything new, did you? I dare say Cain and Abel kept each other warm on a cold night. Brothers do, you know. And there were no girls. Maybe that's the real reason Cain killed his brother. Maybe Abel was holding out—being a cocktease."

Austin's mouth fell open, and he quickly closed it. Was this really happening? "I was going to say 'you're so open,'" he said.

"Oh." Uncle Boden rolled his eyes once more. "Sorry. It's just so nice to have someone here I *can* talk to." He looked at Austin for a moment, as if waiting for a reply. "Austin. My sister sent you to me for a reason. She said you had a mission. All fired up to move to Kansas City to look for some friend of yours. And considering my 'disposition,' she hoped I might be a good influence on you."

Austin nodded. Gram had said something similar to him. Originally, it had been his plan to save up enough money to get his own apartment, but it had been her idea he stay with her brother instead. "Just until you get on your feet," she'd advised. "You'd do him a world of good as well. You're so handy, and you might be able to fix some things around the building. He's the manager, you know. Plus, all his friends are gone. He needs the company. And you'll have so much to talk about—you have a lot in common."

We do? Austin had wondered that day. What would he and an old man have to talk about?

And then, sitting on Uncle Bodie's couch, the light bulb went on.

Oh my God.

Gay.

Gram knows I'm gay.

How? How had she figured it out? He hadn't really known himself until a month ago.

Well, that wasn't entirely true. He'd been figuring it out. He'd known. But not *known*-known. Not for totally 100 percent certain known.

"Are you all right, Austin?" Uncle Boden asked. "You have the strangest look."

He turned to his uncle. *Tell him. Just tell him.*

But he couldn't. It was like his tongue had frozen up or died or something.

"Sherry?"

For a second, Austin thought his uncle was talking to the dog. But wasn't her name Lucille? "Sorry?"

"I thought I would pour us a little sherry."

"Oh. Sure," Austin replied as his uncle stood up. But before he could leave the room…

"I'm gay." God—there it was. He'd said it. Said it out loud.

My God. I said it out loud.

And just like that, he felt a huge surge in his chest. Felt something enormous and infinitely heavy lift off his shoulders. And this tingling. This wonderful tingling all over his body. It felt amazing.

"First time?" Uncle Boden asked. "Saying it?"

Austin gave a nod. "Pretty much."

"Let me get that sherry." He shuffled out of the room in well-worn brown slippers.

Austin ran his fingers through the dark-brown hair hanging on either side of his face, then chewed absently on the tip of his thumb. *Gay. My uncle is gay.*

Just like me.

A moment later, Uncle Boden was back with a tray holding two tulip-shaped wine glasses filled halfway with a honey-colored liquid, as well as a cut-glass decanter. He handed Austin one of the glasses.

"Thanks," Austin said and took a swallow of what turned out to be an overly sweet drink, almost coughed.

"Sip! Sip, my boy. Let it lie across your tongue—absorb it."

Embarrassed, Austin nodded and put his glass down on the coffee table.

"Thank you, Austin."

"For what?" Austin wondered aloud.

"For what you've shared with me. Letting me be the first. Did it feel good?"

Austin smiled slowly and realized he was feeling positively giddy. "It did."

Uncle Boden grinned and looked away. "My God, it takes me back. I couldn't have been too much younger than you are now," his uncle said. "You're around eighteen?"

"Twenty," Austin said. "I'll be twenty-one in a couple months."

"You look younger. I know a young man hates to hear those words, but later in life you'll be glad about looking younger than you are."

Austin shrugged.

"I was sixteen," his uncle said, with a faraway look on his face. "I'd just given a boy my first blowjob—"

Austin's eyes popped. Had his great-uncle Boden—an old man—just said "blowjob"?

"I didn't know that's what it was called. But I knew I wanted to do it. The first time I heard the word 'cocksucker,' I knew that's what I was." He laughed quietly to himself. "Oh, and Jimmy had such a nice cock." The laugh turned into a cackle, and Lucille gave a single happy bark as if agreeing. Austin felt his mouth slip open and he forced it closed with a click.

"What?" Uncle Boden said. "Did you think your generation invented the blowjob too?"

"I guess not."

"I should say not!" He slapped Austin's knee. "You know, I have a picture of Jimmy I can show you." He stood up. Lucille gave a happy bark and leapt to the floor. "No, girl," he ordered. "You stay here with Austin." He pointed to his nephew. "He's our company."

Lucille hopped back on the couch and climbed into Austin's lap as her owner left the room, then stood on her hind legs and leaned against his chest. Austin looked into her joyous, adorable little face—muzzle all white with age—and couldn't help but giggle when she offered him a few sweet little doggie kisses.

"Lucille! Stop," Uncle Boden said, already returning to the room. "Some people don't like that."

"I don't mind," Austin said as she continued to lick his face.

Uncle Boden plopped down next to Austin, and Lucille immediately climbed down from Austin's lap and into his.

"Here," said Austin's uncle, handing over a silver frame.

Austin looked down at a black-and-white photograph, yellowed with age. Two boys, teenagers, with short hair of an indeterminate color—brown? blond?—looked back at him, smiling, happy from some day long ago.

"Jimmy on the right." Uncle Boden pointed. "Hot, wasn't he?"

He was certainly cute, Austin admitted. But so was the other boy. "Who is the guy on the left?" he asked with an appreciative growl.

"Why, that's me. I was hot too, wasn't I?"

Mortified, Austin had to fight to keep his mouth from falling open once again.

"So Austin—this 'friend' of yours you've come to find. Is he—was he—your lover?"

Lover? Austin felt his stomach clench for a moment. "No," he said sadly. "Not really."

"Hmmmm...." Uncle Boden touched a finger to his lower lip, scratched his chin. "Not really? Is he gay?"

"I don't know." Austin moaned in frustration. "I'm hoping."

"You're in love," his uncle sighed happily.

"I-I think I am," Austin replied, felt his heart quicken.

"I was so in love with Jimmy." Uncle Boden sighed again. Then: "Have you two at least been... how shall I say it? Have you two been physical? Have you fooled around?"

"Sorta... I-I...." Austin looked into his uncle's face. The man was elderly, and yet in that moment, Austin realized the man was ageless as well. He saw the boy in the picture. Uncle Boden wasn't just some old man. He was the boy in that picture, wasn't he? Of course he was. The man hadn't been born old. Austin clearly saw that there had been someone gay before him and... there would be someone gay after he was gone.

And suddenly everything seemed better. For the first time in his life, he felt as if there might be a place for him. And maybe, just maybe, everything would turn out right. Anything could happen. And he knew he could trust this man. That they could share intimate secrets. "I gave him a blowjob," Austin said in a rush, before he could change his mind.

Uncle Boden's cheeks pinked and the corners of his mouth flickered upward.

"What?" asked Austin. "Don't you think men do that anymore?"

His uncle laughed. "I dare say they do!" he crowed. "At least I hope they do. Did you like it?"

Austin clutched a hand to his chest and felt his face heat up. "Oh my."

"I know!" Uncle Boden laughed all the more. He glanced down at the coffee table and then reached out and picked up their glasses. He held one out to Austin and then said, "To a new chapter in your life."

"To a new chapter," Austin said happily, returning the toast.

THEY had finished their second glass of sherry, were debating a third, when Uncle Boden said, "You know, we'd better unload your vehicle. I only hope no one has snitched anything already. Let me just quick call Guy."

"Guy?" asked Austin.

"A young man who lives on the third floor. He was gracious enough to move most of the stuff I had in the spare room down to the basement so you would have a place to sleep. Of course, we had to use Miss Hallie's storage space, but she didn't mind. She really wasn't using it. She's a thousand years old and has almost nothing. Imagine. My locker is filled to the ceiling with memories and kitsch."

Uncle Boden left the room and was back in less than a minute. "He's outside already. Can you believe it? Such a nice young man. I hope you two hit it off. He's gay, you know. Peter's aiming to get as many gay tenants as he can without seeming prejudiced."

Guy? Hallie? Peter? Who were all these people? But Austin was sure he'd figure it all out eventually. As in any good play, it would all fall into place.

"Peter is my... boss," Uncle Boden said. "My savior, really. He owns the building. Made me building manager—rent free—even though I can't do much more than collect rent checks and call various handymen when a sink clogs up or a toilet stops working."

"I'm quite handy when it comes to stuff like that," Austin said. "I've got a knack for it."

"So Wilda says. It'll be wonderful to have your help."

"It's the least I can do," Austin said. Before Austin moved to Kansas City, his uncle had insisted he not pay rent, and he agreed only on the condition he help with the building's maintenance whenever he could.

"Anyway, I'm sure you'll meet Peter soon enough."

By this time, they were leaving the building, and sure enough, there was someone pulling the tarp off the back of Austin's S-10 pickup. Tall, dark-haired, and...

Good-looking.

"Guy, I want you to meet my great-nephew Austin. Austin, this is Guy."

The young man approached them, smiling, hand rising from his side—and then he froze. His eyes widened slightly, then narrowed; his full lips parted as if he were about to say something and then forgot what it was. After a beat, he visibly shook himself and held out his hand once more. "Nice to meet you," he replied.

"Likewise," Austin said and took it. The hand was nice, warm, and accompanied by what felt like a tiny shock. Guy was an inch or two taller than Austin, rugged, with close-cropped dark hair and a beard that was little more than a five o'clock shadow. He looked down with milk-chocolate-colored eyes, and *damn*, thought Austin, distracted by flecks of even darker brown. Guy was very good-looking indeed. They were still holding hands, and Austin quickly pulled his away with a twinge of guilt. *I'm here an hour and I'm staring into some guy's eyes. Todd. Todd is who I'm here for.*

"Let's get this done with," Guy said, nodding toward Austin's old red truck. "It's getting chilly."

At least the prediction of snow hadn't come to pass, thought Austin—the reason he'd put the tarp over everything. It might have discouraged people from trying to snitch any of his things as well.

With Guy's capable help, it was surprising how quickly they got Austin's entire world out of the back of the truck and into his new room. It was a tight fit. He had moved into the basement when he started high school. His great-aunt Corvella had needed his boyhood bedroom when she got "the cancer," as his Gram called it. When she died a few months later, he'd never moved back upstairs. If he helped with the laundry, his Gram didn't come downstairs very often. All the tools were down there, but his grandfather hardly ever used them anymore, and so it was a rare day for him to come down either. The basement had become more than a bedroom; it had turned into a clubhouse of sorts for him and his lifelong friend Todd. He'd even given Todd a key to the cellar door.

Which, of course, had led to a complete and utter disaster in the end. One that wound up motivating Austin to leave his home. Correction. His home in Buckman. This little room in Uncle Bodie's apartment was to be his home *now*. At least until he could afford his own place.

They brought in and set up the bed first, and then while Uncle Boden made it, they carried in the drawers of Austin's desk and dresser. They were full due to the fact that Austin had opted to move them as is, instead of packing the contents into boxes and then having to refill the drawers again. The boxes he had packed went up after the furniture—once they had the lay of the land and knew where they could be stacked for the time being. Last of all was Austin's weight set.

"Nice," said Guy, shrugging off his coat. He wore a big baggy Royals jersey underneath. "This isn't cheap shit."

"My grandparents got them for me for Christmas a couple of years ago. I wanted a good set 'cuz I've always hated my body. I'm so crapping skinny."

Guy shrugged. "It looks pretty nice to me," he said with a lopsided grin and the arch of an eyebrow.

Austin felt his cheeks heat up. Guy was flirting. Guy. A real-life gay man.

Todd. Think of Todd. "Th-thanks," he muttered. *You're not so bad yourself*, he almost replied and bit his tongue.

"Another round of sherry?" Uncle Boden suggested when they were finished. "Guy? Join us?"

"No, Bodie, that's just a tad too sweet for me. At least at this time of night. I'll run up and get a beer, though. Austin?"

"Okay," Austin said happily, not sure he wanted any more of the honey-like wine himself and happy Guy had included him in what felt like an adult ritual—even if he didn't particularly like beer all that much. The buzz maybe. The taste he could definitely take or leave.

"I'll be back in a flash," Guy said. "You want one, Bodie?"

"No, that's okay. The sweet stuff for me. Sweets for the sweet," he said with a laugh.

"Bodie?" Austin enquired.

"That's what my friends call me," his uncle explained. "Them that's left. Boden is just so butch. I asked Guy to call me Bodie. Makes me feel real. Young and queer again. I'd like you to do the same."

"Uncle Bodie," Austin said, trying the new name on for size.

"Just Bodie. You can drop the Uncle."

Just Bodie? Austin wondered. No. He couldn't. "We'll compromise, I'll say 'Bodie' instead of 'Boden,' even though I've always thought you had a cool name. But I gotta say 'Uncle.'"

"Fine. Fine," his uncle Bodie yielded. "So what do you think of Guy?"

"He seems nice." Austin swallowed a lump.

"You know, Guy is in the theater? Director. Or is it playwright? Wait, it's both, I think."

"Really?" Austin asked, surprised. He loved the theater. It was a part of why he'd moved to a bigger city. Since he'd graduated, he'd only gotten to do a little community theater, and Buckman Community Theater was less than stellar.

Uncle Boden... Bodie... was nodding. "I saw one of his shows just last week. A crazy version of that movie with Dolly Parton."

"*Best Little Whorehouse in Texas*?" Austin asked. He loved musicals. *God. How did I not know I was gay? What could be more gay than loving musicals?*

"No-no, not that one. The one with the Flying Nun. What's her name? 'You like me, you really, really like me!'"

"Sally Field?" Austin offered.

"Sally Field! That's it! And that stud muffin Tom Skerritt."

Austin started laughing—*stud muffin?*—just as there was a knock at the front door, and Lucille took off like a miniature rocket, barking all the way.

"Lucille!" shouted Uncle Bodie. "Control. A lady needs to show control. I'm sure it's just your Uncle Guy."

Austin wiped his eyes, and a moment later, Guy was back—*damn, he's good-looking*—with two beers, bottles already open. He handed one to Austin.

"Cheers," declared Uncle Bodie, holding his fresh glass of sherry high.

"Cheers," said Guy.

"Cheers," Austin repeated and took a sip, expecting one step above nasty and getting a surprise instead. "Hey," he exclaimed. "That's nice."

Guy nodded, grinning. "I love Boulevard. You haven't had it before?"

Austin shook his head. "I don't know much about beer. If they carried this in Buckman, I didn't realize it or know what it was. The kids I know drink Milwaukee's *Worst* and Pabst."

Guy grimaced and Austin laughed—and took a bigger swallow. It glided down his throat, all malt and hops. "It tastes like liquid marijuana," he said with a snicker.

"We're drinking Double-Wide I.P.A."

"I don't know what that means," Austin admitted.

"Just know it means tons of hops," Guy explained.

"So I was telling Austin about your Dolly Parton play," Bodie interrupted.

"'Dolly Parton Play.'" Guy grinned. "Sounds like a good name for a show, actually. *Steel Magnolias*. You're talking about *Steel Magnolias*."

"I love that movie," Austin said.

"Well, this is the original play, and all the scenes take place in Truvy's beauty shop, and there are no men."

"No Tom Skerritt." Uncle Bodie pouted.

"Really? I didn't know that."

"Did you know the playwright was gay?" Guy asked.

"No, me either."

"His sister died and he wasn't coping—they were really close—and someone said, 'You're a writer, write about it,' and thus we have *Steel Magnolias*."

"Tell him what you've done with it," Uncle Bodie said, all enthusiastic.

"Well, I didn't come up with the idea," Guy said. "But I cast male actors in half the roles."

Austin sat up. "Men?"

"In drag," Uncle Bodie declared.

"I figured since it was written by a gay man, and since I didn't want to rewrite it with gay characters, and since drag is such a part of our heritage—our ancestry—it would be perfect. It's been done. But I hope I did it better. This is the last weekend. Why don't you come Sunday? I'll make sure you get a seat."

"Really?" Austin said. How amazing was that? He loved plays, and here he was, no more than an hour in town, and he was going to a play. "This is the most unbelievable day I can remember in forever," he said, grinning foolishly. "First I get here and find out my uncle is gay—"

"Me too," Guy said.

And wasn't that incredible? If his uncle hadn't told him, had he met Guy on the street, he would never have guessed it. The man was so... normal.

But why shouldn't he be? Austin asked himself. Hadn't he read that one in ten men were gay? Hadn't that been his secret mantra? So what could be more normal than Guy being gay?

"Me three," he admitted, and to his surprise, realized he had said it for the second time in one day. No. Only kind of said it.

"I'm gay," he amended, making it official.

"Your uncle thought you were," Guy said. "And I was hoping."

"You were?" Austin asked, his voice cracking.

Guy's milk-chocolate eyes seemed to bore into him.

"Now Guy," Uncle Boden said. "Stop being naughty. I told you. Austin is on a mission to find his friend, and as it turns out, I was right. Austin looks for his lover."

"Damn," said Guy. "Isn't that always the way? They're either straight or taken."

Austin gulped. "I'm not taken *exactly*." He felt a rush of nerves sweep over him. "I mean—I'm hoping. Sorry. But… but…."

"He's in love, Guy. We must not stand in the way of true love."

Guy looked away—"Of course not."—thank God. Oh, but then those eyes were back. "So how about this Sunday? Will you come and see the play? It should be fun. There's going to be a bunch of people showing up dressed as their favorite character from the show."

"I-I'd love to, but I don't have a costume."

"You're exempt. Tell me you'll be there."

Now those eyes were pleading, and Austin found he had no resistance. "Sure."

"Great! Bodie tells me you're an actor."

Austin found himself blushing once again. Could you honestly call community theater and high school in Buckman, Missouri, acting? "Well. Maybe not an actor, exactly."

"Okay," said Guy. "You're 'not exactly' taken, and you're 'not exactly' an actor."

"He *is* an actor," declared Uncle Bodie. "He was in almost all of his high school plays, and he starred in his senior musical *Little Shop of Horrors*, and the town musical *Big River*."

"I *love* that show. 'I have lived in the darkness for so long, I am waitin' for the light to shine…,'" Guy sang.

Austin chimed in with the next line—all about places beyond the horizon, and beyond dreams—then found himself blushing all the more.

"You've got a great voice," Guy said.

"You think so?" Austin asked and felt his ears burning. "I don't know."

"We do," said Uncle Bodie.

"Thanks," Austin replied, a foolish grin on his face.

Had there ever been a better day?

DESPITE the fact he had been warned, Austin couldn't help but be surprised at the sight. A parade of drag queens. Well, no—not drag queens, exactly. But men in dresses and crazy wigs and outfits, marching right down the sidewalk along Main Street as if such antics were as normal as could be. Hell, maybe it was in Kansas City, but for a guy born and raised in the tiny town of Buckman, it was anything but an everyday sight.

As he stood there outside the Pegasus Theatre, he watched as the men got closer, walking as confidently as if they dressed up like characters from *Steel Magnolias* all the time. Assholes in passing cars honked but inspired nothing but happy Queen-of-England waves from the cross-dressers. At first Austin found the whole thing a bit of a shock, but the closer they got—as he saw the smiles on their faces, the way they held their heads high, as they laughed and poked at each other with umbrellas and, God, was that a shotgun?—he found himself getting caught up in the spirit of it all. After all, these men were coming to see the play *Steel Magnolias*—a production where half the cast were men—so why the hell not?

Austin felt his heart jump. Wasn't this why he'd come to Kansas City? For this kind of magic? That and to find Todd, of course. But in the meantime, why not catch the enchantment? That's what Uncle Bodie had told him to do.

Austin stepped back so as not to be mowed down by the leader of the Magnolia parade, a largish man with a huge blonde-white wig and breasts the size of volleyballs. As a matter of fact, Austin could see that was exactly what they were. Through the thin white blouse, he could just make out that one was orange and the other, green. Austin couldn't help but laugh. The man came to a stop and put a hand, which was clutching a hair blower like a handgun, against his hip.

"What are you laughing at?" said the faux-Dolly Parton as Truvy in a mock-Southern accent.

"Nothing," Austin said, taking a backward step. He swallowed hard and then smiled. "I think you look great."

The Truvy smiled. "Well then! Aren't *you* the one?" He patted his wig and straightened his boobs. "It takes some effort to look like this!"

"Your outfit is perfect." Austin smiled happily. "You look *just* like Dolly. It must have taken you forever to get your outfit together."

Truvy shook his ample hips. "The only thing that separates us from the animals is our ability to accessorize," he quoted.

Austin laughed in delight. "You're brave. I wouldn't have the guts. Not in a month of Sundays."

Truvy's eyebrow shot up. "I don't know. I bet you'd make a great Miss Merry Christmas."

"Move!" shouted a man behind Truvy, this one wearing a horrible brown wig, an ancient fur coat, and holding a stuffed toy St. Bernard under his arm. Obviously, he was supposed to be Ouiser Boudreaux, but truth to tell, as thick as his eyebrows were, they didn't beat Shirley MacLaine's.

"Calm down, girlfriend," said Truvy. "I was just admiring this 'big hangin' man,' here."

Austin laughed uncomfortably. The last thing he'd ever considered himself to be was a "big hangin' man," in any sense of the description.

Truvy grabbed Austin by the elbow with a huge hand and hauled him through the front doors of the Pegasus. "You're coming to see the show, right?" he asked.

Austin sighed. "Well, that was the plan. There was supposed to be a ticket for me at will-call, but they didn't have it."

"Well, hell, honey, let's buy you one. The tickets aren't that expensive."

"The show's sold out," Austin explained.

"Oh no!" Truvy came to a sudden stop, and the man with the toy shotgun crashed into them.

"Hey!" cried the man, and that was when Austin saw the man wasn't a man at all, but a woman dressed as Tom Skerritt—complete with a fisherman's hat and splatters of fake bird poop all over an ugly sweater-vest. At least, Austin hoped it was fake poop.

Truvy spun around again. "Watch where the hell you're going, Tiff!"

"Well, don't stop like that." Tiff/Tom Skerritt tucked a bit of blue hair under her hat.

Truvy pulled Austin out of the way and let the theatergoers pass by.

"You're gonna miss getting a good seat," Austin remarked, nodding in the direction of the passing parade.

"They'll save me a good seat if they know what's good for them. What'll suck is if you miss it entirely."

It had been a surprise to Austin. Guy had said he'd leave a ticket for him. Where was it? Guy hadn't seemed like the type to promise something and not come through. He couldn't help but be disappointed. The play would have been an awesome—if not weird—way to begin his first week in Kansas City. Austin shrugged. "I'm still hoping," he replied. "The guy at the ticket booth said sometimes there are a few seats left for no-shows and I could still buy a ticket. If it's okay with the guy who organized all this."

"Guy? Guy! Guy *is* who organized this." Truvy cocked his head and then scanned the room, pointed, and there was Guy, standing at the far end of the lobby, wearing a thick purple sweater that looked to be at least two sizes too big. "There he is, sugar. Come on," he said, pulling Austin in that direction. "Let's see what the hell happened."

"I-I…. Wait." Austin found he was unexpectedly nervous. He didn't want to be a pest. Maybe Guy had simply forgotten. He'd probably had other things on his mind. It was the last performance of his play, after all. Maybe there hadn't been any seats left. Maybe he'd been too embarrassed to call. Maybe he'd called and Austin had already left. Maybe….

"Guy, this young'un here…." Truvy paused. "What's your name, honey?"

"Austin," he replied, biting his lip.

"Guy, Austin here says you promised him a seat for the show."

"Well, I didn't say he *promised*," Austin said.

Guy looked up from the clipboard he'd been studying. "I'm sorry. What did you say...?" And then those eyes—the color of milk chocolate—flew wide. "Oh shit! Austin. Dammit." He slapped his palm against his forehead. "Wait. Don't move." He dashed over to the will-call window and began to talk to the man standing there. A second later, he returned. He glanced out the window, then leaned out the door and looked down the sidewalk. Turning back, he said, "I think that's it. Grady, are there any people from brunch still coming?"

Truvy looked around at the crowd. "I don't think so. Except for Leonard, who needs a ride because of his broken leg. Hey, Tiff!"

The woman-Skerritt turned around.

"This is everybody except for Leonard and his ride?"

She nodded. "I think so."

Truvy turned back around. "There wasn't quite the turnout for brunch we thought there'd be."

Guy shrugged. "Then you're in, Austin."

"That's awfully nice of you," Austin said.

"No. I owe you an apology," Guy said. "I invite you and then totally mess up. I was sure I called it in, but I have been all nerves. Forgive me?"

Austin smiled, and his heart skipped a beat. "No problem."

"I hope you like the show." Guy smiled back. "Go pick a seat—they're opening the doors right now."

Austin grinned happily. *What luck.* "This is totally awesome. Want me to save you a place?"

"Nope," Guy said. "I'm the director. Speaking of which, I better get backstage."

"Break a leg," Austin said as Guy was turning to leave.

Guy stopped, gave him a sweet smile, and winked at him.

Damn, those eyes.

"Thanks, Austin. Enjoy." With that, Guy was gone.

AFTERWARD, Austin found he didn't want to leave. He felt silly, but he found himself leaning against his truck instead of getting in and driving home. Everything had ended too soon. He wanted it to go on.

The play had been fun. At first, the fact three of the actors were men was a little… well, bizarre. But to his surprise, within ten minutes Austin had all but forgotten that fact. He was pulled into the world the playwright and everyone involved with the production had created. That was Truvy onstage and not an actor, male or female. And sure enough, that was Ouiser. And there was M'Lynn. Soon he was laughing and crying as the story unfolded, the characters sharing their journey, their growth, and their heartbreaks. And then there was the intimacy of the stage. It thrust out partially into the audience, with the seats wrapped around it like a parenthesis. With luck, he'd gotten a front row seat, and he felt like he was practically in Truvy's beauty shop.

Austin loved the play. It was everything theater was supposed to be. It was magic.

When the double doors on the side of the building opened and some of the cast members spilled out—chatting, laughing, smoking—Austin felt his heart race. Actors. They were real actors. Sure, it was a small theater. But it was a real theater. In fact, the Pegasus was popular enough that it had two stages: one called simply "Main Stage," and the second "The Wagner Stage." The play hadn't been some small-town production of *Arsenic and Old Lace* with actors constantly forgetting their lines, or *The Sound of Music* where the star was the daughter of the mayor. The actors had been amazing. How else had three members of the cast, men, made Austin forget—for the length of the play—they were, in fact, men, playing what were generally women's roles?

When one of them looked his way, Austin waved. To his surprise, the actor smiled and waved him over. Heart in his throat, he found himself pulled to them like steel to a magnet. It was only when he got there that he saw what they were eating. "Oh my God," he said, fighting a squeal. "Bleeding armadill'er cake!"

"Want some?" asked the young actress he recognized as having played Shelby.

For some reason, the request made his chest pound so hard he was sure she could hear it. *It's just cake. Why are you acting like such a little kid?*

"I'd love some," he said, grinning.

She motioned for him to follow her backstage. "I noticed you in the audience," she said, heading for a table surrounded by cast members and what must have been crew.

"You did?" he asked.

She nodded. "You're the kind of audience member we love. You had me crying, watching you cry. Thanks. You helped my performance."

Austin laughed in delight. "Really?"

"Oh yes," she said and shepherded him to the table full of food, and yes, right there in the middle of the table, a red velvet cake in the shape of an armadillo, covered in gray icing! She leaned in, cut off a leg, placed it on a plate, and handed it to him.

"Thanks," he said.

"Want a drink?" she asked. "I hear the punch is deadly."

"It better not be" came a familiar voice.

They turned to find Guy standing over them. "We still have a set to tear down today. I knew I should have made people wait to party, but all those drag queens insisted."

"Oh, it won't be all that bad," said "Shelby."

"You want some help?" Austin asked.

"You don't have to do that," Guy answered.

"No, really. I don't mind. It's not like I've never done it before."

"I guess that's true," Guy said with a grin. "If you really don't mind, we'd love the help."

"It's the least I can do, what with the free ticket and all."

"I told you, Austin. It was no bother at all. I wanted you here."

Austin felt his heart jump. *Gosh, the man is sweet.*

"And besides," Guy said. "The seats have all been paid for. I just organized this. Peter bought the tickets, and he wouldn't want there to be an empty seat."

"Peter?"

"Peter Wagner. He's one of the patrons for the Pegasus, and a more stately homo you'll never ever meet. He wanted to make sure a bunch of queens got to see the final performance."

Peter Wagner. As in "The Wagner Stage"? I wonder if that's the same Peter Uncle Bodie was talking about?

"You stick around the Pegasus long enough and you're sure to meet him. They named the second stage after him. The least we could do with all the money he's given to us. You know, I think he's a friend of your uncle. Peter owns our building."

Bingo, thought Austin. He had to be the same Peter Uncle Bodie had been talking about. *Are they lovers?* he wondered.

So those who were willing, after a drink or two, hit the stage and began to strike the set. It was the part of the whole experience that always made Austin feel sad. The end.

Stage sets were the foundation intrinsic to helping him and his fellow actors bring forth their characters. It seemed almost a crime to tear them down. But it had to be done or the cycle could not continue. The old had to make way for the new. Arabian tents or rundown apartments made way for cornfields or a mad scientist's laboratory. Yellow brick roads or the Mississippi River bank for dark forests, ships' decks, and castle keeps. All to help actors bring to life whole new casts of characters.

Bittersweet was what it was.

Luckily, in this case, he had no emotional ties to Truvy's beauty shop, except for what one performance had given him, powerful as it had been. For once, he could see the set as it was, simple sheets of plywood and two-by-fours, garage sale furniture, and fixtures that didn't really work.

He shared these thoughts as he worked with hammer and crowbar by Guy's side.

"I know what you mean," said Guy. "But the worst part for me is the family lost."

"Lost?" asked Austin. "I'm not sure I understand."

"Something very powerful happens with a good play where the actors really connect with their characters and each other and the script. I've seen romances bloom, affairs begin, marriages torn apart. I was involved with a production of *Rocky Horror* where the straight man who was playing Dr. Frank-N-Furter had a wild, kinky fling with the actor who played Rocky. They'd be banging away backstage or in the dressing room—and this 'straight' guy got so lost in it all that he not only had a homosexual affair, but he didn't realize that everybody knew what was going on." Guy laughed. "How could we not know? You could smell it in the air."

"Damn," muttered Austin.

"I mean, acting can be all so *Mr. and Mrs. Smith*. How could Brad Pitt *not* have cheated on Jennifer with Angelina Jolie, making a movie like that?"

Austin didn't know how to answer.

"So all of this powerful family happens, and then? Bam! It's over, and the family that a good script and a good play forged is torn apart, and the actors are scattered to the seven winds as they take new parts and get involved in new shows. I hate cast parties." He waved his hammer over his shoulder in the general direction of the activities in the other room, where some people still carried on. "Too many tears."

"I-I never thought about it," said Austin. "Buckman is a pretty small town. My graduating class was thirty-six people. You're pretty much in all the same plays together. Even in community theater, it's all the same people. How do you do it?"

"I direct." Guy gave him a weak smile and attacked the next section of the set. "It lets me stand back a little bit, anyway. It's like being a teacher at recess. The kids—the actors—they get to play. I watch over them. If everything goes according to plan, they get lots of credit. Of course, if anything goes wrong, it's all my fault. But at least I stop falling in love with my costars." He laughed uncomfortably.

"But what I really love is writing. I get to create the world the actors step into. I give them their words instead of memorizing someone else's reality. I create the identity the actors take on."

"You *sound* like a writer." Austin felt himself get lost in Guy's words. It was potent stuff the man was talking about. "Are you writing something now?"

Guy lowered his hammer and seemed to become lost in thought. He nodded once. "I am." He squatted, getting ready to tackle the base of a flat that formed a wall of the beauty shop.

"What's it called?" Austin asked, caught up even more.

"Right now, I'm still not sure." Guy turned to him. There was a long pause. Finally: "Maybe I should call it *Dolly Parton Play*." He laughed and gave Austin another of those winks. It was an affectation that kept drawing Austin's attention to the man's beautiful eyes. In fact, there wasn't anything about Guy that wasn't attractive. It made Austin wonder about the baggy clothes. Was he trying to hide something? Could someone that good-looking be as uncomfortable with his body as Austin was with his?

Guy looked at him, pressed his lips together, furrowed his brows. "I don't like to talk about it."

"Uh, you don't have to tell me if you don't want to," Austin said.

"I... I.... It's a natural question," Guy said. "People ask me all the time. But I always tell them I don't want to jinx it."

"Sure. I understand," Austin replied quickly. "Don't worry about it. How about those Royals, huh?"

Guy smiled. "It's about a group of people who get thrown together under very mysterious circumstances, and how they come to deal with the situation and each other." His brown eyes grew wide. His smile drifted away and then returned. "Wow. I've never told a soul. And with you, it just slipped right out. I hardly know you, and there it is, right out in the open."

"Thank you," Austin said, feeling honored. He told Guy as well. "Maybe it's because you don't know me. And I'm not a part of your world."

"Not yet," said Guy. "Hang around the theater long enough and someone will hand you a broom. Here you are with a hammer already."

Austin grinned. How about that?

Then Guy seemed to grow thoughtful again. "No, it's not because I don't know you. Something else...."

"What?" asked Austin, wanting to know those thoughts more than he would have expected. What was going on behind those pretty eyes?

"Nothing." Guy shook his head. "Never mind." Guy looked back at him. "Just remember, it's dangerous being friends with a writer. You never know when something you say will end up in his next work."

Austin laughed. "I hardly think I'm interesting enough to be put in one of your plays."

And just like that, Austin saw the shutters to the windows of Guy's thoughts close. *Clack!*

Guy got down on his hands and knees and raised his hammer once more. It made his ass stick out in Austin's direction, and he couldn't help but stare. It was round and looked very muscular. Nothing to be uncomfortable about there.

"Say," Guy said. "After this, you want to have one more piece of cake or something and then cut out of here?"

"Huh?" Austin said, turning his gaze back to where it should be: Guy's face.

"We could go to The Male Box."

"The Mail Box?" Austin asked.

"It's a gay bar. They've got a show on Sunday evening and drinks are only two dollars."

"I'm not old enough, remember?" Then Austin laughed when he caught the pun for the bar's name. The Male Box. Male. Box. He blushed at the implication. But hell, it was a gay bar. And how would that be? Going to a *gay* bar. He felt his heart racing and his stomach clenching at the same time over the idea.

"Okay, then—what if I call a few friends and we have a little get-together at my place? Say eight o'clock? After dinner? You won't have to worry about drinking and driving. I'm right upstairs."

"Just drinking and walking down three flights of stairs." Austin chuckled.

"I'll even escort you. Make sure you get down okay."

Austin smiled. It would be nice. He found he liked Guy a lot, and it would be enjoyable seeing him some more. He hadn't wanted the play to end, and now he didn't want his time with Guy to end either.

Be careful, his inner wisdom warned. *Remember the real reason you came to Kansas City.*

Todd. He was looking for Todd. He needed to remember that.

But it's not like I'm going to sleep *with Guy.* "Sure," he said. "Sounds like fun."

"Then it's a date," Guy said.

A date. Oh God.

A date?

"I'M A little nervous about this," Austin said as he and Uncle Bodie climbed the stairs to the third floor. He had a hand on his uncle's elbow, just in case. The older man got around pretty darn well for someone who was eighty, but why take a chance?

"Nervous? Why?" Then, before Austin could answer, "Is it because Guy is so sexy?"

"Uncle Bodie!"

"Well? He is." Uncle Bodie raised and lowered his thick eyebrows suggestively.

"I—uh—ah—well...."

Uncle Bodie stopped. "Oh. It's because of your friend Todd? Are you worried it's bad for you to find another man besides Todd attractive?"

Austin shrugged.

"How chivalrous." Uncle Bodie smiled, then patted Austin's shoulder. "Attraction does not a cheater make, Austin. And besides, you and Todd are not lovers." He started up the stairs again. "You can't cheat."

Austin shook his head. "God, Uncle Bodie, it's not so much that. It's just the pure fact...." He stopped and after a step, so did his uncle.

"What?"

"I don't even know if Todd's gay," Austin cried.

Uncle Bodie tilted his head, looked at Austin questioningly.

"Uncle Bodie. You and Guy are the first gay people I've ever met. Two frigging days ago it was only me, and now—" Austin snapped his fingers. "—I know gay people. Real gay people. I'm standing in front of and talking to men who have slept with other men. Suddenly, it's all real. It's not just that TV show *The New Normal*. Or *Will and Grace*. It's not just Internet porn." He blushed. "I find my heart starts racing. I can't believe it's not just me anymore."

"Oh, Austin." Uncle Bodie gripped Austin's shoulder. "It was never *just* you. But I get it." He sighed. "My boy, enjoy this time. It's going to go by in a flash. In one year, these days will seem like a century away. All of this will be old. You'll be 'girl friending' it with the best of us."

"I-I will?" It seemed impossible.

"Then again, I hope you don't become jaded. So many gay men turn cynical and bitter so fast. But I look at you and I think that won't be your fate. You'll find your Todd, or not, and I think you will keep your enthusiasm. Seems to be a part of who you are."

Austin had no idea what to say. It felt like he was entering an undiscovered country, and he had no idea what lay ahead.

"You have no idea what lies ahead. Embrace it. All of it. The nervousness too. This, in many ways—even with the very real possibilities of pain and heartbreak—will be the best year of your life."

"ARE all these guys gay?" Austin asked his uncle. He looked around the room and saw about twenty men, not counting himself and his uncle.

"I do not know," Uncle Bodie replied. "But I think that would be a good guess."

Austin found his heart was racing, sweat was trickling down his sides. There were men of every size and shape, although most looked to be thirty or under. In one corner, two men sat close together, heads tilted against each other. Would they kiss?

Pound! Pound! went Austin's heart.

Over there on the couch were three men. Two sat and a third lounged back against them, head in one's lap. God.

Next to the couch was a man in a recliner; another man stood beside him, feeding him a bit of something red off a fork. He then dipped another forkful from his plate and ate it himself. Same fork. And look: it was the bleeding armadill'er cake.

Suddenly it truly was real. *I really am standing in a room full of men who have slept with other men.*

Some of the men were dressed casually, some had on fun and silly outfits, and one was wearing a dress with a blue wig and his goatee painted to match. Crazy.

"Here you go, Austin, Bodie."

It was Guy. He'd returned from the kitchen with a glass of wine for Uncle Bodie and the Double-Wide I.P.A. beer Austin had liked so much a couple of nights earlier. "Oh! Thanks, Guy."

"I picked it up special," Guy said, and then stood close enough to Austin that their shoulders touched. They were both leaning back against a bookcase. He was wearing a big, baggy white sweater with columns of zigzagging cables. *Why wear such baggy clothes?* Yet somehow it worked. Did everything about Guy "work"?

"That was really nice of you," said Austin, unable to keep from smiling.

"Guy," said Uncle Bodie. "Austin was wondering if all your guests tonight were gay."

"Most of them," he replied. "Dave over there in the corner is straight—or *says* he is. He was lighting for *Magnolias*." He nodded toward a tall African-American gentleman who seemed to be holding court over a few listeners in the small dining room. "Why, you got your eye on someone? You want to make sure he's a PNB?"

"PNB?" Austin asked.

"Come on. You're a Dolly Parton fan. PNB. Potential New Boyfriend."

"No," sputtered Austin through a mouthful of beer.

"Don't spit it out," said Guy. "That's alcohol abuse."

Austin coughed a moment and then replied, "That's not it at all. It's just…." He felt his heart begin to speed up again. "If they are… it's so…."

"All those men," Uncle Bodie sighed. "Gay. Just like me…."

"Ahhh," cried Guy. "I get it. Your first time in a room full of gay men."

Austin nodded. Felt his palms grow damp.

"My God, those were the days," Guy replied. "That first time looking around a room and knowing you're not alone anymore."

Suddenly Austin had tears in his eyes. "Yes," he whispered, "it's real and I'm not alone."

"And you never will be again," said his uncle.

"It seems like forever ago," Guy said.

"Tell me about it," said Uncle Bodie.

"I managed to sneak into a gay bar when I was nineteen," Guy said. "It was a weeknight, but it was still busy. I remember looking around that bar and…." Guy let out a long, slow breath. "I knew for the first time in my life it wasn't just me. I was in a room full of men *just* like me. We were all some kind of—"

"Family," interjected Uncle Bodie.

"Family," Austin repeated quietly. That was it. Family.

"I didn't have to worry if I was caught staring at some cute guy," Guy continued. "Or checking out his ass. And maybe, just maybe, I'd get to dance. And I did. Oh, I did."

Austin turned to him, found Guy, his mouth, right there, close enough to kiss. God. To kiss another man. He'd kissed Joan—and hadn't that crapped up everything?—but what would it be like to kiss another man? Would it be different? A stirring in his groin told him it would be. He looked at Guy's full lips. What would they be like? Soft? Strong?

Why can't you be Todd, dammit?

Guy's lips parted slightly, and the pink tip of his tongue slipped out enough, just quickly enough, to wet them and then disappear. "Want me to introduce you?" he asked.

"Huh?"

"Want me to introduce you around?"

"Oh. Oh, sure." Austin swallowed hard.

"I'll start with my friend Tommy over there. He's only here for a few minutes because he's in that show at The Male Box tonight."

Guy took Austin to the man with the blue wig. Up close Austin saw his low-cut sequined gown revealed a pretty darned hairy chest. Between that and the goatee—painted blue to match or not—he wasn't trying to pass himself off as a woman at all.

"Hey guys. This is my new neighbor Austin. He's moved in with his uncle. Austin, this is Tommy—well, tonight he's Dixie."

"Hello," said Tommy, aka Dixie, holding out a blue-opera-gloved hand.

"Hi," Austin replied.

"And this is his boyfriend, Jude," Guy said, indicating the handsome, bearlike man next to Tommy.

They shook hands as well.

Boyfriend, thought Austin. *Imagine. They're boyfriends. Boyfriends!* Would he ever have a boyfriend? Would it be Todd?

"Jude's recently moved here from Chicago. He's a writer too."

"Plays?" Austin asked.

"Romance novels," Jude answered.

"*Gay* romance novels," Tommy added. "Do you read?"

"Well, plays mostly," Austin replied.

"Austin's an actor," Guy explained.

"Oh, that's nice," Tommy said. "Did you see Guy's *Steel Magnolias?*"

"Today," Austin said.

"Isn't it *fab*-ulous?" Tommy drawled.

"I liked it a lot."

"I'm going to try and get Austin to audition for my next show," Guy said matter-of-factly.

"You are?" Austin asked, startled.

"What *is* your next show?" asked Tommy.

"Douglas Holtz's *Tearoom Tango.*"

Tearoom Tango. What could that be about?

"I think you'd be good as The Kid," Guy continued.

"You do?" Austin asked.

"I do." Guy grinned and laid a hand in the small of Austin's back. It felt nice. Warm.

They stood and talked with the couple for five minutes or so until Tommy announced they had to leave. Couldn't be late for work, after all. The show must go on. Jude promised to e-mail Austin one of his e-books.

"I'd love that," Austin said.

"Okay," said Guy. "See those two gorgeous guys over there?" He pointed discreetly and then, with a slight push, guided Austin in that direction. "They *claim* they're not a couple," Guy said, dropping his voice to a conspiratorial level. "In fact, the taller one says he's straight, but you will never, ever meet a more married couple."

He introduced Austin to Curtis and Gavin, and sure enough, the two were practically finishing each other's sentences. In fact, they were the two who had been sharing cake with the same fork. Only a man who was very comfortable with his sexuality could take something in his mouth that had already been in the mouth of another man, Austin thought. They were both delightful, but they made Austin a little sad. They reminded him too much of him and Todd. He could see the love and longing in Gavin's eyes. It looked painful to Austin, and he found himself wishing the two men would find some way to come together. Love was a rare thing and shouldn't be wasted.

Then Guy introduced Austin and Bodie to the three men on the couch—Mark, Tony, and Grant—who were apparently together. "Together?" asked Austin.

"They're a throuple," Guy answered.

"Actually," said Tony, "I hate that term. It sounds like throw up."

"We like the standard 'triad,'" said Mark.

Wow, thought Austin. *Speaking of having something in your mouth that had already been in another man's mouth.* It felt a little unfair, there being three of them. Here he was, single—there were lots of single people out there—and these guys needed more than one husband apiece? And how would such a dynamic work, anyway? Who slept with whom? Did they take turns? Did they all sleep together every night? Was it a mini orgy every time they made love? Despite the weirdness of it, though, as Austin thought about it, he saw how hot it could be. And besides, he'd get twice as much loving.

He noticed the one named Grant studying him, and for a second it was as if the man was reading his mind. Grant shrugged. "It works for us. I couldn't possibly choose between them. Of course, they were together first, and I joined. They were always together for me, right from the beginning."

Before he even realized it, Austin was sitting on the arm of the couch and chatting with them as if triads, or "throuples," were the most ordinary thing in the world. The idea made him nervous, but after all, they seemed happy. And wasn't that all *he* ever wanted? For people to let him be himself?

"Is everyone here together?" Austin asked Guy. "Are there any other *single* people here?"

"I thought you weren't looking for a PNB."

"I'm not."

"Well…. You and I aren't together." Guy winked. He laughed and then, "Okay, okay. Yes, there are single people here. For instance. See him? That's Dean, and he owns this fantastic little coffee shop…."

"WAKEY, wakey, Austin."

Austin jumped what felt like a foot. "Wha-what?"

"You drifted off for a while, and we all just decided to let you sleep."

Austin blinked around the room. Where was everybody? Was he the last one? There were Curtis and Gavin but—nope, they were leaving. And Uncle Bodie had left a good couple of hours ago.

"God, I'm sorry, Guy. Damn, I fell asleep at your party?"

"It wasn't a party, exactly, and you were exhausted. Moving is a big deal. Besides, you looked really cute there snoring away."

"Snoring?" Austin asked, horrified.

"Don't worry," Guy said, flopping down next to Austin on the couch. "Quiet. *Quiet* little snores. Like a puppy."

Austin blushed furiously.

"Geez, Austin, you are so damn cute." Guy placed a hand on Austin's thigh. "And you don't have a clue either, do you?"

Austin looked away.

"Look at me."

Austin turned his head slowly, and there, once more, were those milk-chocolate eyes, making him feel like he might turn inside out. His heart sped up again. It had been doing that a lot the last couple of days. He tried to say something but found he couldn't. Finally, he managed, "I had too many of those beers."

"Did you like them?" Guy asked, leaning in closer.

"Yes." Austin gulped.

"If you're too drunk to drive, you can spend the night here." Guy leaned in even closer.

"I-I live downstairs, remember?" Austin's mouth was suddenly as dry as toast, even as he began to sweat once more.

Guy's face was so near—it was kissing distance again. "Spend the night anyway."

Austin felt a stirring in his pants, let his eyes drift closed, started to lean in himself, and… "No!" He sat back up. "Please, Guy. Don't. I'm… I'm…. Todd. I'm…."

"Saving yourself?" Guy asked, sitting up himself.

Was that teasing Austin heard in Guy's voice? A note of sarcasm?

"Oh my. You are, aren't you? Saving yourself? Shit. You're a virgin, aren't you?"

Austin felt as if his face had caught on fire, and he hated it. "Not exactly."

"You can't *not exactly* be or not be a virgin," Guy replied. "Have you had sex or not?"

"Kind of?"

"Kind of? Were there orgasms involved? Hard-ons? If so, you've had sex."

"There was one orgasm," Austin said looking down at the floor.

"Yours or his?"

Jeez, this man asked some personal questions. "You're being awfully nosy, aren't you?"

"Am I? I am, aren't I? Sorry."

There was a long pause. "His," Austin said finally.

"His?"

"Orgasm. He came. And then he ran out."

"Oh. Shit. That sucks."

"I did. Suck. I sucked him off and then he ran out."

"Oh. That—well, I was gonna say 'blows.' Sorry again. Fuck."

Austin felt his eyes grow wet. *Don't cry*, he told himself. "It was awful," Austin said.

"The blowjob?"

"Oh God, no." Austin turned back to Guy. "No. That was awesome. It was one of the most incredible things that's ever happened to me. I never felt so alive. So right. And his... his...." Did he say "cock?" For some reason the word seemed to degrade Todd. "His erection. It was perfect. I'd seen Todd naked before. Hell, when we were little kids, we'd take baths together and stand up in the tub and wave them at each other. But we never *did* anything. I've heard even straight guys mess around with their buddies when they're young. But not us. Until that night. We were working out, and we were all sweaty, and I'd never been more turned on in my life. Suddenly, I knew I had to have him. I couldn't wait any longer. I'd fantasized about us finally declaring our love for each other, but in that moment, it was all about the sex. I put on some porn I got from my cousin Jimmy and seduced Todd. We were sitting there holding each other's dicks, and it was all I could do not to cum. Then I did it. I sucked his cock, and he came in my mouth, and, oh my God! I was afraid I wouldn't like it but…. Oh. I. Did. He kept cumming and I kept swallowing and then… when he finished…."

"He ran out on you."

"He ran out on me."

There was another long silence. Then Austin buried his face in his upturned palms. "Oh God. Oh God, oh God, oh God. I can't believe I told you that."

"It's okay, Austin."

Austin looked up. "It's not okay! It's horrible. It's *all* horrible! If I had just kept my goddamned hands to myself, Todd would still be there in Buckman. So would I. And it might be—what do you call it? Unrequited love? But I would still have him. And he would still be there."

"And you'd be happy with that?" Guy asked.

"Happier than I am without him."

"Do you think Gavin feels that way about Curtis?" Guy asked, referring to the *not*-couple Austin had met earlier that night. To the man who was in love with a man he couldn't have. "Do you think he's happy loving Curtis from the sidelines? What if he'd just take a chance and do what you did? Everyone knows Curtis is gay. Everyone but him. If Gavin gave him a blowjob, I'll bet anything they'd be married inside a week."

Austin shook his head. "No, it's not the same."

"You don't know that. Maybe—"

"I *know*," Austin yelled. "Because of what I did next with Joan…."

"Who's Joan?" Guy asked.

Austin rubbed his eyes, trying to hold back tears. "Todd's girlfriend."

"Okay," said Guy. "Back up. Todd has a girlfriend?"

"He did. Except I crapped that up too," Austin said and then felt a tear slip down his face anyway.

"Oh, come on. How did you do that?" Guy asked, disbelief in his voice.

"Because I fucked *her*," Austin cried. "And Todd walked in on it. Stood there watching. Joan and I were so busy, and she was making so much noise, we didn't even hear him come in. Didn't know until we were done."

"Shit. This just keeps getting worse," said Guy.

"It was awful. First he runs out on something I thought was the most exciting thing that ever happened to me. And I was afraid to call him. Afraid he hated me. That we weren't friends anymore." Tears began to flow unchecked. He swiped at them. "Then I started getting mad. How *dare* he, I thought. How dare he run out on me?"

Guy didn't say anything.

"Then out of the blue, three days later, Joan shows up at my house. Says Todd won't talk to her. Said that for months the sex was getting worse and worse, and then he started ignoring her. Oh, I hated her. At least she'd been getting Todd. She stole his virginity. She took what was mine. Damn. Crap. Not what was mine. But I sure *wanted* it. And there she was bitching about not getting enough! Then all of a sudden, she's, like, grabbing me. You know, *grabbing* me. I wanted to punch her. Then I thought, oh, what the crap. It was time to finally find out if I was really gay."

"You didn't know already? I mean, you took a load the first time—that can be an acquired taste—and you didn't know you were gay?"

"She was so... soft," Austin said, ignoring the comment. "I kept thinking, *I'm supposed to like this*? But I didn't. I was having trouble staying—" He swallowed. "And right in the middle of this, I started remembering wrestling in high school and how the other guy's bodies felt against my own, all hard, all muscly. I guess—it's stupid—but I guess I just thought she'd feel like that. I couldn't get it up, Guy."

"Until you thought about the wrestling?" Guy asked.

Austin nodded. "Yup. So I just closed my eyes and did it. I thought about wrestling. I pretended I was wrestling naked. I thought about Todd and his cock, and then I was stiff as could be, and I pounded her as hard as I could so I could hurry up and get it done with. And she was loving it. She kept yelling, 'Harder!' And I wanted her to shut up because she was reminding me she was a girl and then—dammit—I felt guilty because I didn't even want her. I was *using* her. I was trying to prove something and, shit. She didn't know. Guy. I was using her!"

Guy reached out and laid a hand on Austin's shoulder. "Austin. It's okay. She was using you too, you know."

"I don't know that." He grew silent again, got his thoughts together. Drew in the tears. He had to finish the story, and he didn't want to start crying again. He took several deep breaths. Clenched his hands into fists. Then slowly relaxed. *Do it. Say it. Hurry.*

"So we finished," he said. "And there's Todd. He's standing there watching us. I don't know how long he'd been there. But Joan and I were both so shocked, and then she leaps up, covering herself, and starts crying, and I'm frozen—can't say a damned word—and Todd runs out. I yell out to him, but he's gone. Joan is, like, hysterical by this time. Crying and crying. And my grandparents have woken up, and Gramps is, like, getting ready to come downstairs, and I'm telling him not to, and Joan is getting dressed, and she's totally freaked out. Guy—I didn't know what to do. Would you think I was scum if I told you part of me wanted to punch her lights out? She started it. If she hadn't, I would have never thought to come on to her, and dammit, Todd ran out on me too."

To Austin's frustration, the tears were threatening again. "Joan called him a dozen times over the next few days. I was too afraid. God, I wish I had. Because then? Then Todd was gone. One day his van was just gone, and his parents wouldn't say where he went. I felt like I had died.

"Joan kept getting worse. She'd show up at my place and want to talk and then start crying again."

Austin shook his head. "But to tell you the truth, it was the talking that did it, Guy. Finally, it hit me. I'd spent all those years being so jealous of her—sometimes even hating her—and God, Guy. She... she was just a girl like... she was just a person like me. She was human—like me. Just wanting love—like me. She was totally, completely in love with him. Had been her whole life. Todd was all she ever wanted. All her life she'd known—the whole crapping *town* had known—that they'd get married and have kids and then grandkids and one day be buried next to each other in the cemetery at the edge of town.

"She started sharing how she knew she wasn't going to college. Her family couldn't afford it. And she hadn't gotten good enough grades to get any scholarships and, crap, that was like me too. She said Todd was all she ever wanted and all she ever thought she'd have. And now he was gone and she didn't know what to do... and she started... looking at me.... And I knew. She was thinking, *Well, maybe Austin.* That's when I told her...."

"You came out to her?" Guy asked surprised. "But I thought—"

"I never actually used the word 'gay,'" Austin said. "I just looked at her, told her I understood, took a deep breath, and told her that I loved Todd too. And when she didn't quite get it, I told her I was *in* love with Todd too."

"God. How did that go over?"

Austin actually laughed. "She didn't say anything for what seemed like forever. And then she just sighed and said she guessed she'd always known."

"Wow."

Austin nodded. "After that, believe it or not, we became... not friends, really... but...."

"Compatriots?"

Austin managed a smile somehow. "Yeah. That's it. Thanks, Mr. Writer. I began to see she was really nice. All those years I'd made her a rival. A villain. Lex Luthor, or Darth Vader, and all she was really was a girl in love with the same guy I was in love with. We started hanging out and keeping each other company. She did most of the talking. It made it all bearable.

"Finally, we heard that Todd had moved to Kansas City. When you live in a little town, you pretty much always find out each other's business. If you don't, people will just make something up instead. I mean, Joan and I were already being teased about being a couple. So I went to Todd's parents' house again—determined to find out the truth. I went there all polite, but assertive, and got his mom to tell me it was true. Then his stepdad showed up at the door, and they claimed they didn't know where, exactly. Said they didn't have a phone number or anything. I found it hard to believe, but with parents like his, maybe Todd really had just run. A week or so later—two days ago—I left."

"And you came looking for him." It was a statement, not a question.

Austin nodded. "That's right."

Guy let out a long sigh and looked away. "Dammit."

"What?"

He glanced back. "Austin, I owe you an apology."

Apology? Austin stared at Guy and saw those eyes of his appeared so—what? Sad? Hurt? "Why?" he asked.

"For coming on to you like I have been," Guy continued. "You're in love with Todd. You made that clear. You come all this way to find him, and I didn't respect that."

"It's okay," Austin said.

"Nope. It's not okay. I was thinking with my dick. I guess I forgot I don't have to sleep with someone to be friends with them."

That made Austin raise his eyebrows.

"I'm a romantic too," said Guy. "At least I was. I fell in love with the theater because of *The Sound of Music* and *Phantom of the Opera* and *Les Miz*. And somewhere along the line, I settled on *Who's Afraid of Virginia Woolf* and *Fool For Love*. Although *Who's Afraid of Virginia Woolf* is about the best play of all time. Still, maybe it's time to start believing again." He stood up, reached out, took Austin's chin in his hand, and lifted it so they were gazing deep into each other's eyes. "If you have a chance to live the Cinderella dream with Todd, I sure as fuck am not going to take it away. As a matter of fact, I know what I am going to do."

"What?" asked Austin. *What?*

"I'm going to help you find Todd."

THE problem with the toilet was a simple one. All it needed was a fifteen-dollar float, and it took Austin all of an hour to replace it. He was glad of that because Guy was coming down for lunch and they were going to begin a plan of attack to find Todd.

Nine apartments. That's what Gatton Point had—nine apartments. According to Uncle Bodie, there was always some little thing or another going wrong in their building, and if he was lucky, all the problems should be so easy as a toilet tank float. It wasn't that there was anything worse about the apartment building than any other, but the building was over a hundred years old. But still, usually the worst problem was a clogged sink or pipe, he'd been told, and there was a snake in the basement that would usually take care of that lickety-split. He might have to replace a garbage disposal or the blade on a ceiling fan. Or maybe change a lock for a new tenant, which rarely happened as most of the people who lived in the old building had been there for the majority of their adult lives. The couple directly above Uncle Bodie had lived there since they married forty-nine years before.

"This year will be fifty," Mrs. Penrose had told him when his uncle took him around to introduce him to the tenants. "How about that?"

"I think that's pretty special," Austin had replied. "I hope I'm lucky enough to find someone and be with them as long as you." Todd, maybe? How wonderful would that be?

"How old are you?" she'd asked.

"Twenty," he'd answered.

"Same age as my Mannie when we got married. I was eighteen."

"You're sixty-eight?" He smiled. "I would never have put you a day over fifty-five."

"Why, aren't you the sweetest thing," she replied while reaching out and patting his cheek. "Such a sweet young man, Bodie. You should be proud."

Austin quickly finished the last of his cleanup, and got downstairs as Guy was coming through the front door. "Hey there, Cinder-fella," Guy said and winked.

Austin crossed his arms. "Wouldn't I be Prince Charming? After all, I'm the one doing the searching. Not Todd."

Guy grinned. "Prince Charming it is." He held up a paper bag. "Hungry? I brought lunch."

"Starving. What'd you get?" His stomach growled at the very idea of food.

Guy laughed. "You are hungry. Isn't Bodie feeding you?"

"Sure," Austin answered, unlocking the door to his new home. "I just ran out without breakfast. Wanted to get a lot done." He waved Guy ahead of him. "I want to do my part."

"You're doing your part," Guy said.

Lucille came dashing into the room, barking her fool head off, apparently surprised she hadn't heard them coming in.

"Lucille! Control!" Uncle Bodie came in the room from the direction of the kitchen. "How many times must I tell you? You need to behave with decorum."

Lucille danced happily at Austin and Bodie's feet. Austin bent and scooped her up, and she immediately began to lick his face.

"Lucille! Some people don't like doggie kisses."

"It's okay," Austin said. "Remember, Uncle Bodie? I told you I don't mind."

"You did? I don't remember." He stepped up and began to scratch Lucille behind the ears. "Oh wait, yes I do." He smiled. "Did you hear that, Lucille? You can kiss Austin, but remember. All things in moderation."

Lucille gave a bark as if accepting the deal and then began to lick at her master's fingers.

"Do I smell garlic?" asked Guy.

"Garlic? Oh. Yes. I'm making spaghetti for dinner. My homemade sauce. Guy, can you make it for dinner?"

"I'd love that, Bodie, except I'm working box office tonight. But speaking of food, I brought lunch. They've started serving sandwiches at The Shepherd's Bean."

"What?" Austin asked. "The shepherd's been what?"

"The Shepherd's *Bean*. It's a coffee shop. Serves the best damned coffee I've ever had."

"Oh. Didn't I meet the guy who owns the place at your party?"

"Yes. You did. He's a great guy. And the new sandwiches he serves there are pretty good too. I guess they're making some kind of trade with a little deli-slash-bakery called Lovin' Oven down by City Market. Sandwiches for coffee."

"Then let's all sit down in the dining room," suggested Uncle Bodie. "I'll get some plates. Anyone want something to drink? Austin, put Lucille down and wash your hands. I would tell you that on the best of days, but Lucille needs a bath badly."

Austin bit back a laugh. The eighty-year-old man was making him feel fifteen years old. He didn't think about arguing, though. He set down the dog, who immediately ran to her owner and wiggled around his feet as he got plates and glasses out of the kitchen cabinets.

"I hope everyone likes turkey and swiss," said Guy. "You're not a vegetarian, are you, Austin?"

Austin shook his head. "Not hardly. I love meat."

Guy winked. "I bet you do."

"I *know* he does." Uncle Bodie eyes twinkled as he began placing plates and napkins on the table. "Anyone want milk?"

"You have ice tea, don't you, Uncle Bodie?" Austin asked, ignoring the teasing.

"I do, son. Although milk is better for a growing boy."

Austin couldn't help but chuckle. "I'm hardly a growing boy anymore."

"Guy. Tea or milk?" Uncle Bodie headed into the kitchen.

"I'll take milk," Guy answered. "I'm still growing."

"When do you start your next show?" Bodie called from the kitchen.

"Casting call is Saturday."

"What's it going to be?" Austin asked. "I think you told me last night, but I'd never heard of it before."

"I'm not surprised," Guy said. "It's not very well-known yet. I hope to help with that. It's a pretty controversial piece called *Tearoom Tango*. Took me forever to talk the board into letting me do it. I saw it at the Fringe Festival in New York a few years ago."

"New York," sighed Austin. What he wouldn't give to go to New York.

"You know, I was serious about you being perfect for one of the parts. The Kid. You should audition for it."

"You really want me to try out?" Austin blinked in surprise.

"You're an actor," Guy said with a wave. "Why not?"

"I-I'm surprised is all." How amazing! He was being offered the opportunity to audition for a play. He hadn't done anything in almost a year. Sure, he'd hoped to do something again, but he hadn't expected anything so soon.

"It'll go into rehearsals in a few weeks and then hit the stage a month after that. Rehearsals start for *The Importance of Being Earnest* tonight."

"Wow," said Austin. "I read that in high school. How come you don't have to be there?"

"I'm not doing it," Guy said.

"You're not directing it?" Austin asked.

"I don't direct everything the Pegasus does, Austin. I'd go out of my mind if I did. We have about a dozen people who direct for us. Most of them only direct maybe one play every couple years or so. I wind up doing quite a few, though. Somehow I've managed to get, like, three practically back-to-back. But it's not normal, and it's not enough to pay the bills. That's why I work part time in the box office and even the concession stand. Gotta pay the rent."

"Well, shit. I guess I thought directing was your full-time job."

"I've got my fingers in a little of bit everything," he replied.

"So I've heard," Bodie said, returning with a glass of milk and one of ice tea. "Austin, your hands. You too, Guy."

Deciding not to argue, both young men washed their hands in the kitchen sink while Uncle Bodie got himself a glass of milk. He raised the glass. "An old man needs his calcium."

"You're not old, Uncle Bodie," Austin said.

His uncle snorted. "I'm as old as Moses's toes and twice as corny."

Austin and Guy burst into laughter. A moment later, all dug into the sandwiches. They were indeed quite good.

After that, Guy began to ask questions.

"ALL right," said Guy, opening a small spiral notebook and clicking a pen. "Let's talk about Todd."

Austin felt a sudden rush of nerves. His stomach clenched. Clenched again.

"Let's start with the obvious. Why Kansas City?"

"What do you mean?"

"You were best friends. You talked. Out of all the places he could have gone, why KC? There's St. Louis. Columbia. Those are just the bigger cities that are close. Why not Chicago or New York or a hundred other places?"

Austin shrugged. "I-I... well...."

"And how about a cell phone? Doesn't Todd have a cell phone?"

"Oh no," said Austin, shaking his head decisively. "There's no way his parents would let him have one, even if he had enough money to afford one on his own."

"His parents wouldn't let him? He's twenty. How could they stop him?"

Austin sighed. "You don't know his parents."

"Not good?" Guy asked, beginning to write down some notes.

"No. Not at all. His stepdad is an asshole." Austin clenched his fists. Tried to will them to relax. "He really screwed with Todd's head. Sometimes Todd would come over to my place after some shit that man pulled, and he wouldn't say a word. And every now and then, he'd just cry." And just like that, the memories brought tears to *Austin's* eyes. "God, I hated the man for hurting Todd. I would promise Todd that it would all be better once we graduated. We could move to Kansas City and find a place of our own, and he'd never have to see his stepdad again."

Austin cleared his throat. Tried to get a grip on his emotions. It wasn't easy. "His mom was cool when he was little," Austin continued. "And his real dad—I can't remember, really. Todd either—but I remember this cool giant of a guy. After he died, his mom married this real creep, and then she changed." He looked up. Guy was staring at him, not saying a word. "That really messed with Todd too. That she remarried."

"That's pretty common, Austin. Kids don't want their parents to marry someone else."

Austin shrugged. Tried to shake off the memories. He couldn't remember his own mother and father very well. "No. Things weren't good with Todd and his parents."

Guy nodded. "And the Internet? Did he have a computer?"

"Yeah. He had a laptop he got off of eBay. I helped him. It was a piece of shit, but it worked and Todd loved it. He had to use dial-up, or come to my place for the Wi-Fi, but he'd get on all the time."

"So he had an e-mail address." It wasn't a question.

"Yeah. But he didn't use it all that much. I was only two blocks away, so he could just run over if he wanted to talk to me. He wasn't into Facebook. He didn't go into chat rooms or anything like that. He used his computer to download stuff."

"Have you tried to e-mail him?"

"Of course, but I guess he deleted his. I got one of those messages back that says 'undelivered mail returned to sender.'" *Because he didn't want to talk to me. Didn't want me e-mailing him.* "I guess he hates me." The tears were back. *Shit.*

"You don't know he hates you." Guy reached out and laid a hand on top of Austin's.

"Then why leave Buckman like he did? Why didn't he return my calls? Why wouldn't he talk to me? Why couldn't we talk it out?" *Dammit. What was with all these tears lately?* Guy was going to think he was a big crapping baby.

"Well, he did catch you having sex with his girlfriend. That would be hard to talk out."

Austin flinched.

"Sorry. I didn't mean to sound judgmental." Guy squeezed Austin's hand.

"You had sex with a woman?" his uncle asked, suddenly sitting up.

Austin shrugged. "*Once.* I wanted to make sure."

"You wanted to make sure of what?" his uncle asked, voice cracking.

"That I was gay." Austin rolled his eyes.

"And you needed to try some poontang to know that?" Uncle Bodie gave a shudder.

"I just knew there would be all those people saying, 'So how do you know you're gay if you've never tried it with a girl?'"

"I don't need to try sticking my arm in a tree shredder to know I wouldn't like it," his uncle responded with a grunt.

"It's okay, Austin. Don't listen to him. I did the same thing. With a girl in college. It was my first time directing. She got this crush on me, and she thought she could change me, and I thought, what the hell? I never dreamed I would like Reubens—what with sauerkraut and corned beef and rye bread and that nasty Thousand Island dressing—and then I tried one, and now they're one of my favorite sandwiches."

Austin shook his head. "You know, sex with Joan didn't exactly win me over as a big fan of heterosexual sex, but I can't believe the two of you are comparing sex with women with Reuben sandwiches and tree shredders. It's hardly a comparison, and it's a little harsh. We are talking about my *friend* here. Now maybe comparing vanilla ice cream with sweet-potato ice cream...."

Guy opened his mouth as if to say something, then seemed to think better of it.

"What?" asked Austin, getting perturbed.

"You're right. Sorry." Guy looked down at his notebook.

"I've never been a big vanilla fan myself," Uncle Bodie said quietly, patting his lap so that Lucille would join him. She did—happily. "Peter got me some sweet-potato ice cream at this Thai restaurant in Westport once. It was simply amazing."

"I think we need to get back on subject, guys," Guy reminded them. "Austin. Tell me some of the kinds of things Todd liked to download."

"Well, he was always watching for stuff about science-fiction movies. Especially *Star Wars*. He even collected the toys. I got him a B-wing fighter for his birthday this year."

"B what?" Guy asked.

"It was the really weird-looking spaceship from *Return of the Jedi*."

"I'm lost," said Uncle Bodie.

"It doesn't matter," Austin said, chuckling. It was all just another part of what made him love Todd, and he decided not to explain. "He likes *Star Wars*."

"So maybe we should look for other sci-fi people," Guy suggested. "There's a group of sci-fi fans who meet in midtown once a month. They all showed up when the Pegasus did *Rocky Horror*. We can check with them."

"Oh wow! You think?" Austin grinned, guilt and tears forgotten for the moment.

"What else?" asked Guy.

"Jokes. Funny stuff. Like those e-cards. You know the ones I mean."

Uncle Bodie shook his head. "I don't have a computer," he said.

"They're these little pastel-colored boxes with old-fashioned drawings, and they say all kinds of funny shit."

"Sure. I saw one on Facebook this morning," Guy said. "It was something like, 'Is your drama going to have an intermission soon? Because I gotta pee.'"

"Yes," Austin said, laughing. "And he likes LOLCats."

"Hmmmm…."

"What is that?" Uncle Bodie asked. "I seem to be getting totally lost."

"Silly pictures of cats with silly captions," Austin explained.

"Kind of creepy," Guy said. "They have the cats speaking this funky baby talk."

"But *Todd* liked them," Austin said, trying not to get defensive. "He loves cats. Well, any animal. But a cat was the only thing his stepdad would let him have. The creep wouldn't even let him have a turtle."

"A cat, huh?" Guy asked.

"Be careful, my boy," Uncle Bodie said, leaning toward Guy's ear.

"Was I about to stick my foot in my mouth again? Austin, I'm sorry. I have a knack for that. Just saying whatever's on my mind."

Like Todd, Austin thought. *No sensor at all. Thought to mouth.* "It's okay," he said, and meant it. "You're trying to help me find Todd."

Guy shook his head. "You are too kind. Todd's a lucky man."

"Lucky?"

"To have someone like you loving him. Now tell me something else he downloads. Jokes aren't much of a clue to help us track him down."

"Well, there was his cooking stuff. He was always looking for some new recipe."

"Todd liked to cook?" Bodie sat up straight. "Was he any good?"

"Oh, yeah," replied Austin. "He wants to be a chef. He was always watching an online show with this woman here in Kansas City. She owns her own restaurant, I think. She makes… box food?"

"Box?" asked Guy. "I don't understand. You mean to-go boxes?"

"No. *Box*. They're these people from France or Spain or something like that. I *should* know, but—"

"Basque," corrected Uncle Bodie.

They turned as one to look at him.

"Basque," Uncle Bodie repeated. "They are a people without an official country. And the restaurant you are talking about is Izar's Jatetxea—"

"That's it," cried Austin, jumping out of his chair. Lucille began barking as if she, too, agreed Izar's Jatetxea was the right place.

"They live in both France and Spain… their home straddles both countries, if I remember correctly."

"Uncle Bodie. How do you know all this?"

The old man shrugged. "It's what comes out of living a long life. That and having a friend like Peter Wagner, I suppose."

"Oh, this is just amazing!" He turned to Guy, barely able to contain his excitement. "I bet he's been there! Maybe he's there right now. He had this dream of going to Kansas City to see if she'd take him on as an apprentice or something. He'd watch that show and then would cook me and my grandparents dinner."

"Well, how thoughtful," said Uncle Bodie. "And you say he's pretty good?"

"He's incredible. Always doing something kind of wacky, like the time he made this pumpkin cornbread. Or he'd add rose petals to salads. Or those orange flowers? Sometimes they're red or orange and they have this black-peppery flavor—"

"Nasturtiums," Uncle Bodie said.

"He even made this sour cream stuff to go on waffles that tasted like roses. Wacky stuff, but it was always good. I don't know what it was about this Jah-texas lady—"

"Ha-*tetch*-a-yah. Izar's Jatetxea is the name of the restaurant," Uncle Bodie corrected, while Austin continued over him.

"—and this Basque food—"

"—the chef and owner's name is Izar. Izar Goya, I believe—"

"—was really good."

"—and yes, it's excellent food. Peter's taken me there a time or two...."

"Of course," grinned Guy. "Peter takes you all kinds of places."

"He's a prince," Bodie explained.

"Even Gram liked it," Austin continued. "And she's pretty much a meat-and-potatoes kind of girl."

"That's true," Uncle Bodie agreed. "Wilda was never an explorer. That's why she stayed in Buckman, and I got the hell out of there."

"Well, that and she was crazy in love with Gramps and had no *reason* to leave," Austin said.

"Yes, she really got lucky with Frawley. He's a man ahead of his time. They never gave me any trouble. Never questioned me. Never judged. Didn't really talk about my life, either, but in those days it was practically giving me their blessing."

"Uncle Bodie...." Austin looked at his uncle, eyebrow raised. A sudden idea had occurred to him, and once it had, he couldn't help but ask: "Are you and Peter lovers?"

Uncle Bodie hooted. "Lovers? Me and Peter? Oh no. Peter's not my type. He's too young for one thing."

"Boys. Boys!" Guy snapped his fingers. "I'm going to have to head for work soon. Austin. I think we've got something here. The sci-fi people and the Basque restaurant. I say we go there tomorrow for lunch."

"Really?" It was all Austin could do not to start jumping up and down. "Oh my God!"

"What a wonderful idea," said Uncle Bodie. "What if I call Peter and see if he'll join us?"

"I told you that you'd meet him sooner or later," Guy told Austin. "It seems like sooner is the name of the game."

Austin began to pace and wring his hands at the same time. "Oh God, oh God. What if he's there? What if this is all it takes? What will I do? What will I say?"

"If you're smart," said Uncle Bodie, "you'll drop to one knee and propose."

"Propose?" Austin giggled.

Guy stood up suddenly, closed his notebook, and put his pen away. "I'll knock on your door around eleven or so tomorrow and we'll head on over. Does that sound okay?"

Austin nodded eagerly. "Yes. God. Tomorrow."

"We'll be ready," Uncle Bodie said.

Guy nodded to both of them and turned to leave, then stopped. "Oh." He gave a laugh. "I hope you have a picture of Todd. To show people?"

"Sure." Austin smiled. "In my cell phone. Want to see?"

"No!" Guy shook his head. "I mean…. No. You can show me tomorrow." And then before either of them could say a word, he was out the door.

"Interesting," said Uncle Bodie.

"What is?" asked Austin.

"Never mind," his uncle said. "Nothing at all."

THAT night, after a delicious spaghetti dinner, Uncle Bodie declared it was indeed time to give his little girl a bath. Austin was surprised when Lucille sat in a sink full of bubbles, seemingly as happy as could be. This was, of course, after they'd done the dishes, Austin washing and Uncle Bodie drying and putting them away.

"Who's my baby girl?" asked Uncle Bodie as his fingers scrubbed up suds in her red fur. "Who's my precious sweet baby girl?"

With a bark, Lucille let him know *she* was his baby girl and no other. Uncle Bodie laughed in delight.

"You know, I never really liked Pomeranians," Austin said. "Yappy little dogs. But Lucille? She's a delight."

Lucille woofed in agreement.

"Poms don't have to be yappy," Uncle Bodie remarked. "People—lazy and irresponsible people—*let* them be yappy. But with a little bit of training, all that noisy behavior can be curtailed. I let Lucille have her say, and then I tell her when it's time to stop. Right, baby girl?"

Lucille barked her concurrence. The adoration in her eyes as she gazed at Uncle Bodie was sweet. She was a very special dog, and Austin told his uncle so.

Uncle Bodie began to rinse her off with the sink sprayer. "Yes. Yes, she is. She is the light of my life. She gives me reason to get up each day, to keep going. After all, what would she do without me?"

And what would you *do without her?* Austin wondered. Such thoughts made Austin remember something he'd been wanting to ask his uncle. "Whatever happened to Jimmy, Uncle Bodie?"

"Ah...." Uncle Bodie looked out the small window over the sink, into the night, seemingly lost in thought or maybe just deciding what to say. Then: "He got married. That's what a man did in those days. Married and maybe had a 'special' friend on the side. And Jimmy was a Halliburton, after all...."

"Halliburton?" asked Austin. "The *oil* Halliburtons?"

"No," said Uncle Bodie. "The cardboard Halliburtons. They were the richest people in town, once upon a time. They owned Halliburton Box and Cardboard before it went out of business. Almost took the town with it—would have if Wallymart hadn't moved in...."

An image of an old factory on the limits of town came to Austin's mind. All the kids had said it was haunted. But that was before it was torn down to make way for the very "Wallymart" his uncle was talking about.

"*Anyway,* Jimmy wanted me to be his 'special' friend. I thought about it too. There was a young woman dying to marry me. It would have been easy. Getting married and having Jimmy on the side. But when I stood in that sanctuary—Jimmy's best man—and watched them promise each other eternal love? Watched them kiss? Not to mention when the minister said, 'If anyone can show cause as to why these two should not be joined, let them speak up now, or forever hold their peace'? Oh, sweet Jesus. My heart was tearing itself out of my chest."

He stopped. Turned off the water. Paused for what seemed forever. Then he began to soap Lucille up again. "I knew I couldn't live a lie. I knew I couldn't be his 'special' friend. I was his best man in every sense of the word, and I wouldn't be anything less. So that night I went home and packed a bag and took the train to Kansas City. Did it on the Halliburton dime as well. I jumped on one of their boxcars—that was back when it wasn't so dangerous—and I never looked back."

Uncle Bodie's words faded away, and the two of them stood there in the silence. Austin wanted to say something. Anything. But what was there to say? There really was nothing to say. Anything would just sound like a platitude. He didn't even want to say "I'm sorry." It would be too much like when people found out his parents were dead. The "I'm sorrys" became meaningless. The "I know what you're going throughs" like dandelion seeds in the wind—puffs floating in the air.

Lucille began to shiver, then whimpered.

"Whew," Uncle Bodie cried suddenly, and Lucille echoed it, stood up in the sink, sat, stood up again, and shook to rid herself of soap and water. Uncle Bodie laughed and grabbed the sprayer again. "Listen to me!" He began to rinse off what Lucille hadn't already doused them with.

"Are you okay?" Austin asked, immediately regretting it. Did it sound as stupid to his uncle as it did to him?

"Of course I'm all right. Shit."

It was the first vulgar word Austin could remember his uncle saying.

"Do you know how long ago all that was? Sixty years. *Sixty years.* My, oh my, I can't believe I've ever even lived that long, plus the twenty more."

The phone rang.

"Will you hand me that towel there and then get that phone?" Uncle Bodie asked, turning off the water.

"Sure." Austin gave his uncle the threadbare and almost translucent old towel and then ran for the other room to answer the phone. "Hello."

"Greetings and salutations" came a cheery answer. "And thou must be Master Austin, Boden's nephew."

"I… I guess I am," he said, confused.

"This is Peter Wagner. Your uncle called earlier and left a message…."

"Oh! Oh my God." *Holy shit.* It was Peter Wagner. "Yes," he cried. "Let me get him." He dashed back to the kitchen as if it were an emergency. He had no idea why the voice on the other end of the line had thrown him for a loop.

Rich. He's rich and he's a patron of the Pegasus and he's Uncle Bodie's friend and….

"Uncle Bodie." He was breathless, even though he'd run no more than ten or fifteen feet. "It's Peter Wagner," he said, the last in a whisper.

"Oh, excellent," his uncle said. "Do you mind finishing drying Lucille?"

Austin nodded and took over with the towel as his uncle left the room. Lucille seemed to be filled with an abrupt excitement and could hardly sit still while he dried her off. She only seemed to grow more animated, and finally, in exasperation, Austin lifted her out of the sink and set her on the floor, worried she would jump down and hurt herself if he didn't. Like a streak, she was in the other room, barking all the way.

"Lucille! Control!" came Uncle Bodie's voice from the other room. "Yes. Yes, it's your Uncle Peter. Now stop." There was one more little yap and then silence. Maybe Pomeranians really could be trained not to be yappy dogs, Austin thought. For some reason, he found himself holding back, staying in the kitchen. Maybe the conversation was private. Why else had his uncle left the room?

A few more minutes later, Uncle Bodie was back. "Bad news. Peter won't be joining us tomorrow. He has to leave town for a few days. Bali, I believe he said...."

Bali? "Bali?" Austin said. "He's going out of town for a few days to *Bali*? Who goes out of town for a few days to *Bali*?"

Uncle Bodie shrugged. "Peter does," he replied matter-of-factly.

Austin shook his head. When was he going to realize he wasn't in Buckman anymore?

"If you like," his uncle continued, "I could stay at home tomorrow. Let you two boys have some time to yourself." He waggled his eyebrows, which seemed to be one of his uncle's things.

"No," said Austin. "It's not a date."

Uncle Bodie shrugged. "I have seen some sparks, my boy. Far be it for me to stand in the way of—"

"Uncle Bodie. I'm looking for *Todd*. That's why we're going to the restaurant, remember?"

His uncle shrugged again. "Yes, I remember. I'm not senile. I just thought—"

"Stop thinking it," Austin scolded. "This is about Todd."

Uncle Bodie nodded. "All right." He sighed. Paused. Nodded once more and then turned to the cabinet. "Sherry?"

"I-I.... Sure. That would be fine." Why was his uncle making these remarks about sparks with Guy? It wasn't the first time. Wasn't his uncle the one who had reminded Guy that Todd was who Austin was looking for?

And yet, as he sat and drank sherry with his uncle, he couldn't help but wonder about his uncle's words. Could he really deny his attraction to Guy? No. Of course not. The man was.... Well, the more he thought about it, the more he realized how much he liked Guy. And how gorgeous he was. Rugged. Not all smooth and varnished, as he'd imagined big-city gays would look—like Bryan Collins on *The New Normal.* Guy wasn't all that different from Todd. But that didn't mean anything. He *was* looking for Todd, after all, and.... Damn. It was confusing. He loved Todd in any case.

Didn't he?

IZAR'S Jatetxea was a lovely restaurant. Open, with one wall of red brick and two others white and bright, inviting the sunlight that poured through a fourth wall of large windows. Along with what Austin assumed was a Basque flag, there were dozens of photographs on those walls; countrysides, buildings, even portraits—perhaps relatives of the owner? Or maybe just Basque people? The ceiling was crossed with thick beams of rough wood that matched the color of the polished floors. White tablecloths made the room even brighter, adding to the feeling of welcome. All of which was nice, but what Austin was not able to see was Todd.

Austin, Guy, and Uncle Bodie were seated quickly and given a wonderful table that looked out onto Kansas City's famous Country Club Plaza and a statue of a boar, his nose polished to a high shine. Guy had explained that people rubbed it for good luck, and it was one of three early reproductions of the famous Wild Boar of Florence.

They were barely seated when a handsome young man with dark skin brought them menus and asked for their drink orders. *Maybe he was Basque?* wondered Austin, although the people in the pictures weren't particularly dark. Water was provided by a busboy. Neither the waiter nor busboy were Todd, and Austin was finding it all but impossible to contain both his anxiety and excitement.

He's got to be here. He's got to be here!

"Why don't we pick something to eat?" Uncle Bodie said.

To Austin's relief, the menu looked vaguely familiar. Not only were the entrees fairly standard, with only unusual names to make them look exotic, but they were the kind of dishes Todd had made him and his grandparents back in Buckman. *Bildotz txuletillak plantxan* translated to grilled lamb loin chops, *txerri txuletak piperrakin* to pork chops with pimientos (and didn't that sound exactly like something Todd would make?), *oilaskoa berakatzarekin laban* was roasted garlic chicken, and *mingaina* was tongue.

"I've never been fond of tongue," Uncle Bodie said while they discussed the offerings. "But I had a bite of Peter's once—"

Austin and Guy snickered.

Uncle Bodie rolled his eyes in that way of his. "His *food*, boys. The *mingaina*. And the pepper tomato sauce was amazing. I might consider it today for once. But oh, I love the *albondigak*...."

Austin was having a hard time choosing, though. Not only was he distracted by his apprehension about finding Todd, but the prices were alarming. He hadn't expected them to be so high. One didn't spend between fifteen and twenty-five dollars for food in Buckman—especially on lunch.

As if realizing what was wrong, Guy leaned over and quietly told Austin today's lunch was his treat.

"Nonsense," said Uncle Bodie. "Peter is buying. His apology for not being here himself."

"How is Peter paying?" Austin asked.

"I have one of his credit cards," Bodie said calmly, as if that were the most normal thing in the world.

Their ice teas arrived, and while there had been milk on the menu, Uncle Bodie had decided against it. "It might not go with what we eat," he said. "Tea goes with almost everything."

Uncle Bodie insisted they have appetizers and ordered something called *txorizo pikante*, which turned out to be grilled sausages on a bed of pimientos. They shared, wanting to make room for lunch. It turned out to be delicious, made of pork and beef, garlicky, peppery, yet not the least bit hot.

"When do we ask someone about Todd?" Austin asked. The longer he waited, the more nervous he was getting. Too nervous to really enjoy his food, for even that reminded him of Todd.

"You have those pictures ready?" Guy asked.

"Sure." Austin yanked out his cell phone and in less than a minute was showing his uncle and Guy his collection.

"You sure have a lot of them," Guy said.

"I do?" Austin asked, embarrassed. Were there that many?

The first showed Todd in his jacket—autumn jacket, really, but the only one he had. Austin had tried to give his friend a heavier one once, but he'd refused. And Austin knew it was because of his frigging stepdad. Something about not accepting charity. In the picture, he was looking away—he hated it when Austin tried to take pictures. "I love how his dark-brown shirt brings out his eyes." Austin sighed. "And his scruff. He would have a short beard in less than a week when he got lazy and didn't shave." Austin loved that. What would it be like to be kissed by someone with a beard? Even just a little fuzz, like in the picture....

Uncle Bodie cleared his throat.

Austin looked up, startled, felt himself blush all the more. He clicked to the next picture, this one of Todd cooking. He was frying something—Austin couldn't remember what. He clicked again, and this time Todd had his arm around Joan.

"Who's that with him?" asked Guy. The look Austin gave him made his eyes widen slightly and then ask Austin to show him the next picture.

It was of Todd lifting a dumbbell, his bicep popping nicely. Austin felt a stirring in his jeans at the sight. God, he'd loved working out with Todd. It had led to him finally seducing his friend. Maybe the biggest mistake of his life.

Uncle Bodie cleared his throat again, and Austin looked up, feeling guilty. He swallowed hard, went to the next picture, and instantly felt his face blaze. It was of Todd, asleep, one arm over his head, chest bare and blanket barely covering his genitals. He'd masturbated to the picture ten dozen times, and he was sure his red face broadcast it to the table. He'd been so tempted to pull the sheet down, take a picture quickly, and then pull it back up. But what would Todd have done if he'd caught him? It was bad enough he'd taken the picture he had.

He quickly went to the next picture, but of course, it was too late.

"How'd you get that one?" Guy asked. And was that a slight smirk on his face?

Austin was sure by this point he was so red his hair would catch on fire. "Sleepover," he muttered and put the phone down on the table, upside down.

Their lunch arrived then, saving Austin for a while at least. He'd ordered the *gambak berakatz eta limoarekin tximinoiak*: shrimp sautéed in butter with garlic, parsley, and a touch of lemon. It was a safe choice, and delicious besides. Uncle Bodie had elected to have the *albondigak*, which turned out to be tangy meatballs served with a brown sauce and peas.

It was Guy's meal he scrutinized suspiciously. It was *txipiroiak bere tintan*—baby squid cooked in their own ink. The entrée arrived in a casserole dish swimming in a thick and murky puddle of sepia, and it looked a bit gross to Austin. Guy assured him it was rich, and even though a steak knife was provided, the squid was tender enough to be cut with a fork. "You sure you won't try it?"

Austin shook his head vigorously.

"Bet you would try it if *Todd* made it."

Austin wasn't sure if that was true. Maybe only so he wouldn't hurt his friend's feelings. He elected not to try the dish or take a taste from Uncle Bodie's plate, either. It made his excuse that what he had was plenty a little more credible.

When a woman came out onto the floor—dark hair pulled tightly back, dressed in a white chef's coat—Austin suddenly decided he'd waited long enough. He realized she must be Izar, the owner, as she walked from table to table, smiling and checking with the customers. She had no sooner arrived at their table when he had his phone in his hand and was pulling up Todd's picture.

"Good afternoon," she said, radiant despite the fact that beauty was not a word Austin would use to describe her. Her skin was quite pale, making her red lipstick all the brighter. "Are you enjoying your meal?"

"Everything is wonderful," his uncle said before Austin could open his mouth.

"You're a friend of Peter Wagner's, aren't you?" she asked.

Peter again? Who was this guy?

"Yes, I am," Uncle Bodie said.

"Well, any friend of Mr. Wagner's is certainly a friend of ours. Anything I can help you with? You know, let me get you some *Txakolina*. Do you all drink?"

"What is Tax-a... colin?" It was the closest Austin could manage. All the consonants, especially those Xs, were tricky.

"*Txakolina* is a fizzy white wine. I am sure you will love it. And it's on the house."

"That would be marvelous," Uncle Bodie cried.

She smiled and had turned to leave when Austin stopped her. "Excuse me... Miss... Izar?"

She came back to the table. "Izar is my first name, and please feel free to use it." She stopped their waiter, who was just passing, and asked him to bring a bottle of the wine.

"I'm looking for a... a friend of mine. He's kinda disappeared."

"Oh dear," she replied.

"He's talked about you and your restaurant for as long as I can remember, and how he was hoping he could be your student one day—"

"I don't take students," she said, interrupting him.

"—and I was hoping maybe he had stopped by?"

Their waiter, already back, placed three tall glasses on the table and opened the bottle as Austin held up his cell phone. "Can I show you anyway, just in case?"

She pursued her lips, and her annoyance was obvious. The change from cheerful host surprised Austin. She shrugged, glanced down at the small screen at the picture of Todd in his coat, and then shook her head. "Sorry," she said and turned away.

"Jesus," Austin said. "What a—"

"*Austin*," his uncle warned.

"I can't help it. She didn't even look and—"

"Excuse me," said their waiter.

They looked up as he poured the pale-green wine into their glasses from a surprising height. He then scanned the room quickly before bending slightly toward Austin's ear. "I've seen him. I couldn't forget him. *Very* cute."

Austin sat bolt upright in his chair. "What? When? Where?"

The waiter scanned the room again quickly. "He came here asking for Miss Goya to teach him, just like you said."

"When?" Austin repeated, ready to leap from his chair.

Another look over his shoulder. "She threw him out. She was pissed. Bitched the rest of the day about how audacious it was of him to ask. She went on and on about how many chefs had begged her to teach them, and here he'd just walked in off the street and thought he could become her student."

"Damn," cried Austin, suddenly disliking the woman and not wanting to touch another bite of his food. "What a bi—"

Uncle Bodie cut him off once again. "When was this?" he asked.

"About a month ago. More or less. Look, I need to check my orders."

Austin felt like he might cry. *No!* So close and so far away.

"Did he fill out an application or anything?" Guy said, breaking his silence.

The waiter shook his head. "I don't think so. I'm pretty sure he didn't."

"Can you check? Isn't there a law that a business has to hold onto an application for a while? A year, I think. Maybe there's something in the office?"

The waiter's eyes went wide. "I couldn't go into her office. At least not to snoop around."

"You sure?" Guy asked and slipped a twenty-dollar bill on the table.

The waiter swallowed hard, looked around once more, and snatched the money off the table. "I'll try. You got a number or something?"

Guy nodded, pulled his wallet from his jacket pocket, fished out a card, and handed it to the young man.

"Don't expect me to call back soon. This isn't going to be easy."

Guy nodded while Austin shook in his chair. "I understand."

The waiter turned and fled.

"Fuck," muttered Austin, a word he rarely used, especially out loud. He reached for the wine, despite the thought he didn't want anything more to do with Izar Goya's hospitality. He slugged it down in a few quick gulps, barely tasting it. "I-I don't believe it."

Guy reached out and laid a hand over Austin's. "It's okay, Austin. Don't worry."

Austin stared at their hands, right there on the table, and... froze. He didn't know what to do, what to say. There was a part of him that wanted to jerk his hand away—this was a public place. And yet? And yet there was a part of him that was suddenly and deeply amazed at the sight. Those two hands. Male. They were two men, touching in a way he had only seen men and women, boys and girls, touch before. His heart was unexpectedly racing. He glanced up into Guy's face. Guy: rugged, so male, hair cut almost military short, brown eyes, nose large and masculine, and with a shadow of beard across his jaw. Handsome.

Why can't you be Todd? he wondered. Quite suddenly, he saw that while Guy was older, his face not as wide, he shared a lot of Todd's attributes. Dark hair, brown eyes, masculine, the slightest bit scruffy.... *God. My type.* He almost laughed at the thought. *I have a type. Imagine.*

"We'll find him," Guy said then. "Either that waiter will help, or maybe at that sci-fi group or just driving around looking for him."

Austin nodded. "You think?"

"I know." Guy squeezed his hand. Strong. Protective.

That's how Austin felt, suddenly. Protected. It was nice. It was how it was supposed to feel. There was a... masculine energy. It felt amazing.

Shit. Now what?

Now I wait. Go according to plan. I find Todd. One way or the other. Find out if I have a chance. And if not? He looked into Guy's eyes. *Who knows? Anything could happen.*

AUSTIN kept himself busy over the next few days. Word that Austin had moved in spread quickly, and the tenants were warm and friendly. Apparently, they liked his uncle a lot, and while he had only lived in the building about ten years, not the lifetime most of them had, and while he was gay to their straight lives and marriages, they considered him one of their own. It seemed any nephew of Bodie's had a place in their hearts.

They found things to keep him busy. Things they'd been reluctant to bother an old man with were not too insignificant now that there was a young man in the building. Plus, Austin suspected they all wanted to meet him, see for themselves who he was. He was the first new thing that had happened to most of them in quite a while.

So he moved refrigerators so kitchens could be cleaned like they hadn't been in years, replaced an electrical outlet with only one working socket, substituted new light bulbs in the high stairwells, shaved the top of a door that wouldn't close correctly due to decades of the building settling, and even changed the spark plugs in Ortisha Walker's car.

He had enough to do that he almost forgot the tryouts for Guy's play. Or maybe he'd wanted to forget? The whole idea was turning to a stone in the bottom of his knotted stomach. This play wasn't going to be performed for a high school of under two hundred students, or for the community theater for two weekends in a town of less than 3,000 people. Kansas City had a population of half a million people, over two million if you counted the metro area. Guy had told him that a play performed at the Pegasus might be seen by up to 3,000 people, 150 in one night. People who loved plays and saw them all the time, not small town people who were thrilled with the cracking, sometimes flat voice of the mayor's daughter.

Damn. Could he do it? Did he even have the balls to try out, let alone perform in front of such audiences? And what would Guy think of him if he stank? Sure, Austin had standing ovations. But that was by classmates. People who had known him all his life and loved his grandparents.

As a matter of fact, Austin had all but decided he wasn't going to audition for the play after all; he would find an excuse. He was too busy with the work he was doing for his apartment building. Something.

But then Guy called the night before and filled the phone with his rugged voice, and Austin had pretty much melted. He couldn't refuse.

"Of course you're going," Uncle Bodie told him. "Not only that, you're going to get your first part. And I am going to be your number-one fan."

Austin couldn't help but smile, despite that brick in his stomach.

It was with great trepidation that he arrived at the Pegasus that Saturday afternoon, barely a week after his first day in Kansas City. How could your life change so fast, he wondered.

But then, he knew how fast life could change. What was the cliché? Life changed on a dime? That was true. Because one day, not all that long ago, he had been best friends with a boy named Todd Burton. Then, in one evening, in less than an hour, less than fifteen minutes, he'd given his best friend a blowjob. And that was the end. Suddenly, everything had changed. Not for the better, either. Then three nights later, he'd had sex with a girl. Todd's girlfriend. It had lasted all of half an hour. That thirty minutes changed his life again. He was no longer a virgin to heterosexual sex. He had used someone in a way that made him ashamed. And he had lost his best friend for sure.

One day he had a best friend.

Three days and thirty minutes later, he didn't.

Had a blowjob been worth it? Had sex with a female been worth it? Had surrendering to his base nature been worth turning his life upside down?

Life did turn on a dime.

Who knew what direction it would turn today?

"AUSTIN!" A huge smile spread across Guy's face the minute he looked up from that clipboard of his and their eyes locked. He strode across the room and gave Austin a hug. "So glad you made it."

"Thanks," Austin said.

"I want you to meet someone." He placed his hand low on Austin's back and guided him over to a woman standing nearby, reading from a sheaf of papers. She was short, looked to be in maybe her late forties, and had curly black hair. "Jennifer? I want you to meet my friend Austin."

She looked up with large dark eyes through wide red-and-black glasses. Her smile was dazzling. "So nice to meet you. You're all Guy's been talking about lately." She held out a hand. "I'm Jennifer Leavitt."

"Pleased to meet you," Austin said, his nerves ramping up a notch or two. He was all Guy had been talking about lately?

"Jennifer is the Producing Artistic Director of the Pegasus." He turned to Jennifer. "How many years now?"

"Almost thirty, thirty next year."

"Thirty?" Austin exclaimed. "Did you start when you were ten?"

Her eyes went wide. "Listen to you! You didn't tell me how sweet he is," she said to Guy. "I first started working with the Pegasus when I was twenty-two."

Quick math in his head told him that meant she was fifty-two. "Wow. Do you have a painting in your attic somewhere that ages without you?"

Her grin intensified. "Damn." She started to laugh. "Hardly. And just to let you know, flattery gets you nowhere in an audition, okay?"

"Oh no! That isn't what I was trying to—"

"Take it easy, kid. I'm just playing with you. Sit down. Relax. We're just about to start."

He gave her a little nod and turned back to Guy, eyes wide.

Guy just laughed. "Come on," he said. "I can't wait to see what you can do."

Austin nodded, felt a buzzing in his ears, heard his heart pounding. When he turned to the circle of chairs, saw the twenty or so men, the sound leapt to a trip-hammering in his chest.

The men ranged in age from eighteen or nineteen to fifty, maybe sixty. And it was only men. What kind of play was this? He knew he should have googled it, but he hadn't really planned on auditioning. *Dammit! What's wrong with me?*

Austin sat down in an empty seat between a guy about his age—quite pretty and almost effeminate—and a powerhouse of a man with amazing muscles and just beginning to gray at his temples. He might have been forty, but no older. He was quite attractive. Austin nodded at them both, and his nervousness rose several notches. Usually, he wasn't so tongue-tied. He could talk to anyone. But of course he knew, at least by face, almost anyone he'd ever talked to. Living in a small town, you might not know everyone personally, but you got to a point where there was rarely a strange face.

So what did he say to the strangers next to him?

Were these amateurs like him? Professionals? He had no way of knowing.

He felt the tickle of a drop of sweat as it rolled down his side. God. This sucked. It was enough to make him want to leap up and run out of the room. He was about to do just that when Guy walked into the middle of the circle of chairs.

"Afternoon, everybody, and thanks for showing up. First things first. I want to make sure you are here for *Tearoom Tango* and not *Good People*. Both are fine, and I welcome you to it. But they are decidedly different plays."

There was some laughter. Austin swiftly felt like there was some joke he'd been left out of.

"You got that right," said Jennifer.

"Jennifer here is directing *Good People* and will be taking auditions starting in… about an hour?" he asked her.

She nodded. "Yup. But I had to see what was going on in here."

"And that's Jennifer—fingers into everything."

"They don't call me Producing Artistic Director for nothing," she said.

"And thank God the Pegasus has her. She is *the* main reason the Pegasus has such a good reputation."

"All this flattery today." She laughed and winked at Austin.

Guy stood for a moment, looking in the faces of the actors around him. Then he nodded. "Well damn. I expected at least a few of you to leave. It's surprising how illiterate some actors can be."

More laughter.

"Okay, then," he continued. "You all know this is a gay play, right?"

Austin froze. Felt himself blush as surely as he'd felt it the other hundred times he'd blushed in Guy's presence. Gay? The play was gay?

Guy began to walk around the circle of chairs. "Or maybe it isn't gay. What it's really about is men who are lost, men who are afraid, men who are addicted, men who need *something* visceral to feel alive. Some of them find a sense of... reality in what they do in this play. Of feeling real. Of ego. I've known a few straight men who don't care where they get their blowjobs. It makes them feel alive to have even a man suck them off...."

Austin's feelings of reality faded further away. What? What was Guy saying? Blowjobs? What?

"*Tearoom Tango* is about anonymous sex between men in public restrooms."

What? What?

"I am sure you all remember, or most of you do, a few years back when George Michael was arrested for 'lewd behavior' in a public restroom. The story varies if he was alone or if he was having sex with someone, but it doesn't matter. Mr. Wham! is—or was—addicted to public sex."

Austin's stomach lurched. Sweat broke out across his forehead. What the hell had Guy asked him to get involved in? Public sex? Sex in public? In a bathroom? Sure, he'd heard of it, knew the stories told of the rest stop about a half hour outside of Buckman. But he had never quite believed it. Men really had sex in public restrooms? He sure hadn't seen any sign of it when he'd stopped at that selfsame rest stop on his way to Kansas City. Nothing more than a few sentences scrawled on one wall in one stall.

Guy continued around the circle, looking into each man's face. "There are all kinds of reasons why men engage in what is potentially such a dangerous practice. Some just need to get off and don't care how they do it. Some find their identity in being nothing more than a sex toy. Only feel real when they've got a cock in their mouth."

Austin's mouth fell open, and then he quickly snapped it shut, begging the Universe that no one had seen him do it. What might they think?

"Some feel they aren't worth anything, that they aren't worth more than being just an outlet for the pleasure of other men—a cum-dump, they call it. Sex like that can be degrading—and maybe they feel they should be degraded.

"It can also be liberating. Telling the world to fuck off and indulging their sexual needs and not caring what it thinks. But like anything—drinking, drugs, gambling, food—it can be extraordinarily addictive and it can *destroy*." When his gaze locked with Austin's, it was like his eyes were bottomless. Not milk-chocolate brown, but black holes.

As Guy walked on, all Austin could do was wonder. What did that look mean? He couldn't help but think he saw sadness in the man's eyes. A deep sadness.

"I saw *Tearoom Tango* at the Fringe Festival a few years ago in New York, and fifteen minutes into it, I knew I wanted to do the play. Knew I wanted to present my interpretation of the story." He stopped in the middle of the circle of actors and heaved a deep sigh. He grew by inches with his indrawn breath and seemed to shrink twice that with his exhale.

"I think this show is important. And I think its time has come." He nodded emphatically. "There are six characters. The Cop, The Loner, The Married Guy, The Romantic, The Slut, and The Kid. They're all quite different, despite the tribe to which they all belong."

Austin closed his eyes. Oh God. What had he let himself in for?

"I've asked a few of you here myself. For those I would like you to just do a cold reading from the script. The rest of you can do your prepared monologues, and we can see what part might be best for you."

The one thing Austin was grateful for in the next moment was that he was not called first. After all, he was one of those who had been asked to read for a particular part. What was it again? The Kid? Yes... The Kid.

"Asher? I am seeing you as The Cop."

The big man next to Austin gave a grunt and stood.

"I don't want to give you any direction at this point. Just read. We'll see what happens." Guy started to hand the muscle man a script, then paused. "I will say that it is unclear just who The Cop is trying to convince in this scene. Us. Or himself."

Asher nodded and took the script. It was apparently open to his part. He looked over it a moment. Two. Nodded again. Closed his eyes. Opened them. He stood up, sauntered into the middle of the circle, tilted his head—*looked* at each of them.

"I'm sure some of you have seen the scribblings on toilet stall doors or on the wall above the urinals," he read. "Not the limericks or the phone numbers of women who can show you a good time, but the other graffiti. Sometimes it's just two words. 'Date? Time?' This is usually a good indicator that you are relieving yourself in a t-room. The *T* stands for *toilet*. It's got nothing to do with old ladies sipping Earl Grey while a symphony sedates them into their later days. In here, beverages generally aren't served. Exact location is not important. Let's just say it's an average men's room at your very own neighborhood park, truck stop, government building, university campus, Walmart...."

The actor's voice was strong, powerful. He read the words as if he'd read them a hundred times before—as if he instinctively knew what was coming next.

How is he doing it? Austin wondered.

"Huh. Can't believe it's still empty." Asher looked around the room, a curious/surprised look on his face, and Austin almost found himself *in* that rest stop outside of Buckman. He could picture it. Smell the piss.

"Just as well." Asher pretended to light a cigarette. "I'm sick of this fuckin' job. This is why I became a cop?—to chase a bunch of cocksuckers out of the park every night? I don't know why they even bother havin' us come out here. They're never going to stop it. They send in crews to paint over the graffiti and it's back in a couple days. Like cancer. Why do they even fucking bother? I've busted guys only to see them back in a week...."

The words faded away at that point. They became lost in the roar in Austin's ears. He closed his eyes. The words were powerful. And they were about sex. About sex and how much trouble it could get you into. And boy, did he understand that.

Use it, came some inner voice. *You know the trouble sex can get you into. How it can ruin you.* Hadn't that been what Guy said this was all about?

The thought was what made him able to stand when it was his turn.

"YOU'RE The Kid, Austin. Young. Pretty. They all want you. You're powerful. You know it."

What happened to "no direction"? Austin wondered, and he reached out and took the script Guy handed to him. Like Asher, he took a deep breath, closed his eyes, forced everyone to disappear—it was only him and the words on the page.

You can do this, he told himself.

He cleared his throat.

"'Sup?" he read. "Name's uh—well, whatever. I been comin' here for I don't know... a while now." Austin took a breath. "Since I was a kid. Like fourteen or somethin'. Get out of the city for a while. I mean, we're *in* the city, but we're not, ya know?" He swallowed hard. *Keep going. Don't let them see how scared you are.*

"When I first took off I came to this exact fuckin' park. I couldn't believe all the dudes out here getting' off 'n' shit. It was awesome." He smiled. Winked. Tried to imagine what The Kid was feeling. "And, shit, when I walk in I'm always the main attraction!" *God, what would that be like?* "Was from *day one.* They even give me shit. One guy paid me a hundred bucks 'cause he wanted to drink my pi...." Austin's eyes went wide. *What? Drink what?*

He looked up. Guy's eyes were on him. In fact all eyes were on him. He saw Jennifer watching and his stomach clenched and he knew he didn't want to embarrass Guy. *I'm all he's been talking about! Shit. Fake it. Skip the word. Pretend it's part of the script.*

"A hundred bucks," Austin cried. "That's more money than I ever had in my whole life. I end up surrounded by eight or nine guys, rubbin' me down, strokin' my cock...." Austin gulped. Cock? Eight or nine guys stroking his cock? Was he really supposed to say this out loud? And in front of an audience? *Keep going!*

"What the fuck? I got a nice dick," he continued. "You wanna see it?" Then froze again. Shit, was he supposed to.... Relief hit him when saw the directions called for him to only begin to open his pants, that he was supposed to stop before then. So he did it. He unsnapped his pants, made a move to start unzipping them. "Oh, yeah." He stopped. "Not here. Right." He snapped them up again. "You'll just have to come by sometime. I'll definitely make it worth your while. These dudes love the hell outta me...."

Austin stopped. Suddenly saw himself in front of a room full of people. Saw his uncle in the front row. Saw his grandparents sitting next to him.

He looked toward Guy.

I can't, he thought. *I can't*. He saw Jennifer standing there, her expression unreadable. Looked at the men around him.

"I can't do this, Guy...."

Guy's brows came together. Those eyes seemed to grow even darker. "Sure you can."

Austin shook his head. "You want me to say this stuff in front of people? Strokin' my dick? Tell people I've got a nice one?"

Guy shook his head. "Not *you*, Austin. The Kid's. You're an actor. You know it's a part. It's not you...."

Austin looked around the room. Saw the faces of the other men who were preparing to try out for the play. Saw instead that first row of an audience and his grandparent's faces as clearly as if they were really there.

He turned back to Guy and shook his head. "No, Guy. I can't." For some reason, tears sprang to his eyes. "Maybe I'm not an actor after all. 'Cause I can't do this. I can't."

And with those final words, Austin ran from the room.

"HOW'D it go?" asked Uncle Bodie as Austin sped through the living room and straight to his room.

A moment later there was a knock. "Austin?"

Austin didn't answer, which was stupid and he knew it.

"I take it that it didn't go well?"

He doesn't deserve to be ignored, Austin thought and went to the door. He opened it only a few inches. "Sorry, Uncle Bodie. I just need time alone, okay?"

"Of course. But maybe leave the door open a crack? Unless, of course, you're going to...."

Oh God. Only Uncle Bodie.... "Sure. A crack," he replied, and did just that. The narrowest possible crack. Then he lay on his bed, staring at the ceiling, wondering why he was being such a drama queen. Knowing suddenly that this was exactly what being a "drama queen" was all about.

Why had he been so embarrassed? No. Why had Guy even suggested he audition for that play? A play about public sex? Had his new friend really thought he could stand up in a room full of people and say something like "eight or nine guys, rubbin' me down, strokin' my cock...."? How could anyone? Who could have written such words?

It was only then he realized he still had his copy of the script. He picked it up, glanced over what he'd read and the next page or so. Saw the line "I'm like God here. They get on their knees and worship at my cock."

Holy shit. He would have been expected to stand on stage and talk about men worshipping his cock?

He fell back on the bed and ran his fingers through his hair. Worshipping. Cock. God. He closed his eyes, and immediately the image of Todd's erection sprang to his mind. So beautiful. Slim and gorgeous and pulsing with need. And his balls had been so hairy. Sexy. And when he had finally taken that erection in his mouth, had anything as erotic ever happened to him? He'd wanted to fall onto his knees in front of his friend.

Worship. Oh God. That is what The Kid was talking about!

But to stand in front of God knew how many people and talk about that? Admit it? Say such personal and private words?

Impossible.

Plus, was there any doubt his grandparents would come to town to see him in a play? There was no frigging way he could let them see him in such a show, hear him saying such words. They accepted him. As amazing as it was to think of, they accepted him, accepted that he was gay. But to talk about worshipping cock? About letting a man pay him to drink his…?

Impossible.

Then, to his surprise, he found himself reading the entire play….

A few hours and a restless nap later, there was another knock on the door. "Should I shove your dinner under the door?" came a quiet voice.

Austin went to the door, still confused over the cacophony of thoughts and voices going on in his head. He opened it to find his uncle standing there, holding a plate. Chicken-fried steak and mashed potatoes and gravy. It smelled wonderful. But at the same time, his stomach clenched. Could he eat?

"Thanks, Uncle Bodie." He took the plate, and then, feeling stupid, followed the man back to the dining room table. He sat and picked at his food.

After a while his uncle broke the silence. "You gonna tell me what's wrong?"

Austin sighed. "That's what is so dumb. I can't even pin it down."

"Start anywhere. The audition didn't go well?"

Austin slumped. "It was a disaster, Uncle Bodie. You wouldn't believe the script! It's all about these men who have sex in bathrooms. Guy wanted me to play the part of this beautiful kid who men just paw all over. There is, like, simulated sex and everything. Right on stage."

Uncle Bodie nodded. "I guess that isn't the kind of thing Wilda was expecting to see you in...."

"No," Austin said, horrified. "Grams would die!"

They ate for a while, neither saying anything.

"I guess I was just expecting that when Guy said the play was controversial, it was going to be more like *Who's Afraid of Virginia Wolff* than *Men Addicted to Blowjobs in Public*."

"And that's all there is to it?" Uncle Bodie asked. "That's all the play is about? Guy is an impressive young man. I wouldn't expect him to be interested in just shocking an audience. Teaching them, maybe. Showing them a side of the world they'd never seen, even. But porn?" He shrugged. "Doesn't seem his... what is the word? 'Style'? It doesn't seem his style."

Austin slumped a bit more in his seat and picked at his mashed potatoes. Took a bite. They were good. Not instant for sure.

There was a knock at the door, and of course, Lucille, who had been hiding somewhere, shot for the front door—a red streak—barking all the way.

"Lucille! Good girl," Uncle Bodie said, rising and shuffling after her. "Good girl. Thank you. But enough. Control. A lady must always maintain a level of dignity fitting her station in life."

Please have it not be Guy, Austin begged the Universe. *Anyone but Guy. I'll unclog a toilet. Just don't be Guy.*

It was Guy.

Crap.

"Guy. Are you hungry? We're having chicken-fried steak, and I made plenty."

Austin couldn't quite make out the reply but wasn't surprised when he looked up and saw Guy approaching. He closed his eyes. *Crap.*

"Hey, buddy." Guy pulled out a chair, turned it around, and straddled it. "You okay? You ran out of there like your pants were on fire."

Oh God oh God oh God! Austin took a deep breath. "I'm okay."

Guy reached out and laid a hand on Austin's knee, gave it a squeeze. The grip was so strong. Once more, Austin couldn't figure out if he wanted to pull away or just let it lie there. The warmth seeping through his jeans from that hand felt good. He looked up into Guy's face—his handsome face—looked into brown eyes filled with concern.

"I'm sorry," Austin said. "Sorry I ran out. But my God, Guy. I can't believe that script."

Guy raised a shoulder and let it drop. "What about it?"

"What do you mean 'what about it'?" Austin asked. "Jeez, Guy. Did you really think I was going to be able to stand in front of a room full of people and talk about people worshipping my caw.... My... c...."

"Cock?" Guy said, providing the word.

Austin looked away. As always, he felt his cheeks heating up over something Guy had said. Guy had a way of making him feel like a little kid one moment, and more of a man than he'd ever felt at others. This was one of those kid times.

"What about it?" Guy asked. "The script. Not your cock. Not that I wouldn't mind seeing—"

"Lucille," Uncle Bodie broke in. "Shall we retire to the boudoir?"

The little Pomeranian barked happily and dashed out of the room.

"I am going to read a book, boys. I'll get up and do the dishes before I go to sleep."

"Don't worry about it, Uncle Bodie. I'll get it." Austin stood up, Guy's hand slipping from his leg.

Uncle Bodie hugged them both—whispered a "Good luck" in Austin's ear—and headed off to his bedroom.

Austin watched him go, trying not to look at Guy, and then went into the kitchen. Guy followed him.

"What about the script, Austin?" he asked again.

At least he isn't talking about my dick, thought Austin.

Austin went to the sink and started the hot water, then headed back to the dining room to get the dishes. "Did you want something to eat?" he asked.

Guy shook his head. "What about the script," he said a third time.

Austin froze, then spun around. "What's wrong with the script? You want me to say that some guy paid me to drink my piii...."

"Can't you even say the word?" Guy shook his head. "Everyone does it, Austin."

"Everyone doesn't drink...." He stopped, strode out of the room with plates and silverware.

"*Water*sports, Austin. Golden showers. Some people are into it."

"Well, I sure as crap aren't," Austin cried.

Guy shrugged.

Austin took a step back. "Are you?"

"I would think the only reason you would need to know that would be if you wanted to do it with me" was the reply.

Austin's eyes went wide. "Well I don't!" He spun around and practically threw the dishes in the sink, only then worrying about breaking them. It was a relief to remember they were Corelle.

"The point is," Guy said, "that it doesn't matter if you or I are into it. It isn't about you or me. It is about a character. It is about The Kid."

"A kid who has sex in public restrooms, Guy. Jeez! What made you think I would want to play such a part? When you said controversial, I thought you meant more like your production of *Steel Magnolias*. When you said the show was called *Tearoom Tango*, I was picturing people having tea and maybe lots of screaming like in an Edward Albee play."

"Sorry, Austin. The T stands for toilet in this case and not something old ladies and English people drink."

Austin shot him a look. "Yeah. I remember what Karl said. How could I forget—"

"I thought about you because you're an actor," Guy answered, eyes flashing. "I thought of you because you liked *Steel Magnolias* and didn't get all freaked out that half the characters were played by men. That it meant you were open to something different. I thought about you because *since* you're an actor, you *knew* it wasn't *you* that you were playing on stage, but a *character*. Were you playing you or Seymour in *Little Shop of Horrors*? Were you playing you when you did *Big River*, or were you Huckleberry Finn?"

Austin's eyes narrowed. "The Kid can frigging *hardly* be compared with Huckleberry Finn," he shouted.

Guy stepped close. "Austin, I thought of you in the part because The Kid is stunning. Beautiful. In my mind he has to be *shockingly* beautiful."

Austin's mouth dropped open. *Wait. What did he say? Wha...?*

"Close your mouth, Austin."

"Beautiful?" Austin finally managed.

Guy let out a long breath. Gave a single nod. "Yes," he said, his voice almost a whisper.

"You-you think I'm—"

"Beautiful," Guy finished.

Austin felt a tremor run down through him, then a jolt. He turned to the dishes, the first sink now nearly overflowing, the bubbles foaming over into the second. *Beautiful?*

Guy took another step. He was close. Almost kissing distance. "Beautiful," he said again. "You're one of the most beautiful men I've ever seen in my life. Like one of those tropical butterflies."

"Me?" Austin said, his voice cracking.

Another step. Guy's body was touching his, and Austin trembled again. He could feel the heat of the man against him. Then Guy's hand was resting at the middle of his back. Austin closed his eyes. God. A man was touching him. He opened his eyes, turned to the man he'd been shouting at, finding now he couldn't even speak.

Guy reached up with his other hand, cupped Austin's cheek, let a finger slip over the rim of his ear. A tiny moan escaped Austin.

"Yes," Guy said. "You."

Austin closed his eyes once more. Leaned toward Guy an inch, two. *Kiss me*, he thought. *Do it. Kiss me. Please. Kiss me. Take the choice away. Do it.*

Then Guy was stepping away and Austin looked up, saw a different flash in Guy's eyes. Almost dangerous. And it was all he could do not to moan again.

"I'm sorry if I upset you, Austin. I didn't want to. Sorry we weren't on the same page."

Austin opened his mouth to reply and found he still couldn't talk. The words wouldn't come. He didn't know what to say. There were so many things he wanted to say. "I…. Sorry I messed up. I messed up."

"No you didn't. I did."

Austin stepped toward Guy, but he was already turning away. "I gotta go, Austin. I'll see you. Soon." Before Austin could say another word, Guy left.

Crap. Crap, crap, crap!

"SHERRY?"

Austin was sitting on the balcony, watching traffic, when his uncle stepped out to join him. "What the hell," he said. "Why not?" What he wanted was one of those beers of Guy's, but he certainly wasn't going up to the man's apartment to ask for one. That and he had no idea where to get some on his own. Boy. Life turned on a dime. A *dime*. He laughed. Lack of money was one more reason he didn't need to be out getting beer.

Uncle Bodie was back a moment later with tray and glasses and decanter once again, Lucille swishing around his legs like a cat.

"You know, you're going to drop all that stuff one of these days. You could just bring out a couple plastic cups with the sherry already in—"

"Good heavens, boy." He began to pour. "It is the finer things in life, traditions, cut crystal decanters, that separate us from the animals."

"I thought it was our ability to accessorize," Austin responded, taking an offered glass.

"What?" Uncle Bodie thought about it a moment and then started to laugh. "Oh! Guy's play."

"Yeah," Austin sighed. "Guy."

"Hmm," his uncle said and sat down.

Austin shot him a look. "Don't 'hmm' me."

Uncle Bodie looked out into the street. A bus had stopped, and an old lady was struggling to get off while a young man waited to get on.

"Look at that," his uncle said. "Young people. My mother would have slapped me if I had just stood there, mouth hanging open like an idiot, with that poor old woman needing help. Help her." Uncle Bodie stood and leaned over the balcony. "Help her! You! Young man. Help that lady!"

Both looked up, surprised. The woman had finally managed to get down, along with her little pull cart of groceries, and the young man first gave Austin's uncle a look of surprise, then flipped him the bird. "Fuck you!" he called, then pushed past the woman and up into the bus.

Uncle Bodie turned and gave Austin a wide-eyed look. "Did you hear that? That youngster cursed me!"

Austin could only clap a hand over his mouth. His uncle never ceased to surprise him.

Uncle Bodie sat back down, shrugged, and took a drink of his sherry. "Oh well. Think of something nice…. I love the fact I have a balcony. Most first-floor apartments don't. They either have a little patio or nothing at all. But of course, we aren't really on the ground level, right? Those eight steps make us just high enough to safely have one—we don't have to worry about someone breaking in, that is. And are you going to tell me what happened with Guy?"

For a second, Austin missed it. "Crap, Uncle Bodie. Just leave it, okay?"

His uncle shrugged. "Whatever."

"I messed up. Okay? I did. I went in there and started to read that part, and I freaked out. Then he comes over here to find out how I'm doing, and before I knew it, I thought we were going to kiss. I *wanted* him to kiss me. Can you believe it? I am here looking for Todd, and I was going to let him kiss me."

Uncle Bodie took another sip. "So do you think it is a bad thing to be attracted to another man besides this Todd?"

"I-I don't know," Austin replied. "It feels like I, I don't know, like… cheating."

"It's not, you know," his uncle said. "My God, Austin. You don't even know if this boy is gay or not. It sounds like 'not' is a possibility."

Austin shook his head. "No. I think he is. You should have seen him that night. I've played it out over and over in my mind. I think it was his stepdad. The son of a bitch was always accusing Todd of being a fag, and Todd hated it. I think he didn't want his stepdad to be right, you know?"

Uncle Bodie didn't say anything.

"What?"

Uncle Bodie still didn't say anything.

"Are you thinking about Jimmy? Is that it?"

Nothing.

"Jimmy got *married*, Uncle Bodie. To a woman. Todd didn't."

"But he ran away. He wouldn't talk to you and ran for the hills." He turned to Austin. "All I am saying is Guy is here, and he is obviously interested in you. And you are interested in him. You have no idea where Todd is, and you don't really know if he is even gay. Lots of straight men have had sex with another man. It doesn't mean they're gay any more than you having sex with that girl made you straight."

"A bird in the hand is worth two in the bush? Did you really just say that?"

His uncle fell silent again.

"Arrgh," Austin cried, gripping his long hair.

"Take a drink of your sherry."

Crap. Why not? Austin did as his uncle had suggested.

Silence.

"He's so damned tempting," Austin muttered.

More silence.

"And he's here," Austin said. "He's *real*. God. He's gay. He's a gay man. The only gay man I ever knew before you and Guy was Mr. Tanson—"

"Gary Tanson?" Uncle Bodie asked. "The town librarian?"

"Yeah. And I wasn't sure—"

"He's gay," Uncle Bodie said.

"How do you know?"

"I know." Uncle Bodie laughed.

"I swear, Uncle Bodie. What all has been going on my whole life that I didn't know about?"

"Give it time, Austin. You'll begin to see it. Your eyes will learn, and you will see what was always right there in front of you the whole time. You'll say, 'How did I not see that?' and kick yourself. But it's okay. It's all a part of that journey you've set yourself upon. Enjoy it. Remember what I told you—you have no idea what lies ahead. And don't become jaded."

"I thought you said you didn't think that would happen to me."

"I like to think not."

"And you also said I would find Todd. So shouldn't I wait?"

Uncle Bodie let out a long breath of air. "Yes, I did, didn't I?"

"So?"

"So what?" his uncle asked.

"So what do I do? Wait for Todd?" Or... Austin felt his heart skip a beat. "Or go for the bird in the hand?"

There was a scraping at the balcony door.

"I think Lucille wants to join us" was his uncle's only answer. He stood and opened the door, and the little Pom ran out and immediately, jumped into Austin's lap, and reared up so she could lick his face.

"Oh, Lucille." Austin giggled. "Enough, sweetie. Control. Remember?"

His uncle joined him in laughing.

"No one can resist you, Austin. Your beautiful face."

Austin turned to his uncle in surprise. "That's what Guy said."

"What?"

Austin found himself blushing. "Beautiful. He said that about me."

Uncle Bodie shook his head. "And you didn't jump his bones?"

"I might have. But that was when he left."

"Ah, well, Austin. A lesson learned. Carpe diem."

"Seize the day...."

"Yes. Or perhaps *carpe mentulam*...."

"What's that?" Austin asked.

"Seize the penis," Uncle Bodie said, and they both burst into laughter.

They lapsed into silence for a while, and then suddenly, Uncle Bodie sat up in his chair. "Oh! I forgot!" He stood up and pulled a piece of paper from his back pocket, and when he handed it over to Austin, it turned out to be an envelope.

"What's this?"

"Well, look" came the reply.

Austin opened the envelope and was surprised find a check. A nice check. "Wh-What's this?" he asked.

"A check," said his uncle.

"I can see that." Austin looked again, eyes wide, saw the signature. "Peter Wagner did this? Why?"

"Because of the work you're doing around here," Uncle Bodie explained.

"But the agreement was that I was doing the work because I'm not paying rent."

"That was between you and me. Peter doesn't care that you're not paying rent. And Austin—I don't pay rent. That's part of me being building supervisor. And that money he gave you? Do you know how much a plumber costs? Peter came out ahead."

"I don't know. This is a lot of money," Austin cried. He still couldn't believe it. He hadn't done that much. Light bulbs, a toilet fixed, a garbage disposal…. "This is too much. Jeez, I've only been here a week."

"But you know how much more quickly problems were taken care of in that week? You saved Peter time. Peter is grateful to have good tenants. He wants them happy. And paying you keeps you doing the job."

Austin slipped down in his chair. "Gosh."

"Take the money and be happy."

"Oh, I'll take it," Austin said, grinning.

"And be happy."

"I'll work on it." Austin nodded. "I'll do my best."

"COFFEE?"

Austin backed out from under the sink, bumping his head on the way out. "Ouch."

Guy squatted down beside him. "You okay?"

Austin rubbed the back of his head. *Where the crap did* he *come from?* Austin wondered. "Ah—yeah. Sure. What did you ask me?"

"I wanted to know if you wanted to go for coffee. I'm about to get real busy with the play. It's gonna be crazy. Six days a week of rehearsal, plus all the other stuff I'll be doing for the Pegasus: grant requests, organizing a trip to see some new plays…."

"I'm not really a coffee person," Austin said. The truth, of course, was he wasn't ready to sit over coffee with Guy. The man made him feel all confused. He didn't think clearly when Guy was around. Something about his eyes, his presence, his… energy. His intellect. And of course, there was the fact he was a real, live gay man and, oh-oh how Austin had wanted the company of gay men. He'd wanted it even before he could really acknowledge it. To want something you saw online was one thing—to take the plunge and enter a gay community? That was reality. That was something else.

In retrospect, he could see so much. Hindsight really was twenty-twenty.

"Let me guess," Guy said. "Your grandmother makes Folgers—or God—is it Taster's Choice instant?"

"Maxwell House," Austin corrected.

Guy made a gagging sound.

"I don't get it." Austin put his wrench in his tool kit and then grabbed a dirty towel—one obviously not used for the bathroom—and began to wipe up water that had gathered on the floor. "Coffee's so damned bitter. I love the smell. Why can't it taste as good as it smells?"

"Maybe you're just drinking the wrong coffee," Guy suggested. "Remember the beer?"

Austin sat back on his heels and raised an eyebrow. He had to give Guy that.

"The Shepherd's Bean has the most amazing coffee I've ever had. And I've already talked to your uncle. He says he doesn't have anything else for you to do this morning."

"Thanks, Uncle," Austin muttered under his breath.

"Come with me? If you don't like it, I'll drink it. I'll be happy to share your germs." Guy winked.

Austin smiled. "You must really like coffee."

Guy nodded.

Crap, thought Austin. *He's not going to let me out of this.* "Fine," he said.

"Good." Guy crossed his arms and leaned back against the bathroom threshold.

"What?" asked Austin.

"Nothing. Just waiting."

He wants to go now? "You want to go now?"

"Yup."

He wants to go now.

Guy crossed one foot in front of the other.

"Okay. Okay!" Austin jumped up, smacked his hands. "Let me take this"—he held up the tool box—"to the basement and get washed up."

"I'll meet you out front in… fifteen?"

Austin sighed inwardly. "Okay. I'll see you in fifteen minutes."

THE Shepherd's Bean sat back from most of the shops on the block. Which included a hair salon called Shear Fantasies, a comic book store, a place that sold used CDs and records (real vinyl!), and an impressively large metaphysical/new age store. Austin was surprised there was even a no-kill animal shelter called Four-Footed Friends right around the corner. Most of the shops had cheerfully painted concrete exteriors, except for the coffee shop and its nearest neighbor—some kind of scrapbooking place—both of which were of old red brick. In fact, the patio area in front was paved in the same brick. Three trees grew there as well, their branches providing shade for its patrons.

"It's really pretty," Austin said.

"Wait until you see the inside." Guy opened the door and waved Austin in ahead of him.

"Wow," Austin said as he walked through the door. As with the outside, red brick was the predominant feature of the room, but there was also a lot of wood—reminding Austin of Izar's Jatetxea. The floor was wood, along with the long customer counter, a half-dozen tables, and a ledge wrapping around the room, just wide enough to sit and enjoy a cup of coffee or sandwich. What caught his interest, though, was a series of paintings—like illustrations in a children's book—that ran around the plaster border by the ceiling. Apparently, they featured a story of a shepherd boy and his goats.

And of course, there was the aroma, the heavenly fragrance of coffee. *If only it tasted half as good as it smells,* thought Austin. "Come on," Guy said, nodding toward the counter.

"All right," Austin replied, still doubtful.

"Hey, Poindexter," said Guy, approaching a short woman with huge black glasses.

"Hi, Guy," she exclaimed, lighting up and transforming a nondescript face into the very definition of adorable. "What can I do for you today?"

"Well…." He grinned. "You can help me show my friend Austin here just how wonderful coffee can be."

Poindexter's smile grew even wider. "All right! Austin, let's start by asking you what you like."

"Tea," he responded.

"Oooo," she said, eyebrows high. "Okay, let's rephrase that. Do you like strong, dark, light, floral—"

"Floral?" he asked. "You mean like flavored?"

Poindexter's brows furrowed, and she let out a long hiss and raised pointer fingers on both hands to make a cross.

Austin laughed. "I think I said something wrong."

Poindexter looked around wildly, obviously teasing him. "No flavors," she whispered. "Evil. Flavoring evil."

"But I *like* hazelnut," he said. "And pumpkin. My gram always gets pumpkin-flavored coffee about this time of year." He pouted. "No pumpkin?"

"No pumpkin," she stated.

"Well, what's this floral thing?" he asked.

"It's one of the qualities coffee can have," she answered. "We have coffees with a black tea character, berry and spice aromas, coffees with a creamy mouth feel. There are fruity characters—like orange or cherry, and even beans with a nice cocoa or even olive oil finish."

He looked at her, a little disbelieving. "I've heard about that kind of thing before. I've heard it about wines too. And I've pretty much thought of it as bullcrap."

"Okay." She gave a nod. "A doubting Thomas. I can respect that. But I bet I can find you something you'll like. Since you enjoy—" She paused and dropped her voice to a whisper. "—flavored coffee"—she raised her voice again—"I'm going to bet you want something light roasted and a little sweet. I'm going to make you the Papua New Guinea Goroka. It's funky. I know you'll like it."

Austin shrugged and then watched something he hadn't expected. Poindexter began to go through an unusual ritual he'd never seen before, certainly not concerning making coffee.

All Gram did was open up a can of Maxwell House, scoop out some ground coffee, and put it in the filter basket in the top of her Mr. Coffee maker. The press of a button, and soon there was a pot of coffee. In contrast, Poindexter weighed out actual beans on a small scale, ground them in a contraption that hung on a wall, and poured the fresh grounds into what at first appeared to be a ceramic coffee cup. On closer inspection, it looked a lot like the funnel-shaped filter basket that was a part of the typical coffee maker. She placed the ceramic "cup" on top of a beaker, and then began pouring steaming-hot water in a slow spiral fashion onto the grounds. The scent that rose up with the steam was wonderful. Finally, as the last of the hot water made its way through the ceramic drain, she poured the hot coffee into an actual coffee cup. There was still some left in the beaker when she was done and—wow!—she handed both to him. *Not gypping me out of what won't fit in the cup.*

"Sugar?" he asked, looking around and not seeing any. When he looked back, Poindexter was grimacing.

Oh, for goodness sakes. "No sugar? How about Sweet 'N Low?"

The grimace intensified.

"Guy," he said spinning on his friend.

Guy looked amused. "If you don't like it, I'll get you something else."

"Why do they call you 'Poindexter'?" Austin asked.

She looked up through her huge glasses. "'Cause that's my name," she said.

Austin blushed.

She gave him a wink, then nodding said, "It really is."

Now through all of this, Poindexter had been making Guy's separately: different beans, different filter, different beaker. Then before Austin could even try, Guy was paying.

"Wait," he said. "Let me."

"Nope. I insist."

"But…." *I have money*, he wanted to say. *A nice amount of money, thanks to Peter Wagner.*

"No buts. I asked you out for coffee. And you say you're not even going to like it. By the way, I can get you some tea if it turns out you don't." He motioned Austin to the front door.

"You don't want to sit in here?"

"It's warm today, for this late in the year. They've forecast snow later in the week. Let's not lose one of the last days we'll get to sit outside." He held the door for Austin.

"Okay." *Why not?*

"Plus," Guy said as they sat, "what I want to say, I don't really want anyone else hearing."

Oh boy. What's this going to be about? Then, changing the subject: "I don't get why they don't have sugar."

"They want to teach people to appreciate real coffee," Guy explained. "It's their whole philosophy. Their mission. They go to a lot of trouble to pick the right bean, the right crop. Some of the harvests are so small, they'll only manage to get a certain variety for a week or two."

"Really?" Austin asked, curious. "How come? Somehow I've always envisioned coffee fields going on and on, like in the movie *Out of Africa.*"

"And there are some like that. But the owner of this shop knows farmers from all over the world. He met them traveling when he worked for some of the Big Monster companies back when he started out in this business."

Austin could almost hear the capitals in "Big Monster."

"Of course, the big guys wanted *huge* crops, but by then Bean—that's his nickname—had made connections, and when he finally started this place, he knew where to get the best coffee on the planet."

"Wow." Austin looked down at his coffee. *Why not?* he thought, and took a drink—at the same time hearing his uncle's advice about sherry. *Sip! Sip, my boy. Let it lie across your tongue—absorb it.*

He discovered something unexpected, something he should have known from Todd's obsession with flavor. Sometimes you had to give something a chance. Even if you were sure you wouldn't like it.

Austin found his coffee was everything Poindexter had said it was. Mellow, funky, and with a sweetness to it. It was a sort of... melon sweetness that emerged across his tongue after he swallowed. "Gosh." He took another drink, and yes, there actually *was* a sweet aftertaste. Far better than the bitterness he was used to—and all without the benefit of sugar.

"You like?"

Austin could hear the hope in those two words. "Yes," he replied. "I do."

Guy's face lit up.

Naturally, that made Austin's heart skip a beat. *Why do you have to be so good-looking?* "I like," he managed, not sure if he meant the coffee, or Guy. He shivered.

"You cold?"

"No, I'm fine," Austin lied. *I'm anything but fine.*

"If you're cold...."

"I'm *fine*."

"If you're sure...."

"Yeah, yeah," Austin said and held back another shiver. It was a nice day, but he should have brought a jacket. He'd imagined they'd have their coffee inside. With the breeze, it was a tad chilly under the trees, where they were still in the shade even though the trees were starting to lose their leaves.

"You can wear my jacket if you want," Guy said.

Had Guy just looked into his mind? He felt a little jolt. Guy had offered him his coat, like a gentleman did for a lady. Yet it didn't feel like Guy was feminizing him at all. Was this one of the rules gay men got to break? A man could offer another man his jacket. It was exciting for some reason. Like he had joined some kind of club.

And to wear another man's coat—one Guy had been wearing and that would hold his warmth. Why, the idea was delicious. Austin blushed. "No, that's okay. I don't need it." *Even though I kinda want it.*

"Well, let me know."

Austin nodded, carefully not looking Guy in the eyes. "I think Gram would really like this coffee too," he said, changing the subject.

"You know," Guy said and took a drink of his coffee. "You always talk about your grandparents, but I haven't heard you mention your mom or dad. You lived with…."

Ah. The question, thought Austin. He was surprised it hadn't come up before. He took a deep breath. "My parents were killed in a car accident when I was little. Drunk driver. What else? It's a miracle that I'm alive. They had me in a car seat. Neither of my parents were wearing their seatbelts."

"Shit. Open mouth, insert foot. I didn't realize…."

Austin looked away, not wanting to see the usual expressions on Guy's face. Surprise, embarrassment, pity. "There's no reason why you should have."

"Oh, Austin. I don't know what to say. Words are so empty when it comes to something like this. I'm sorry sounds so… stupid. I am just glad you had your grandparents. It sounds like they're pretty special."

Austin looked at Guy, whose face was totally open. He saw only kindness and support in those eyes. It brought tears to his own. "Yeah," he managed. "Thank God for them." He cleared his throat, willed the tears away. "You know, it was the whole parents thing that drew me and Todd together in the first place—why we became so close. He lost his dad when he was a kid, and I lost both my mom and dad."

"I can imagine," Guy replied. He reached out and laid his hand on Austin's.

There. It was happening again. Austin tried not to look around to see who might be watching, but he couldn't help it. The other two tables were occupied now, but the three women at one were far too busy with their own conversation to notice. Then, when he glanced at the other table, he saw something he would never have expected. Two men sat there, very close, heads almost touching, and one of them was looking at him with a smile and a nod.

Gay. They're gay. And that guy.... He's telling me it's okay. Austin felt a wonderful tingle rush across his skin, down his back.

Part of a club.

He *was* part of something. Something new and sensational and wonderful.

He was no longer alone.

THEY sat for a while, neither saying anything, but then after a bit, Guy began to fidget. Finally, "Um, about the play."

Oh God. That play. Austin had been hoping if they had to get serious, it would be about their almost kiss the other night. They could talk about anything. The coffee. The gay couple at the next table. But why the play?

"I'm sorry that it upset you—"

"What upset me," Austin snapped, "was that you thought about *me* when you were casting a sex-crazed, disgusting pervert."

Guy flinched.

"I mean, for goodness sakes. You actually wanted me to say"—he dropped his voice—"'worship my cock.' And 'drink my *ppp*....' Well, I can't even say it. What kind of men have sex—*sex*—in a public restroom? How sick is that? How sick are they? Who would...?" He stopped.

Guy was looking away, his expression.... Well, what was his expression? It was hard to read. There seemed to be several emotions warring for control of his face.

"Guy?"

"I would...," Guy said quietly. "Did. *Did*. Not now. Not in a long time. But. But *I* did, Austin. I was one of those sex-crazed, disgusting perverts. Maybe I still am?"

Austin's mouth fell open. *Wait. What? What was he saying?* "G-Guy?"

"I'd like to think I'm not, but…. But sometimes, even today, if I have to use a public restroom—and I try to never to use one—I'll walk in and suddenly I'm breaking out in a sweat, my gut clenching… I'll even get dizzy. And it's been *ten* years." Guy closed his eyes, and when he opened them again, he was staring down at the table. He took a big gulp of his coffee, seemingly unmindful of the heat, as if it were alcohol. Almost desperately.

Austin sat frozen. He was stunned into an inability to think properly. Oh, there were thoughts, but they kept crashing into one another before they could go to any kind of logical conclusion or become fully formed. It was as if Guy had claimed he was really a woman, or as crazy as if he said he came from that planet Luke Skywalker came from in Todd's favorite movies. The place Austin could never pronounce. Tattoo-Toonie or something like that. Why, it all made as much sense—which was to say, no sense at all.

"I was sixteen the first time. My mom and I were shopping for school clothes." Guy laughed. "Isn't that funny? Such a normal, normal thing to do. Something normal that normal moms and normal kids do. Except I got my first blowjob that day."

Guy took another drink, this one a little less desperate. "I had to go to the bathroom, you see? Normal, right? I told her I had to go 'number two' so I'd be a little bit, and we should meet in—oh hell, I don't remember—shoes or jeans or some damn thing. So I'm sitting there minding my own business, you know, *doin'* my business, when I see this hole in the stall wall. A circle about yay wide." Guy held up his hands making a circle by touching thumb tip to thumb tip, forefinger to forefinger.

"I can remember thinking, 'Gosh, someone might see me using the bathroom!' and getting all anxious and nervous. And then the strangest thing happened. This finger appeared for just a second. Kind of ran around the edge of the hole and vanished. I was so startled, I jumped. Someone might as well have shouted 'Boo!' Then after a minute, it happened again. My heart started pounding. It reminded me of this Stephen King story called 'The Moving Finger.' The third time, though, I saw it was really only a normal old finger, and before I even knew what I was doing, I leaned forward and peeked through the hole, and there was this man with a big old boner."

Guy stopped talking for a moment, and Austin wasn't sure if he was glad or if he wanted Guy to continue. He was riveted to the spot, as shocked as Guy must have been all those years ago. How many? Ten—that's what Guy had said. At least ten? Guy had been sixteen back then? Was he twenty-six now? Austin had figured him a little older than that.

"That's when I heard this voice," Guy continued, interrupting Austin's musings. "The guy in the next stall said, 'Stick it through,' and me—being sixteen—said, 'Stick *what* through?'" Guy gave a half laugh. "So the man says, 'Your dick, kid. Stick it through and I'll suck it.'

"Austin, I sat there stunned for a minute, and then he asked me again, and damn if I didn't have a hard-on. Of course, when we're that age, almost anything made us hard, right?"

Austin had a sudden memory of a Snickers commercial several years ago, where two men were eating the same candy bar and accidentally kissed. Hadn't that made him hard as could be—right there in the room with Gramps? He hadn't been able to stand up for ten minutes.

"And the guy asks again," Guy continued. "Practically begs me to let him suck me, and before I knew it, I was standing and—well, you know—sticking it through."

Guy closed his eyes. "Then I felt it for the first time. You know? That warm wet heat, a tongue, lips…."

Austin didn't know. Todd had refused to return the favor. He could only guess at how it would feel. And dammit. Was this turning him on? He felt another shiver.

"It was fucking intense, and it was over in a minute," Guy said, his voice almost a gasp. "I remember this moment of panic when I realized I was going to cum in his mouth, and I started to pull back and he grabbed me and then I was doing it. I thought I would pass out. My knees almost went out from under me. I finally collapsed on the toilet, and I was trying to apologize for not pulling out, and to my complete shock, he said, 'Thanks kid. Your cum tastes great!'"

Guy opened his eyes, and Austin could see he was embarrassed. "I ran. I ran out of that stall, and I am surprised I waited long enough to pull my pants up. I just couldn't believe it. I'd gotten a blowjob. I went looking for my Mom, sweating like crazy and just sure she would know what had happened. But no. She didn't even notice I was wigging out.

"We went home, and I took a long shower. I kept washing my dick, worried that I might have caught a disease or something, and beating myself up. Wondering if I was some kind of sicko. A pervert."

Austin looked away, embarrassed himself. Wasn't that exactly what he'd said? But when he tried to imagine that sixteen-year-old boy, he couldn't think of him being a pervert. Guy had succumbed to his hormones. He might have done the same thing in Guy's place.

"I *hated* myself, Austin." He let out a long sigh. "But that night, I had to jerk off at least twice before I could go to sleep. And a week later, I was taking the car to that mall and getting another blowjob. It was just too much to resist. At first I would feel so guilty. But God, the way the men practically attacked me. It was like in the script for *Tearoom*. I was like a god. They did worship me. Some paid me! They did. That made me feel guilty for about as long as it took me to buy something in the mall. After a while, I started justifying it. They weren't complaining. Hell. They were begging. Why not take a little money? Or sometimes they would just buy me something. Ask me what I wanted and I would tell them, and they would suck me off and then take me into a store and buy me things. It was so fucking powerful. At school I was a nobody. A nerd. The kid who liked to star in the school plays. But when I went to the mall? I was a totally different kind of star and they *wanted* me."

Guy looked up, and Austin could see something else in his eyes. Not embarrassment this time. Fear? Was it fear?

"I did this for almost two years." Guy looked away again, took a breath, looked back. "Jesus, sometimes it doesn't seem real. It didn't seem real then. There were times I wanted to stop so fucking bad, but I would get horny and—*bam*—I was right back. It just felt so good. And I was young. Sometimes I would get off a couple, three times. I was hooked. I didn't know it, but I was, like, one step from total addiction. Maybe I was addicted." Guy shrugged. "Then one day I got arrested."

Austin gasped.

"Tell me about it," Guy said. "I wasn't eighteen, so of course, they called my parents."

"Crap." God, poor Guy. It must have been horrible. Beyond horrible. Austin shook his head. He wanted to reach out and hug that poor kid from years ago. What would he have done if it had happened to him? What would his gramps have done? What would Gram have said? Yes, it turned out they were accepting, but what would they have done if he got arrested for having sex in a bathroom?

"They had to get a lawyer and everything, and the only reason I wasn't registered as a sex offender for the rest of my life was that I was underage."

"God." Austin wanted to say something else, but what did he say? Platitudes. That is all it would be.

"It was bad. *Really* bad. Worst year of my life. At least to that point. They dragged me to church and people prayed over me, and I lied and told them I wasn't gay. Got them to believe I was the total victim and that I had never done anything like that before. I was still sort of pretending I wasn't gay, even to myself. A little bit. I mean, I knew. I didn't have the least interest in girls. It was boys. But in all that time, I'd never sucked a dick myself. I wanted to. God, I wanted to. But I was afraid I would get AIDS—no one was sure if you could get it from sucking back in those days. Those days." He laughed. "Twelve years ago, I think?"

Austin shivered again, and now he wasn't sure if it was the cold or the picture Guy was painting with those words of his. Those writer's words.

Guy paused. "You okay?"

"Am I okay?" Austin asked surprised. "I've been wanting to ask you the same thing."

"Are you disgusted?" Guy grimaced.

Disgusted? Truth to tell, he wasn't. He was disgusted men used a boy, an underage one at that. But disgusted with Guy? No. He shook his head. "No. I'm not."

"Really?"

The look on Guy's face. It broke Austin's heart. Yes, it *had* been fear he'd seen on Guy's face. Fear and worry and shame, maybe? "Really," he said. "You were a kid."

"Not much younger than you are now," Guy said. "And it was part of why I thought of you for the part *of* The Kid. I *don't* think you're a pervert, Austin. Not at all. It was your innocence that made you perfect. The combination of worldly words you would be speaking, but the air of innocence that surrounds you. Radiates out of you. That contradiction. With how beautiful you are, you would have been perfect for The Kid."

Austin found he was blushing for about the thousandth time in Guy's company. Which was embarrassing and only compounded the problem. Beautiful? Why did Guy keep calling him that? He'd looked at himself a million times in the mirror, wished he weren't so young looking, so girly. He kept growing a short scruff of a beard, trying desperately to look more like a man than a boy. Like Todd. Like Guy.

"I'm not all that innocent," Austin replied, not wanting to talk about his looks. "You know that. I've told you the things I've done."

"Innocent," Guy repeated. "And God, I hope you can stay that way. It's part of what I love so much about you."

Love? Austin's heart skipped a beat. *Now what did he mean by that?*

"What I wouldn't do to recapture my innocence. But it's gone. You know, after getting arrested, I still didn't stop? My parents took my car, or at least made sure I didn't drive it anywhere except for school and work. But that didn't stop me. I talked this girl who had a crush on me into taking me to the mall. I was a lot more careful, of course. That's how I found out about this rest stop. Some guy who blew me told me about it. He said it was a lot safer, that cops never went there. So I would skip school every now and then and spend like a huge hunk of the day there. It would take me nearly an hour to ride my bike out there, and I almost got home late several times. It was so easy to lose track of time. Especially on those days the T-room was slow and I had to wait to find someone to… you know. I came really close to finally sucking dick myself, but I didn't. Played with a lot of them, but I didn't suck one. Then one day it started hurting when I pissed—"

"Hurting? You got a bladder infection? I had one. It is the worst—"

"I got the clap. Gonorrhea."

"Oh crap."

"Right again. What was worse is it never occurred to me that was exactly what it was. I was a total moron. I did all that online research about HIV, but it never occurred to me to be worried about gonorrhea or syphilis or chlamydia or even herpes. So I just, like, went to Mom and told her it was hurting really bad when I peed. I figured I had what Tom Hanks had in that movie *The Green Mile*. So she took me in, and of course, that isn't what it was, and of course, the doctor had to tell her."

Austin bit off saying "crap" yet another time and elected to stay quiet instead.

"And that was it. I had just graduated, and they said I was old enough, and they kicked me out. Said they didn't want me to spread my evil nature to my younger brothers."

Austin felt his face fall, his mouth want to drop open.

"And I had no place to go. They gave me twenty-four hours, my car, and a hundred bucks. Told me never to darken their doorstep again. They actually said that. Darken their doorstep. How frigging cliché can you get?"

Now Austin could see the tears gathering in Guy's eyes.

Before he realized what he'd done, he was up and then down on one knee, and had gathered his friend in his arms. Guy dropped his head to Austin's shoulders, stifled a sob, then slowly put arms around him as well. For a long time, Guy didn't say anything. Austin glanced over Guy's shoulders, saw the two gay men looking but with concern on their faces.

Something happened to Austin then. It was as though he had passed through a doorway into another country. It was Guy's story of countless sexual encounters with other men. Stories of men wanting other men. It was the way Guy would place his hand on Austin's, even when people could see. It was holding this man in his arms. It was the smile and now the concern on the gay men's faces at the other table.

Even inside the ugliness and pain, Austin felt joy—like a tiny bird fluttering in his chest. Pain or no, he saw, totally and clearly, he was not alone. This was not Buckman, where he was the only gay man. Or at least the only one he knew of. Then he thought of Mr. Tanson, Buckman's librarian. Damn. He'd never been alone.

He nodded at the couple at the next table, mouthed "It's okay," and.... Oh. They nodded back and went back to their business, giving Austin and the man he held—in public—their privacy.

Not alone.

Then he did something else before he even realized it. He kissed the side of Guy's face. Then his cheek. His forehead.

Guy pulled back and looked at him. They gazed into each other's eyes, and with a sigh, Austin went with it.

They kissed.

Nothing big. Nothing long. No tongues. Just a kiss. Like one he might have given to a relative. His gram, maybe.

No. It was more than that. Austin felt the tingling again. The unique feel of the stubble on Guy's face against the slight growth of beard on his own.

I'm kissing a man.

And it's not Todd.

He leaned in to kiss Guy again, this time knowing he would go all the way.

Except that Guy shook his head, pulled lightly out of Austin's arms. "No," he whispered. "Not yet."

A small moan escaped Austin's chest. "Why...?" A word like a whimper.

"Not yet," Guy repeated. "You have to find Todd."

Austin shook his head. "I don't care about—"

"Yes, you do," Guy interrupted. "And when, *if*, I really get to kiss you, it's going to be the way I *really* want to kiss you."

AS THEY walked back to their apartment building, Austin found the chill was beginning to get a grip on him, and to his embarrassment, his teeth began to chatter. He knew it hadn't been *that* cold when they walked to the coffee shop, or he would have worn his crapping jacket.

"My God, you *are* cold," Guy said. "I knew it. I'm such an ass." He whipped off his coat; it reminded Austin of a magician with a cape, the way he whirled it off his own body and behind Austin's own. "Here."

"It's okay…," Austin said, and felt that little thrill.

"Do it," Guy said, and helped Austin into it.

And yes. It was warm. Warm from Guy's own body heat. He felt a stirring in his pants and marveled that was all it took. It was like he was wrapped in another man. Wrapped in Guy. It was incredible.

And when Guy put his arm around his shoulder, drew him close, it was even better.

Now this is when you'll find Todd. Or he'll see you. He'll drive by and see you walking down the street with a man's arm around you.

And weird. It was the only reason Austin didn't like the thought of anyone seeing him walking like this with another man. There was something almost exhilarating about walking proudly down the street like this. Everyone who saw them probably figured they were gay. How amazing.

How thrilling!

Because I am gay. I. Am. Gay.

He turned to look at Guy. This man next to him, with an arm around him, he was gay too. Austin found he suddenly wanted to shout it out to the universe. *I'm gay, everybody! And you're not!*

He dropped his head so it rested on Guy's shoulder. The man was such a nice height. A little taller, but not real tall. Tall enough so if they were standing, looking at each other, and they were going to kiss, he would have to lift up a bit and tilt his head back to kiss the man. Just one more little thing to remind him Guy was a man. Like he needed a reminder.

Austin shivered, but this time it didn't have anything to do with the cold.

I can't believe I am doing this. I mean... God, it's great. It feels so unbelievably amazing! For so long, it's all been a fantasy. And now it's real. He looked around him. Saw the cars passing by, saw people on the streets. Maybe one or two had a frown on their faces, but the others weren't even looking. *No, wait. That woman over there is. And she is smiling.*

He nodded to her, felt a sense of pride swelling in him that he couldn't remember feeling in a long, long time. He looked at Guy again. How could he have been so mad at this man? All over a play.

A very sexual play. His eyes went wide for a moment.

A play about sex in public bathrooms. And he was being held by a man who'd had sex in public bathrooms. It seemed so impossible. Guy seemed so... masculine. No. Manly. Dammit. That wasn't right either. Moral? Chivalrous?

How could Guy have such a past? The disgust Austin had felt about the play was melting away. Who was he to judge this man? *Does it make me any better than someone who might judge me for being gay?*

Of course not.

"Guy.... This play of yours. *Tearoom Tango.* I'm sorry. I overreacted."

Guy looked down at him. "No, you didn't. I should have realized you might not be ready. Small-town boy and all."

Austin laughed. "Don't make me out to be a hick."

Guy rolled his eyes. "I can't win for losing with you, can I?" he asked.

"Sorry," Austin said, and this time what came out of him was more like a giggle.

"It's okay." Guy gave him a squeeze.

"So… why did you want to do *Tearoom Tango*?" Austin asked. "I would think it would dredge up all kinds of crap. Painful crap."

"Oh, Austin. You don't even know."

"Then why?" *I don't understand.*

"*Because* it dredges it up. Makes me confront it and exorcise my demons. And the piece is so damned honest. Brings into the light something that stays in the shadows. That so many men can only be themselves in a sleazy, pissy, shitty restroom."

"Don't forget dangerous," Austin added, thinking of the final scene of the play. That scene had taken his breath away.

"Exactly," Guy replied. "I love the brutal honesty. The emotions. The way it makes you feel, no matter what it is it makes you feel. It made you feel something and you haven't even seen it."

"Don't remind me," Austin said, suddenly feeling self-conscious.

"No. No, it's okay, really." Guy gave Austin's shoulder a squeeze. "Art is supposed to make you react. And we aren't all going to react the same way. I think the script is brilliant. I got to meet the guy who wrote it after I saw it. Crazy guy. Crazy in a good way. He's so impassioned. He feels life so deeply. I admire his courage in writing it. We shared a lot that night…."

"A lot…?" Austin asked, feeling a silly burst of jealousy.

Guy nodded, thankfully oblivious.

"He inspires me. Makes me want to write with the same ruthless honesty."

"So your play…. It'll be controversial? Sex? Addiction? That's what it's about?"

"No. Yes. No." Guy shook his head, then nodded. Laughed. "All the above. It's sort of science fiction—but only sort of. Five people wake up in a steel room, and they have to try and figure it all out. How they got there. How to get out. How to get along. Alliances formed and broken. It's about human nature. And there's a gay character. I named him Perseus because he's my favorite mythological character, and I wanted him to have a really different name. Because all the characters… they're all people I know, but not *exactly*. They're each these… amalgamations of people I know or have known."

"Should I be worried?" Austin said with a laugh.

Guy froze in place, and Austin almost stumbled. He turned. Saw what looked like panic on his friend's face. "Guy? You okay?"

He watched as Guy visibly gulped, then nodded once. "Sure."

"What's wrong?"

"Nothing." He began to walk again, this time faster. "Everything."

"What's that supposed to mean?" Austin asked.

"Later," Guy answered. "Look. There's your uncle." He pointed, and Austin looked and saw Uncle Bodie on his balcony. He waved to them, and Austin raised a hand in response.

And wondered what could suddenly be bothering Guy.

ACT *TWO*

THE days passed and it got colder. Autumn had hung on bravely as long as it could, but all things change, and the seasons pass one into another. Winter arrived. The last fiery leaves fell, leaving bare branches like fingers reaching for a sky that had gone from blue to gray.

Austin didn't see much of Guy in those weeks. He tried to keep himself busy, and of course, Guy was involved with *Tearoom Tango*. Austin found his thoughts returning to the play many times. He'd read it as well. Over and over. But it was the first time he got all the way to the end that really shocked him—as he was sure it was supposed to. It seemed The Kid, the very character he was supposed to play, wound up killing the police officer. Apparently in self-defense. Austin had found himself crying when reading those final lines, knowing the desperation and fear The Kid must have been feeling. And he wondered—picturing himself on a stage—if he would have made the audience cry.

But he'd never know now, would he?

Thinking of *Tearoom Tango* invariably made Austin think of Guy's significant admission and his sexually misspent youth. That led to confusion. Austin didn't know what to think.

His heart broke for Guy. As a young man, Guy had lost his innocence in an underground of sexual anonymity and promiscuity. No love. No sweet first kisses. No lovers discovering making love together. No romance.

Obviously, Austin saw his blowing Todd in the basement, and subsequently fucking his girlfriend, was hardly romantic either. Who was he to judge? Had he narrowly escaped a similar experience with that notorious rest stop not far from Buckman?

The idea made Austin break out in a sweat. Would he have been able to ignore the siren song of such immediate gratification, had he known the full truth Guy had revealed to him? Had he discovered it himself? At a time when hormones were raging and a mere breeze could give him a hard-on?

There was a distinct possibility he could have fallen into the same kind of trap Guy had. Hell. His hormones were raging right now. He was nearly twenty-one and had never had a blowjob himself. He'd given one—and God, loved it—and he'd had... intercourse with a female. The latter could only allow him to guess how receiving oral sex might feel. The world Guy had conjured up in Austin's mind was at once disgusting, appalling, and to his discomfort, exciting. Would a blowjob through a hole in the wall be better than nothing at all? Austin hoped not. He liked to think his romantic fantasies were the stuff that made the world go round.

Austin had discovered websites on the Internet. Gay sites. He'd seen pictures and videos of what men could do to each other, and it hadn't taken long for him to realize he wanted to try almost all of it.

He'd found the story sites as well—tales written to jack off to—and he'd done a hell of a lot of jacking off reading them. He'd read all kinds of stories. About high school and college students. Accounts of older men with younger men. Incest stories. Adventures of men submitting themselves to Masters and Doms, and conversely, stories told from the other point of view. Reports of first times. And yes, even stories about glory holes, watersports, and worse.

And dammit! Hadn't some of those stories been as wild as anything in *Tearoom Tango*? Was there anything in that script he hadn't read before?

Crap!

Had he overreacted?

Of course, the difference was when he'd read those stories online, it was at night when his grandparents were asleep, and he'd been horny as hell and he had been all alone. *Tearoom Tango* asked him to stand, proudly, in front of 150 people and say that stuff out loud.

Finally, though—to be fair to himself—weren't the stories he loved the most the romantic ones? Making love by candlelight, midnight skinny-dipping with a buddy, losing virginity during a campout in a pup tent with a boyhood crush?

Hadn't there been campouts with Todd in the middle of nowhere? How many times had he lain there, Todd next to him, snoring peacefully, and he—Austin—wide awake, cock hard as steel, wishing he had the guts to tell his friend how he felt? Oh! Why hadn't he? Wouldn't that have been better than a blowjob by the light of porn on his old TV? It might have made Todd face what happened afterward. It was harder to run away in the woods at night than from a basement. Crap it all. If only he could go back in time and do it again. Or if he could go back in time and rescue Guy. Save him from a life of degradation, even if it had all been filled with pleasure.

Maybe Guy would still have a family? If they had discovered their son was gay slowly, under more favorable circumstances?

Might it have made a difference?

"Oh, sweet Guy," he mumbled under his breath. Guy's face came to his mind. Those eyes, so beautiful; and his hands, big and masculine; and a body, mysterious, hidden by such baggy clothes. Of course, Austin had seen that butt, so round, even covered by jeans.

"You okay?" Uncle Bodie asked him one evening when he'd come in from playing with Lucille in the courtyard of their building. He'd caught Austin staring deep and long into a bubbling pot of pasta. Austin had jumped as if he'd been goosed.

"Huh? Wha—"

"I asked if you were all right. You seem faraway and long ago."

Austin shrugged. "I'm all right."

"You missing Guy, or Todd?"

Austin jumped again. How did his uncle do that?

"Both?" his uncle asked.

Suddenly, Austin felt like crying. He nodded. "Yes," he whispered. "Both."

"He's pretty special, isn't he?" Uncle Bodie opened a cabinet that got Lucille to prancing.

"Who? Guy or Todd?"

"Well, I don't know Todd. I can only go by hearsay, although naturally I trust you. You wouldn't fall for some deviant or serial killer. At least, I hope not. But I was talking about Guy."

Austin sighed. "Yes. I miss him too."

"Well, Austin, he lives right upstairs. You know where *he* is, after all." Uncle Bodie pulled out a bag, and Lucille began to dance, even pirouette. "Who's hungry?" he asked.

"Yap!" Lucille answered. She was hungry, Dad!

"And remember something else, my boy. No one wants to be second choice. Would you? He might put up with it for a while. He knows why you came to Kansas City. But... would *you* want to be a consolation prize?"

"Crap," Austin said.

"Indeed."

"What the hell do I do?" He had to admit, he was finding himself drawn more and more to his upstairs neighbor.

"I'm not going to tell you what to do. I just know Todd is a fantasy. And Guy? He's so close you can almost touch him."

"I know, Uncle Bodie, but... he's gone all the time now with his play. Gets home late from rehearsal—"

"And what hours do *you* keep? You aren't a nine-to-five kinda girl, are you?"

"I'm not a girl at all, thank you."

"Give it a little time...." Uncle Bodie picked up Lucille's *I Love Lucy* ceramic double bowl. One side—for water—had a painting of Lucy, and the other—for food—had Ricky.

"Never!"

His uncle tsked him. Then: "Have you thought about going out and getting some of that beer you both like and meeting him at his door one night?"

"How will I know when to be there? Sometimes he comes home right after rehearsal, and others he goes to that Male Box place."

"Speaking of which, you're almost old enough. Let's go there for your birthday. It's on a weekend this year, and isn't that fortuitous?"

Austin smiled. "Could be fun." *His first gay bar!*

"We'll go to the Liddle Awful Annie show that's all the talk right now. And that boy Tommy—the one who was wearing a blue wig a few weeks ago? He'll be there. I hear he's very funny."

"But is he supposed to be?" Austin asked. He'd watched a few episodes of *RuPaul's Drag Race* with his uncle, and some of those queens took themselves very seriously.

"Honey, he wears a blue wig and doesn't shave. He's *supposed* to be funny."

GUY did keep his promise and took Austin to the sci-fi group one Saturday. They called themselves KaCSFFS—pronounced Kaks-Fis—or the Kansas City Science Fiction and Fantasy Society. They were nothing like Austin had pictured. No *Star Trek* costumes, no lightsabers, no hairy rubber hobbit feet, although there were a few *Big Bang Theory*-type wallflowers.

As it turned out, science fiction and fantasy fans had a decided dislike of the word "sci-fi."

"What do you call it, then?" Guy had asked.

"SF" was the standard answer, and one member of the club added that "sci-fi" looked like it should be pronounced skiffy and gave an exaggerated shudder. Who would have known it would be such a big deal, especially when there was such a popular network channel with the very name they so disliked?

Otherwise, the members of the club, for the most part, seemed to be pretty regular people. During the meeting, they talked business and how to keep the club viable in such tough economic times. Afterward, they discussed politics—seemed most were strongly for gay marriage, even though the majority of them appeared to be straight. That was pretty cool. Evidently, "SF" fans were very open-minded. Like any other group of people, several went on ad nauseam about sports, in this case The Chiefs, the Kansas City football team. Pretty normal stuff.

Sure, they were impassioned about whether Peter Jackson should have added so much material to his adaptation of *The Hobbit*. "But I suppose," Guy said afterward, "it's no weirder than actors getting all upset about the changes Hollywood makes when it adapts a play into a movie. Boy, can I remember how upset some of my friends got over what Christopher Columbus did to *Rent*."

But what had really been significant about the club members was that none of them knew Todd. When Austin showed the pictures on his cell phone, and he made sure not to show the near-naked one this time, not one of them had seen him. Austin couldn't help but feel a crash in his spirits. Both their leads—the Basque restaurant with its obnoxious owner and the SF fans—were busts. The waiter from Izar's Jatetxea still hadn't called back. Which was horribly frustrating, because Austin didn't know if that meant Todd hadn't left an application, or if the waiter just plain hadn't bothered.

"We'll find Todd," Guy said. "If we have to drive up and down every single street looking for his van. It was a van, right? Isn't that what you told me?"

All of which made Guy's absence all the harder. Not only had he still not found Todd—and it was appearing more and more likely he wouldn't—but now Guy might as well be missing himself, for all Austin was seeing him. Austin had just begun to realize he was crossing some magical threshold into the gay world when his guide to that world was gone. Or at least, too busy.

Should he show up at Guy's door with flowers and a six-pack?

No. The more he thought about it, the more he knew that wasn't going to happen. First, he didn't have the guts. Second, he wasn't old enough to buy beer. And third? What the crap would Guy think of getting flowers? Was that anything *but* a courting gesture? A message saying "he loves me, he loves me not"?

Correction!

He *wants* me, he wants me not.

Todd.

Guy.

Todd or Guy?

How had Guy even become a consideration? Wasn't Austin in love with Todd? Wasn't he? Wasn't that what his move to Kansas City was really all about? Wasn't the big city and the opportunity to be who he really was of secondary importance?

So many crapping questions!

Was that what growing up, becoming an adult, *being* an adult was all about? Would life ever calm down?

"Not really," his uncle explained when Austin finally asked him. "There's *always* something going on. Something to figure out, something you messed up that you have to fix. Life is change. The only thing you are *really* in control of is your attitude, how you face your problems. Be hopeful. Expect the best, and you'll find it. And remember this—*anything* can happen."

Anything?

Then he was going to hope he found Todd. He had time. There was very little Guy in his life right now. He could get his head straight. He laughed at himself for the thought. *Get my head together*, he corrected.

Because what if he did fall into Guy's bed, only to find Todd—a Todd who loved him as well? Wouldn't that be the worst thing that could happen?

Anything could happen?

Then he would wait. If the fantasy happened, there wouldn't or couldn't be anything better than that.

AUSTIN answered the phone on the third ring, not even bothering to check the caller ID. "Hello," he said.

"Happy Thanksgiving" came the cry from the other end of the line.

"Gram! Happy Thanksgiving," he exclaimed. "God, it's good to hear your voice." He sat down at the small kitchen table and, shifting the phone to his other ear, began to peel the potatoes Uncle Bodie had left for him.

"And how is life in the big city, son? We never hear from you."

Austin felt a stab of guilt. He was nearly twenty-one, and damn, she could reduce him to a six-year-old in an instant. "Gram, I'm so sorry." He did call, just not as often as she might have wished. "It gets so crazy and—"

"I know, dear. But you gotta remember. You've always been here. Twenty years you were underfoot. Some of those years literally. When you was in the basement. Now you're gone. It's not easy gettin' used to."

Were those tears in her voice? God.... "I miss you too," he confessed. And he did. She and Gramps had been his whole world. Loving. Supportive always. And now he knew how much that meant.

"I wish you were here," she replied. "First Thanksgiving you've been away in twenty years."

"Second, Gram. Remember the year I went with Cousin Jimmy to Florida?"

"I remember. I still wish you was here."

"Sorry, Gram." He and Uncle Bodie had talked about it, driving to Buckman, but in the end decided to have their first Thanksgiving together. A symbol of Austin's new life and all that was opening to him.

"So, have you... *met* anyone yet?"

"I've met lots of people. Great people! I would love you to meet them. I think you'd approve."

"Yes. That's nice. But... are you... *seeing* anyone?"

It took Austin a second to get the implication, but when he did, he smiled and blushed at the same time. She wanted to know if he was dating a man. "No, Gram. I met this nice... person. But I gotta find Todd first."

"Ah.... Of course. No luck, then?"

"No," he said, and felt sadness sneaking up on him. No! This was Thanksgiving! It was not time to think about what he *didn't* have, but what he did.

"I ran into Mrs. Sandburg the other day...."

Mrs. Sandburg. *Todd's mother?* "You did?"

"I asked her how Todd was doing, and she wasn't very friendly. Told me he was fine, and when I asked her where he was, she said she had to go."

Austin felt his heart expand, and the threatening melancholy was thrown back into the dark. Leave it to Gram to make him feel surrounded with love. He really was lucky.

"I asked her if she'd spoken to him, if he really had moved to Kansas City, and she just walked away. The bitch."

Austin's eyes popped and he burst into laughter. "You didn't call her that, did you?"

"Not exactly. But I did say things an eighty-two-year-old grammy lady shouldn't say."

Oh my God! What did she say?

"How's that bird coming along?" Gram asked, just as Uncle Bodie came into the kitchen and opened the oven, pulled out a roasting pan, opened it, and began to baste the small goose Austin had bought for the occasion. They'd been shopping, and he'd insisted he'd pay, despite his uncle's protestations. He wanted to do something to show how much he loved his uncle, and to show his thanks. Wasn't that what Thanksgiving was all about?

Austin had never had goose—his grandparents thought it was too greasy—but he was willing to give it a try. His uncle was no Todd when it came to cooking, but he could give his friend a good run for his money. The smell was certainly wonderful.

"Why don't you ask Uncle Bodie," he said, letting her off the hook, but still wondering what she'd said to Mrs. Sandburg. It could be almost anything! "I'm in charge of the side dishes."

"Some of them," his uncle corrected. "*Not* my stuffing."

Austin handed him the phone.

"Hello, Wilda, dear," he said, not taking his eyes off the goose. "Why yes, it looks heavenly…. Yes, I know you think goose is greasy. That is why I am making it for Austin and myself. You know we have more sophisticated tastes."

Austin clapped his hand over his mouth. *Dear God. What was he saying?*

"True. There is no sweet-potato pie that touches the miracle of yours. Maybe you could mail us a couple pieces?" He laughed. "Awww.... Thank you, Sis.... No.... Really...?"

Uncle Bodie closed the roasting pan and slipped it back in the oven.

"I miss you too.... It has been quite a while.... Christmas?"

Uncle Bodie stood up straight. "Why... that sounds interesting. I'll discuss it with Austin, but I don't see why not." A slow smile crept over his face. "Wilda... that sounds wonderful." His smile grew. "Yes... You too, Wilda, dear. Love you too. And Austin is doing great. You'd be proud." He laughed. "Good-bye, dear."

He hung up. "Guess what?" he asked.

Austin had an idea, and he hoped he was right. He'd stopped peeling potatoes as he began to figure out what his grandmother and uncle might be talking about. And he liked the idea. A lot. "Tell me," he said, crossing his fingers.

"Your Gram has asked us to come up for Christmas. Spend a couple days. What do you think of that idea?"

Austin gave a whoop of joy. "I say yes!"

"AUSTIN, before we eat...."

"You want to say grace?" Gram always insisted on Thanksgiving grace. It amused him because Thanksgiving, Easter, and Christmas were the only days dinner prayers were important to her, and he'd never really known why. They weren't churchgoers. He used to tease her about hedging her bets.

Uncle Bodie shook his head. "No. I don't really do that, you know? Pray? To some old man sitting on a throne up there in the clouds somewhere?"

"You don't believe in God?" It was only a question. Austin wasn't sure where he weighed in on the subject himself.

"I don't believe in some Zeus- or Odin-inspired deity," he replied. "I think there is probably 'something,' but I don't think I am privy to what *It* is. I mean, It must transcend anything we can understand if It created the entire universe, eh? And has lived forever? I think it's foolishness to attribute any qualities we can comprehend to such a being. And I refuse to believe It micromanages us or cares who we sleep with."

Austin gave a nod. Uncle Bodie's words surprised him. His uncle didn't talk about things like the nature of God. How did he respond to such words?

"But I do believe It responds, especially to gratitude. *So*, before we eat, let's say—or I will, anyway—what I am grateful for. Will you indulge me?"

"Sure," Austin said. In fact he was pretty sure he would indulge his uncle in anything.

"All right, then." His uncle smiled. "First and foremost, I am grateful for you. I am thankful for your presence and your company. I was getting quite lonely, despite my dear little Lucille."

Lucille, curled up on a pillow not far away, perked up her ears at hearing her name. She was keeping half an eye on what they were doing and looking for any dropped morsels of food.

"I needed someone who answered back when I spoke—in human words, that is. It's been a long time since I've lived with anyone."

Austin felt his heart expand. Who would have known this old man could move him so deeply? Now and so many times since he'd moved in with his uncle. How had someone become so important to him so quickly? A few weeks ago, he had hardly known the man, hadn't seen him in a decade. And now? Uncle Bodie was a friend. A man who had given him freedom. "I don't know what to say...."

"Don't say anything. That's not what this is about. This isn't about you needing to thank me. This is about *me* thanking you. This is about me being thankful for you."

"Oh," Austin said quietly, not having a clue what else there was *to* say.

"Austin, I am thankful for your service. I am grateful for your youth—for reminding me that life goes on and that new generations will come, are coming, and it's getting better. The world is becoming a better place despite the foolishness of some. I look at you and see a young gay man who is stepping into a gay world that now is no longer terrified or ashamed to be a part of the greater world around it...."

Uncle Bodie smiled and did that thing he occasionally did—he seemed to go away. To another place, perhaps another time?

"I am thankful I had Jimmy—the love of my life."

Austin felt a jolt, a crack, a hurting. Jimmy? From—what?—sixty or more years ago? Jimmy was the love of his life? But Uncle Bodie was eighty. Had he been alone all that time?

But then he saw the smile on his uncle's face. It was beatific. As if he were looking at an angel only he could see. No sadness. No regrets. If Uncle Bodie could feel these things, shouldn't he as well?

If only I could think of Todd that way.

Maybe he could?

"And!" his uncle cried, startling both Austin and Lucille, who leapt to her feet and began barking, head pointed to the sky, one eye on her master. "And I am thankful for Lucille! She is the *light* in my life, aren't you, girl?"

With a mighty double bark, she let him know she knew that very thing, thank you very much, and she was proud of it. Uncle Bodie laughed in delight. She ran to his side and stood on her hind legs, front paws on his thigh, and barked once more. He scratched the mane on either side of her face vigorously, and praised her and made sure she knew she was his reason for living. Her entire back end was wagging so hard Austin didn't know how she didn't fall over, and he joined his uncle in laughter. Lucille was a joy.

"Okay now, girl. Get down. Back to your place. Soon you will get some of this Thanksgiving feast for yourself."

Lucille danced back on her hind legs, reminding Austin of a tiny horse, front feet waving in the air. She spun around, ran to her pillow, and threw herself down.

When the laughter died down, Austin decided it was his turn to speak. "Uncle Bodie.... My turn."

"Really? You don't need to."

"Of course I do," he said, knowing this was more than merely indulging an old man. "The first thing I am grateful for is that I'm gay."

"Outstanding!" Uncle Bodie clapped.

"Over the last few days, I've had this growing feeling. It sounds weird, silly maybe, but it feels like I've been... well... *chosen*. I know *I* didn't choose *it*. I would have been too stupid. But it's like gay chose *me*."

"Oh my," Uncle Bodie said with a happy sigh. "Oh, Austin."

"I feel like I'm standing on a ridge, looking down into this gorgeous valley, and it's my... my..."

"Promised Land," Uncle Bodie offered.

"Yes," Austin cried. "Yes, that's it."

"And you have a lifetime to explore it. The rivers and creeks, the oceans and tributaries. The fields and forests and plains and mountains. It is yours by right. Sometimes there will be deserts and rattlesnakes and scorpions. But for the most part, there is joy, my boy."

A rush swept over Austin, taking his breath away. For a moment, he couldn't speak. And when he could... "I am so grateful—" He paused. "Uncle Bodie? I'm grateful that I had Todd as my best friend for most of my whole life. No matter what happens next—"

"Even if something is over, it doesn't undo how good it was," Uncle Bodie supplied.

Austin nodded. "—I will always have that." He smiled. "I'm thankful for coming here, to Kansas City. For meeting actors. *Real* actors. I'm thankful for my new life. For my grandparents. But most of all—" Suddenly, his eyes were welling up with tears. "—I'm grateful for you. I'm grateful that you're gay—but that doesn't matter. I'm thankful that I'm related, that I'm *friends*, with you."

Uncle's Bodie's eyes glassed over as quickly as Austin's had, and it was apparent he was one step from crying. "Th-thank you, Austin," he said, voice cracking.

Austin's smile grew and a tear slipped down his cheek. "This isn't about you thanking me," he said. "This is about *me* thanking *you*."

THE dinner was wonderful. Yes, indeed, the goose was greasy, as Grams claimed. It reminded Austin vaguely of the dark meat of a chicken, but multiplied. It even tasted a little like chicken livers to him. "Strong."

"Gamey," said his uncle. "They say there's things to do about that, but hell. A goose is a game bird, after all. I like that flavor. I grew up on it. So did Wilda, I guess, but then again—like I told her—we homos have more sophisticated palates."

Austin couldn't help but grin.

Uncle Bodie's stuffing was as good as promised. And Austin was pretty proud of his green bean casserole. He'd used one of Todd's tricks—sour cream and fresh-cooked mushrooms instead of a can of mushroom soup, with green *and* yellow beans. And the mashed potatoes turned out surprisingly like home—Grams had taught him to leave in some diced peeling and add at least a stick of butter.

He didn't even attempt Todd's pumpkin pie, though. That had been art. Somehow his friend had added a clear layer over the top, like a glaze. Then, right when it was time to serve, Todd had taken a large serving spoon and wacked it right it the middle, causing it to look like a shattered frozen pond. Beautiful. It had been a candy recipe, apparently, one that involved lots of Karo syrup, candy thermometers, watching it all boil, and never looking away for one second because the temperature was critical and… way more than Austin was going to try. So store-bought was the solution, with a pecan pie as well.

"Too much for two people, but both will hold over quite well in the refrigerator," Uncle Bodie had said while they shopped. "It'll be an excuse to get Guy down here later, don't you think?"

Austin hadn't said anything.

"Did I tell you?" Uncle Bodie said when Austin brought the pies to the table. "Guy is going to make your birthday party."

"Really?" Austin asked, cutting a large piece of the pumpkin pie. "What about his play?"

"He'll be getting out of there about the same time we're starting," his uncle explained.

Austin placed his pie on a plate and sat back down. A smile slowly spread across his face. What a nice birthday present. He took a bite of pie. Delicious.

"I take it the idea pleases you?"

He felt a heat spread across his cheeks. He nodded. "It'll be nice."

"I was hoping you'd feel that way."

"Why wouldn't I?" Austin stomach gave a pleasant flutter.

"Well, good. I wasn't sure how you were feeling lately. I wasn't sure how things stand with you two."

"I'm not sure either. But I guess I'll find out Saturday."

"Good. Excellent. And if all goes well, I have another idea."

"What's that?" Austin forked up another bite of pie.

"I think we should invite Guy to Buckman with us."

Austin froze, the piece of pie halfway to his mouth. "Huh?"

"The poor boy has no one. His family has rejected him. He shouldn't spend Christmas alone."

"But...." The idea simply stunned Austin. "I just figured...."

"You just figured what?" Uncle Bodie scooped out another spoonful of stuffing from its casserole dish, dessert apparently not on his agenda yet.

"Well," Austin managed. "I, ah.... He didn't want to have Thanksgiving with us, so I just figured he wouldn't want—"

"That's because he and a bunch of his actor friends who couldn't go home because they're in that play are eating together. As director, he felt he needed to lead it with his boss. I forget her name...."

"Jennifer," Austin supplied, and felt a wave of... something. He wasn't sure what. Jennifer Leavitt was the woman who had heard he was all that and a box of crackers, and then he'd made a fool of himself in front of a roomful of people by running away.

"Lesbian? Very sweet woman? Single too, I think...."

"You sure do know a lot, don't you?" Austin asked, barely stifling a barb in the process. Why did his uncle insist on bringing up things he didn't want to talk about?

"I do, don't I? Now about taking that boy to Buckman. Good idea? I think it is."

"I-I... I mean, do you think he would even want to go?" Austin wondered aloud.

"I don't know. I know it would be sad for him to wake up on Christmas morning all alone—and to maybe spend the day alone as well. Wouldn't that suck a big glass of Tang?"

Austin swallowed hard. "Yeah. It would." It would suck bad. So why did he feel like he was about to break out into a sweat? Take Guy home to Buckman? What would that be like? Spending real time with him? Hours and hours on end, several days in a row. Austin felt a shiver. It reminded him of the day Guy had let him use his coat. Austin's heart started beating faster. To spend real time with Guy would be nice. To really get to know him, even better.

"Okay," he said. "Why not?"

"Why not indeed?" Uncle Bodie asked.

IT WAS with great excitement that Austin passed over his next big threshold—and that was his entrance of The Male Box, his first gay bar.

His first thought?

Are all these guys gay?

Guy saw the look on his face and, as if reading his mind, said, "Honey, you ain't seen nothin' yet. The gays don't even show up until at least ten, and that's only because they want to get good seats for the show."

But Austin's thoughts remained the same. Ahead of him and slightly to the right was the main bar, which stretched the length of the room. It was a good thirty feet long, and almost every stool was occupied. To the right was at least one pool table—it was hard to see from where he was standing—and three men were gathered around it. Immediately in front of him were several round tables, tall enough to need barstools as well, and patrons claimed half of those. To Austin's left was a set of stairs leading to where he did not know, but four or five guys were heading up them.

It was quite a few men, and.... *Are all these guys gay?* Austin's heart started beating even faster. *Are they?*

Farther to Austin's left was a slight drop and the stage area. It was there that Guy and a handful of others guided him. Rows of chairs and small tables had been set up, and as they approached, Austin saw three of the tables had been ribboned off with "Reserved" signs. Several helium balloons rose above each table, held in place by brightly decorated weights.

And how many chairs have been reserved? Austin wondered. Was that nine? Ten? People Guy had invited, apparently. Which was nice since Austin really didn't know many people in Kansas City yet, especially those who would want to go to a gay bar. Most of his acquaintances at that point were the senior residents of his apartment building.

"Which one of you is the birthday boy?"

They turned around, and Austin's mouth fell open. Standing before them was a young man—one who didn't look old enough to be in the bar—wearing little more than a black leather vest, jock, and matching army boots. He was very thin, but with a respectable little set of pecs, and was smooth as smooth could be. He didn't even seem to have hair on his legs. He did, however, have long dark hair touching his shoulders, and a very pretty face. Pretty as a girl.

"This is the one you're looking for," Guy said, stepping behind Austin, resting his big hands on his shoulders and giving them a squeeze. Austin shivered.

"You cold?" Guy whispered in his ear, so close he could feel the heat of the man's breath.

Definitely not cold. "I'm fine," Austin managed. He gulped. Between the nearly naked young man with the surprising bulge in his leather jock and Guy so close behind him, breathing against his neck, a stirring had begun in Austin's jeans.

"Well, Happy B-day," the youth said and leaned in and gave Austin a kiss that somehow managed to be chaste and sexy at the same time. "The management of The Male Box has asked me to say that we all hope you have the best birthday ever."

"Th-thank you," Austin stammered, feeling his cock shift even more.

"And..."

Just then another man appeared, dressed—or undressed—like the youth. This one was much more muscular, though, with a thick, hairy chest. He was carrying two buckets filled with ice and a bottle of Champagne apiece, one in each hand like dumbbells, biceps popping deliciously. Austin's eyes went wide at the sight and his crotch stirred even more. This new waiter—after putting the buckets down—pulled him close, clutched his ass roughly, and licked his cheek. "Happy fucking birthday," he said, and then turned and sauntered off. Austin could only stare at his retreating hairy butt.

"Happy birthday, Austin," said Uncle Bodie.

"Huh? Wha?" Austin asked as that muscular ass disappeared in the crowd.

"I said, 'happy birthday.'" His uncle laughed.

A little zing went through Austin, one he'd been getting all day. *Twenty-one.* He was twenty-one! Legal. Now, at least, he could do whatever he wanted. He'd never understood why he was old enough to die for his country at eighteen, but not allowed to drink for it. It seemed wrong somehow.

"Thanks, Uncle Bodie." He threw his arms around his uncle. He'd done that a lot today. "I love you." He stood back, then pointed at the Champagne. "Did you do all this?"

"Don't look at me. Guy did most of the organizing."

He looked over at Guy. "Thanks." He hesitated a moment, then gave the man a hug. And yes—*Zam!*—he felt that rush go through him again. *Why can't you be Todd?* he thought for the hundredth time.

"No problem. It was fun. But I didn't do the bubbly."

"You didn't?" Austin asked. "Then who did?"

He pulled a card off one of the bottles and looked down at the lovely script. "For Austin," it said.

"Go on," said Uncle Bodie. "Open it."

Austin waited a moment longer, and then tore it open in a rush. "Gosh," he said. "Happy Birthday—sorry I couldn't make it—hope your day is an adventure—Peter Wagner." He looked up, astonished.

"Peter really is sorry he couldn't be here," his uncle said. "He's in Germany. I should have given him more warning we were doing this; he probably would have made it. Sorry, son."

"No," said Austin. "It's okay, Uncle Bodie. I just can't believe he did this."

"Do you want these bottles opened?" asked the younger waiter, who was still standing there.

"Let's wait just a tad," suggested Guy. "A few more people are going to join us. Is that okay with you, Austin?"

"S-sure."

They sat and Guy ordered a round of drinks. "What'll you have?" he asked Austin.

Austin shrugged. "I don't know. They probably don't have that hoppy IPA stuff, right?"

"Nah, it's a specialty beer. And I sure don't want you to drink the Box's house specialty—Pabst."

The waiter shuddered. "God, no!"

"What are you having, then?" Austin asked.

"I'm a Cuban-Lesbian fan myself."

"Excuse me?" Austin was confused.

"A Cuba Libre," the waiter said. "Rum and Coke with lime."

"Oh, I love lime," said Austin. "That sounds good. Extra lime, please."

"I'll just have some white wine," Uncle Bodie said.

"Okay, then, I'll be right back in a shake." He turned, shook his impossibly round bare ass, and winked over his shoulder.

"Oh my God," Austin exclaimed as he sat down. This was what gay was?

"This is all a *part* of being gay," Guy said, once more seeming to read his mind.

How does he do that?

He looked around him. A few men and women were sitting at a nearby table. *Are they gay?* he wondered. He was sure the young waiter was. So pretty. Not really his type, but….

Like that, the waiter was back with a tray and their drinks. He placed them on the table, and Guy asked if he could start a tab.

"If you leave your credit card," the boy-man said. Boy? Man? If it weren't for the bit of pecs, and what may or may not be a fairly big dick in that jock, he could be a girl, Austin thought. He was that pretty.

Guy dug it out of his back pocket and handed it over.

"Hey, you can't do that!" Austin said. "I've got money."

"And it's your birthday," Guy replied. "Tonight, you don't pay."

"I'll take this to the bar," boy-man said and strode off, wagging his ass once again.

"Damn." Austin couldn't help but stare. He'd never seen men stroll around like that outside a locker room.

"I'd tap that," Guy said, laughing.

"As would I, in another time and place," Uncle Bodie said appreciatively.

"He's a little pretty for my taste," Austin replied.

"You wouldn't kick him out of bed for eating crackers, would you?" his uncle asked.

Austin blushed and they all laughed. "I guess I like my men a little more… hairy." And he blushed all the more.

"Listen to you," growled Guy. "So you liked Mr. Muscles?"

Now his face was positively flaming. "I guess. But someone in between the two of them would be best." *Like you*, he thought, looking into Guy's handsome face.

Todd! Remember Todd!

"LOOK," said Uncle Bodie. "Why don't we drink a toast to Austin."

"Sounds good," Guy said.

Austin smiled shyly.

"To Austin's twenty-first birthday. As Peter said so wisely, may it be an adventure."

"Hear, hear!" Guy raised his glass, and Bodie and Austin clinked theirs against his and drank.

"Whoa!" Austin's eyes nearly popped out of their sockets. "Did they put *any* Coke in this glass?"

"Very little," said Guy. "These bartenders depend on tips. You even give a dollar and you know all the ones you have after that will be killer."

"Plus, I imagine they know you well here," said Uncle Bodie.

"Not *that* well, my friend," Guy protested.

"You spend too much time in places like this."

"You make it sound like I'm an alcoholic."

"I never meant to imply that at all," said Uncle Bodie. "Only that you could come home a *little* more often in the evening. We've missed you. Of course, my bedtime is nine anyway. But Austin doesn't know many people in our fair city and could use a little company now and again. The poor boy is alone almost all the time."

"Oh." *Is that an uncomfortable look on Guy's face?* Austin wondered. He hoped not. *Change the subject*, he thought. Tonight was supposed to be fun. "I'm not alone," Austin told his uncle. "I have you and Lucille and a building full of tenants."

"People four times your age are hardly the company you need, my boy." Uncle Bodie took a drink of his wine. "And speaking of being alone, what are you doing for Christmas, Guy?"

He shrugged. "Nothing really. Probably hang out in the evening with a few friends. Here probably. It's packed here on Christmas evening. All the fags who've had to spend 'quality' time with their family all day. Macho bullshitting with dads and uncles and cousins. Being asked when they're going to get married by moms and aunts and more cousins...."

"See what I mean, Austin? He's going to be alone all day. And then spend the evening with drunken fools. And you, Guy. Telling me you don't spend too much time here."

"Well, Bodie. I'm playing the cards I was dealt, you know?"

Austin cleared his throat. *Good time! We are supposed to be having a good time.*

"Well, what if I dealt you a different hand?" Uncle Bodie asked.

God. Uncle Bodie is going to do it. Crap! He felt his stomach knot up. What would Guy say?

"Austin and I are going to go home to Buckman for a few days for Christmas. We wondered if you would go with us."

The question obviously startled Guy. "What?"

"We'd have to take your car, of course. There isn't room for the four of us in Austin's pickup. But we could get away for a few days. And you could relax and have a real Christmas for once."

"I-I... I don't know what to say. This is such a surprise."

Guy at a loss for words? Austin thought. *Will miracles never cease?*

But before he could answer, some of the first guests arrived. It was the triad he'd met at Guy's little get-together weeks ago. Thank God they introduced themselves, because there was no way he remembered all the names of the people he'd met that night, even if they were as unusual as a "throuple."

Tony, the big, bearded member of the little group, went to get drinks.

"That's Tony for you," said Mark, a handsome man just starting to go salt-and-pepper. "Too impatient to stick around long enough for a waiter."

"While Mark will wait until the end of the universe to be served," said Grant. He was the one who'd said he was the newest member of their little family, Austin remembered.

"Damn right," Mark said with a wink.

Austin put on a grin and tried to talk. He wanted to meet people, but coming from a town where he knew nearly everyone, he didn't really know how to go about it. He found he was as nervous as hell.

Tony came back with three small pitchers of beer, and Austin couldn't help but goggle.

"It's really only about two, two-and-a-half glasses worth a pitcher," Grant explained. "It's cheaper, and you don't have order as many times."

"Oh," said Austin. That made sense.

"We make you uncomfortable, don't we," Grant said quietly, leaning in.

Austin shrugged. "A little, maybe."

"I understand. Believe me. I never expected to be with *one* man, let alone two. But I fell for both of them. Hard, Austin. I fell in love with them, *as* a unit. And miracles of miracles, they fell for me too. And got me out of a bad situation."

"What kind of situa—sorry. None of my business," Austin apologized.

"It's okay. It's not like you couldn't read about it if you wanted."

"How in the world would I do that?"

"A friend of ours. Jude. He's a writer. He used to live in Chicago, and once when the three of us were vacationing there, we met him and were talking and he asked if he could tell our story. It was pretty cool."

"He wrote your story?"

Grant nodded. "And then it was a surprise when he moved into our neck of the woods. We were all amazed when we bumped into each other here one night. I think he'd forgotten we live so close."

"Where are you from?" Austin asked.

"Terra's Gate. It's a college town about forty-five minutes west of here. Anyway, I was married to a woman for twenty years."

"A woman? Twenty years?"

"I was fighting it. Being gay. Did a damned good job of it until they moved in next door."

Austin nodded but didn't fully understand. Twenty years? One hour with Joan—no, five minutes, and he'd known he was gay for sure. He could never have married. And certainly not for twenty years. He looked at the man, tried to imagine him married. And funny—just like that—the triad/throuple thing was okay. Not because there was anything wrong with a man being married to a woman. But not *this* man. *This* man *needed* to be gay. And if it took a couple to bring him out of himself, so be it, and he was happy for the three of them.

It still made him curious how it all worked, though.

"Speaking of Jude," cried Grant.

Just then Jude, the cute bearish guy who had been with the pseudo drag queen at Guy's party, walked up and pulled up a chair. "Hey, everybody. Hey, Austin. Happy birthday."

"Thanks," he said and felt the zing again. *I'm twenty-one! I'm actually twenty-one at last.* "Where is your boyfriend?" *Boyfriend.* He was asking a man about his *boy*friend. Jeez, was there anything more thrilling? He would never get tired of asking a man about his boyfriend. Never.

"Tommy's backstage, silly boy," Jude answered.

"Duh!" Austin rolled his eyes and felt silly indeed. Of course. Pseudo drag queen. Drag show.

Then Jude cringed. "I mean, Dixie. Please don't tell him I said 'Tommy'! They take this very seriously."

"I won't," Austin promised.

"And the show's about to start. Five minutes."

EVERYONE was getting their second round of drinks when two things happened. The first was that Jennifer Leavitt arrived.

Oh no! Austin closed his eyes, willing her to be an illusion. *Guy! How could you? I humiliated myself in front of this woman.*

But no, when he opened his eyes, she was still there. She had on an even wilder pair of glasses and rings on almost every finger. *Why not? She's an artist, isn't she?*

"Hey there, Austin. Happy birthday. It's good to see you again."

"It is?" Austin said, feeling mortified.

She reached out and ruffled his hair.

"Ms. Leavitt. I am so sorry about my audition."

She looked at him as if someone had goosed her. "But why?"

"I made such an ass of myself...."

She shook her head with great fanfare. "No, you didn't. You found out a part was not for you. Guy had made a mistake. I admit you are pretty enough for the role—"

Pretty? Pretty?

"—but if you couldn't identify with the character, then you were smart to leave. Yes, I would tell you to walk away next time instead of running—"

Austin thought he would die.

"—but you did the right thing. And even just the little part you did read showed me you can act."

Austin fell back in surprise. "It did? I can?"

"Oh yes. And I insist you audition for us in the future. Promise me, all right?"

"I-I...."

"Promise!" She pointed a finger with great authority right in his direction.

"I-I...." He smiled. Grinned. Wow! And instantly felt a weight lift from his shoulders. "I promise."

"And you were worried," Guy whispered in his ear.

He turned to his friend, and was immediately lost in his eyes. He found himself wondering what it would be like to kiss those eyes, kiss that mouth, when sudden loud music blasted out over them from hidden speakers.

"And now, ladies and gentlemen, it's time for the Liddle Awful Annie Show!"

The crowd went wild. Apparently this was something pretty awesome, thought Austin.

Then that famous ballad, "Tomorrow," from the Broadway musical *Annie,* bombarded them at even higher decibels. "Starring—Liddle—Awful—Annie!"

More cheers.

"Also starring Dixie Wrecked, Gena Talia, Dharma Greggs, and Billy the Bear!"

By now the whooping and hollering was drowning out even the music, and that was saying something. "And now that filthy filly, that sleazy slut, that temptuous tramp, Liddle—Awful—*Annie!*"

And like a tornado, she appeared. For a moment Austin assumed she was a drag queen, a "he." But that thought didn't last long. Annie was every single inch a woman—and her extraordinary cleavage was just part of it.

"The queers will throw up, tomorrow!" she belted in a spoof of the lyrics to the famous song, her voice powerful and crazy. "'Cause they drank themselves silly at the bars! All night looooong. Just dreamin' about… cock-sucking… got them horned up, oh so bad, they drank like fools!"

It was the "Tomorrow" song—and it *wasn't*. Like she was Little Orphan Annie, and she was most assuredly wasn't. Sure, she had red curly hair, but it was huge and bouncy, reminding Austin of a Halloween afro wig a friend in school had worn one year when pretending to be a hippy with his girlfriend. It was simply gigantic. She had a red dress with a white collar—but said dress also included a corset, which took her already ample breasts and thrust them up and out in a straight man's—or lesbian's?—fantasy. She had even painted her eyelids white, so that when she closed them, it gave her the creepy blank stare of the famous newspaper strip. But this *wasn't* Little Orphan Annie, oh no. This was Liddle—Awful—Annie! And Austin saw right away what all the fuss was about. She was awesome.

"The queers are all out, tonight and, bet their bottoms need fucked well, all night!"

By then Austin was laughing until tears were running down his face. He shouted with the audience and knew something else magical had happened. It was more than looking around a room and wondering,

Are all these guys gay? It was more than knowing that, yes, all these men—or most of them—were gay. In the cheering, he knew without a doubt he was a part of something bigger than himself. And he truly was not alone. He never would be again. By that point, he didn't know if his tears were from laughter—or from joy.

Annie's song came to an end, and she bowed to more applause. Austin clapped until his hands hurt. He was having that much fun. His worries, at least for now, were forgotten.

"Hello, everybody!" she shouted jubilantly into her mic.

"Hello!" screamed the crowd.

"Are we ready to par-*tay* tonight?"

The audience let her know they were.

"I can answer that myself just by asking you this: Does a fish have a watertight asshole?"

Of course, everyone let her know that fish do indeed have watertight assholes. They screamed it from the rafters in fact.

Annie stood up proudly, thrust her tits out, and said, "Well, we have one fuck-a-doodle of a *great* show tonight. You aren't going to know whether to shit or wind your wristwatch by the time we're done. And you know what else? We have a very special birthday tonight! We have us a new gay! And what could be better than that?"

"Oh crap," cried Austin and looked all around him. If he only lowered himself in his chair, maybe the audience wouldn't know which person in their group she was referring to. That hope vanished very quickly.

"Mike? Alyn? Go get our birthday homo and bring him up here on stage!"

"Crap," he exclaimed again. By then it was too late, and Annie's sexy cohorts were on him, dragging him up on the stage to the approval of the packed room.

But while that was happening, Liddle Awful Annie came down into the audience. "Hey, Guy. How's my favorite director?" she asked into her mic.

"I'm good," he answered when she thrust said mic into his face.

"These Sham-pag-nee bootles aren't open yet—how's a why?"

Mic back in his face. "We were still waiting for a couple people."

"I assume they're fags?" she asked.

Mic in his face again. "Indeed."

"What?"

"Yes, they are."

"And you didn't know they would be late?"

The audience laughed.

Austin watched all this from the stage, wondering what the hell was going to happen next.

"Hey, Grandpa," she said to Uncle Bodie. "Aren't you cute?"

"Not nearly as cute as you," Uncle Bodie replied for all to hear.

Annie smiled. "You are a sweetheart. May I ask you a question?"

"You may," he replied.

"Are you here because you support your friends, or because you are a homo-so-sexual?"

"Baby girl… I am as gay as a Catholic priest."

"Hurray," she cried, and many hoorays followed.

"Are you family or friend?" she asked.

"I am both. At least I like to think so."

Annie turned back to the crowd. "This is awesome!"

She turned back to the three tables, still with a few empty seats. "Mind if I take one of these here Sham-pag-nee bootles? I mean, considering some of the birthday boy's guests are late. I will make it fun."

"My lady," Uncle Bodie replied. "I would not dare tell you what you can or cannot do during your own show. But please do take note that Champagne is *not* Andre."

Annie pulled one of the bottles from the bucket and read it carefully. "Oh my. This isn't the cheap shit, is it?" She spun back on the group. "I still promise it will be a birthday he will never forget, *bien*?"

Uncle Bodie nodded. "Then be my guest," he said. "In honor of once-in-a-lifetime birthdays," he said with a nod.

Austin stood transfixed, watching what was going on below. How the hell was this happening? How did they know it was his birthday? Well, the reservations must have clued them in a bit, he realized. And the leather boys did ask whose birthday it was.

I am screwed!

Annie sauntered up to the stage, bottle in hand. "Austin," she said. "I want to ask you something."

Austin gulped. "Yes?" he replied.

"Out of my two boys here—" She pointed at the young one. "—Alyn—" Then she pointed at the bigger of the two. "—or Mike. Which one flicks your Bic?"

The crowd began to chant, some of them saying one name, some of them saying the other. Both men began to hump against Austin, running their hands up and down his body, thank God avoiding his crotch. *Please don't let them touch my dick!*

Annie stuck the mic in his face. He looked down at his friends once more, saw them all grinning and chanting with the audience. "I guess Mike," he gasped.

There was much applause.

"Okay, then, Mike. *You* do the honors, all right?"

Mike gave Austin a lascivious grin, snatched the bottle from Annie's hand, and stepped deep into the birthday boy's personal space.

Crap, thought Austin. Muscles on muscles. He'd never been into that more-than-military buzz cut, but it worked on Mike. The man was a shadow away from being bald, but God, it was hot. He began to make a great production with the Champagne bottle. He rubbed it against his bare chest, licked it like he was about to give it a blowjob, and finally popped the cork so it flew across the room. Then quick as a flash, he pointed it at his own chest, and when the Champagne foamed out, his muscles were instantly covered in bubbles. The crowd went insane. Then he grabbed Austin, and shoved his face between his pecs.

Oh, what the crap, Austin thought, and to the bar's approval, he began sucking and licking the expensive wine off the man's body. It was a mess. By the time he was done, or that Mike was done with him, *he,* too, was a mess. But when they finally let him go back to his seat, he knew it was a night he would never forget.

THE evening turned into a series of montages in Austin's mind after that. The alcohol flowed pretty freely, after all, and the drinks were strong and everyone was buying.

The show was a blast. Tommy Smith, aka Dixie Wrecked, came out and did several numbers that had Austin nearly falling out of his seat, they were so crazy. What really impressed him was that Tommy/Dixie sang instead of lip-syncing, including his version of "Supercalifragilisticexpialidocious." Instead of the Mary Poppins classic song, Dixie came out on stage whirling a long double-headed dildo over his head like a baton and singing….

"Because I was a pervert back when I was just a lad
My father gave my butt a spank, and told me I was bad
But then one day, I bought a toy to soothe my aching hole
The biggest toy you've ever owned that you can even blow!
Super-phallic-realistic-double-ended-dildo,
Even though the sound of it will give you such a thrill-oh!
If you use it long enough, you might come on your pill-oh!
Super-phallic-realistic-double-ended-dildo!"

The song brought the house down.

Guy got rather possessive. Mike the waiter and backup dancer tried to move in on Austin again, but Guy wasn't having it. He scooted his chair right up next to Austin's, put his arm around his shoulders, and glared at the man. Austin couldn't believe it. Part of him wanted to say, "Hey, whose birthday is this, anyway?" Having a hairy muscle man flirt with him was pretty hot. But the other part kind of liked Guy's surprising possessiveness. And so he snuggled closer and pretended. Why not? It felt nice.

More people showed up to fill the empty seats they'd reserved—including Grady, the big man Austin had met dressed up as Truvy Jones the day he'd seen *Steel Magnolias*. The rest were mostly people Austin didn't know, but that was okay. Grant went to the car and brought back a gift, which turned out to be a sexy pair of underwear. "Now make sure we get to see you in it," Tony said, and Grant elbowed him hard. More laughter.

Jennifer gave him four passes to the Pegasus, which pleased Austin immensely. She leaned in and whispered, "Use at least one of them to see this show of Guy's," and winked at him.

Jude and Dixie gave him a fifty-dollar bar tab, which stunned him. "You can't do this," he protested. "We hardly know each other!" But they assured him the bar manager had put in half, and that made him feel a little better.

And Guy got him a T-shirt with a rainbow-bar logo and words that decreed: "Sorry Girls, I'm Gay." Austin's eyes went wide in surprise.

"Hope you don't mind," Guy said. "I wanted you to have your first gay shirt. I know you might not be ready to wear it down Main Street, but you'll have something for Gay Pride at least."

"Gay Pride?" Austin asked, a tad nervously.

"Of course," Guy said. "You're going next year, right?"

Austin thought about it for a minute, and then let the Cuba Libre do the thinking for him. "Sure," he said. "Why not?" and got a little cheer from his guests.

"I got you something else," Guy said.

"You didn't have to do that!"

Then Guy pulled out a colorful envelope from his jacket. "Here," he said.

"What's this?" Austin asked, surprised.

"Open it," Guy said.

And so he did. It was an autographed copy of the playbill for *Steel Magnolias*. "Oh, wow," he said.

"Everyone was thrilled to sign it," he said, "although I had to track them all down."

"Look," Austin said, holding it up for all to see. "This was the first play I saw in Kansas City. And Guy directed it."

Everyone agreed it was a pretty cool gift.

"It's very nice." He went to Guy and hugged him. "Thank you. Thank you so much."

WHEN the show was over, everyone went upstairs, and he discovered where that staircase led. There was a fairly large area for dancing with huge video screens on two walls, and the music was loud and the choices perfect for a fun time. Guy dragged him out onto the floor, where Austin found himself dancing with another man for the first time. Sure, it was disco dancing, but he *was* dancing with a man. And not the high school jock version either.

It was a song Austin knew, thank God. Ke$ha's "Die Young," and Austin found himself lost in the irony of lyrics about how it was a shame he was here with someone else instead of the one he loved. He wasn't—not physically. Boy, Todd was always there in his head, along with that fantasy of holding out.

But there was Guy and those lyrics telling him he should make the most of the night. Guy was dancing sexy, giving him deep smoldering looks, and dammit... the man was doing it again. Making his heart slam in his chest. Austin felt himself begin to sweat, felt that shifting in the crotch of his jeans. Would Guy notice?

Guy noticed.

And now I am crapping blushing again!

Then, to Austin's surprise, the music took a very abrupt change in tempo and speed. It was a slow song, and while half the dancers left the floor, the rest fell together as couples. Austin froze, looked around him. Now it really *was* men dancing together. He couldn't believe what he was seeing, and he was caught up in a whirl of emotions. What amazed him the most was how beautiful the same-sex couples looked—like it was the most natural thing in the world.

Yet, wasn't it?

He looked back at Guy, who stood there looking deep into his eyes, arms held out in offering. Austin panicked for a minute and glanced to where his uncle had been standing a few moments before. Uncle Bodie was there—and he was nodding. "Yes," he mouthed. He nodded again.

Austin turned back to Guy, and before he knew what he was doing, he stepped into the man's arms.

Guy pulled him close and then began to rock in an easy slow circle, knowing somehow that Austin had no idea how to slow dance. With one hand, Guy drew Austin's head against his chest, and he marveled at the muscles he felt. The eternal baggy clothes weren't hiding a body he should be ashamed of. It was all corded steel, covered in sweet human flesh. He could smell Guy as well. He'd chosen the tiniest bit of cologne, so it accentuated instead of hiding the man's natural manly scent. Austin shivered, marveling how it felt to be held by another man, happy tears threatening again.

"I know you aren't cold now," Guy whispered, and the warmth of his breath tickled Austin's ear in the most delightful ways.

Austin pulled back just enough to look into Guy's beautiful dark eyes. He overheard a line in the lyrics—something about somebody being so beautiful, and how the singer couldn't believe his eyes. He knew the feeling, because wasn't Guy beautiful? He'd thought it funny Guy used that word to describe him, but now he saw how clearly it applied to Guy. Handsome and sexy, yes. And beautiful. His heart began to pound. Surely, Guy could feel it? Feel it through his chest and their clothes. Surely, Guy could feel the hard length of Austin's cock pressed against him? Austin shivered again.

"Not cold," he said, realizing the man in his arms was hard as well.

Kiss me, he tried to say with his eyes. *Do it. Please. Kiss me. Kiss me in front of all these people. There'll never be another moment like this.*

Guy did. Austin felt a tremor run through him as those lips touched his, so lightly at first, as if waiting to see how he would react.

Austin did not pull away. He closed his eyes and pushed his mouth against Guy's, and then Guy was pressing back, his opening only the tiniest bit—his tongue touching Austin's lips, softly at first, then demandingly. *Oh God!* thought Austin as he opened his mouth to Guy, gave that questing tongue entrance. He let Guy show him because he really had no idea what to do. Austin experimented with running his tongue against Guy's, and he trembled again, and Guy moaned into his mouth. *This is what it is supposed to be like*, he thought. *This is it.* The most natural thing in the world. *And if he asks me back to his apartment, I'll go....*

LOUD music took over again, and they parted. Austin was given yet another drink, and his head was buzzing and the world swimming. He remembered Uncle Bodie hugging him and leaving—taking a taxi, he said, and Austin offered to go with him, and the old man laughed and told him it wasn't anywhere near time for him to end his adventure.

Somehow, he found himself with several of his new friends in the leather shop and being encouraged to try on a black vest. He consented and started to slip into it, but Tony was having no part of it.

"Without that shirt," the bear of a man said. "That's how you'll know if it's right." He reached for Austin's buttons, and then Guy was there, batting the hands away, pushing the man aside.

Guy unbuttoned the top button, his eyes looking into Austin's. He stopped. "Do you mind?"

Austin swallowed hard and shook his head. He didn't trust himself to speak. He trembled again as Guy slowly undid each button, then gently pulled the shirt out of his jeans, letting it fall open and exposing his chest.

"Dear God," Guy said. "Austin. You're so beautiful."

That word again. Beautiful. Austin couldn't believe the words. Skinny. That's what he was. He'd worked out for hundreds of hours with his weights, and the best he could say was that his chest was bigger than the little man-boy's from downstairs. Skinny except for a bit of gut, and he covered it, suddenly self-conscious.

Guy pushed the hands away. "You're beautiful, Austin."

"Frigging hot is what he is!" Tony growled.

"Tony, I feel like dancing," said Grant. "What do you say, Mark? Shouldn't we all three dance?"

"You're right, Grant. We should," Mark said, and they dragged their lover away.

Then Guy was slowly pushing Austin's shirt back off his shoulders, his fingers touching bare skin, and Austin thought he might cum in his pants. Gooseflesh broke out over his back and down his arms as Guy stepped behind him and helped him into the leather vest. Guy gently guided him over in front of a mirror, and Austin gasped.

Sexy. I look sexy.

"I'm buying this for you, Austin. You have to have it."

Austin started to protest, but Guy wouldn't hear it.

"But I do want you to put your shirt back on," he said. "Otherwise they're going to be all over you when we get back out there."

"Over me?"

"Yes," said the man behind the register. "If you weren't so obviously with this guy, I'd be breaking all kinds of rules about not touching the customers."

Austin ducked his head, embarrassed. He couldn't believe it. People were making such a big deal about him. At first he'd chalked it up to it being his birthday. Tony had been flirting, but his lovers were keeping him on a leash. And now this shopkeeper? It seemed impossible.

Guy helped him back into his shirt, even buttoning it for him. Was it an accident when those fingers grazed his nipples? They tightened into hard knots instantly, and more goose bumps rippled over Austin. He tucked his shirt in by himself and then shrugged back into the vest. A quick look in the mirror showed it looked good either way, but now he saw the appeal of the bare flesh and wondered how Guy would look dressed the same way.

So they danced some more, and Austin let his buzz and his youthful energy pull him through one song after another, with new dance partners among his friends taking over when the last one stepped away. It all became a blur of pounding music and flashing images and bodies. He let himself get lost in it—the wondrous power of it all. Lady Gaga's "The Edge of Glory" slipped into the Scissor Sisters singing "Let's Have a Kiki," which made way for Gossip's "Move in the Right Direction." It was like Rihanna and Carly Rae Jepsen and Swedish House Mafia were serenading him and him alone.

He felt infinite.

FINALLY, they all decided to go out for breakfast and wound up in a place called Chubby's, which looked very fifties but didn't have the fifties prices. But there was no worry—even though Austin could afford it, no one was letting him pay. He couldn't decide what he wanted—pancakes or biscuits and gravy or eggs and sausage and hash browns—so his new friends ordered him the latter and then shared their meals as well. He got at least a taste of everything he'd wanted.

What's more, Guy held his hand under the table, and it was all he could do not to giggle. This was what it felt like to those kids in high school when they went on dates at the local soda shop. This was what he'd been missing. The hand felt so good in his. So strong. A man's hand. Austin wanted to shout out his bliss, and he left feeling stuffed and as content and fulfilled as could be.

When he and Guy finally got home, his stomach turned into a clenched fist. What would happen now? Would Guy simply walk him to his door? Or invite him upstairs?

I'm drunk, he thought. *Good. Invite me upstairs. Please. Do it. Do it!*

"Did you want to go to bed?" Guy asked him as they let themselves in through the two sets of doors and into the building proper.

Your bed, he wanted to say. There was no way he had the courage, even with all the rum and Cokes. Maybe the huge breakfast had sobered him up more than he realized.

"You're probably tired, huh?"

Austin shrugged. "I don't know," he said. It was the best he could do.

"Or you could come up…," Guy offered, almost shyly.

Austin nodded. "Sure. I'll come up," he said and could barely hear himself answer because his heart was slamming in his chest so hard.

Guy smiled, and it only made Austin's heart beat all the harder. Guy's smile was simply gorgeous. He followed Guy up the stairs, watching the muscles of his round ass flex through his jeans, and he wondered if he would see it naked before the night was over.

"Beer?" Guy asked as he let them into his apartment and flicked on the stand-up lamp just inside the door.

"Do you have any of that—"

"Double-Wide I.P.A.?" He nodded, winked. "Of course I do. Sure you're not too drunk already?"

"Breakfast is taking my buzz," Austin said.

"Well, we can't have that, can we? Sit down." Guy waved at the couch.

Austin sat as Guy left the room and then came back with a beer and a Pepsi.

"You're not drinking?" Austin asked.

Guy gave a half shrug. "I want to maintain my senses."

"Oh?" Austin wagged his brows in a way he hoped was sexy and took a big gulp of beer, desperate to retrieve that warm, floaty feeling.

"Yes, indeed. Because I am fighting jumping your bones this very minute."

Austin's mouth went dry, and oh-oh-oh, that warm, floaty feeling was back. *What do I say? I have no idea how to do this.* He relaxed back into the cushions, let his legs fall open, rested his arms across the back of the couch—hoping all these gestures were enough to say what was on his mind. *Do it. Jump my bones.*

"Goddamn, Austin…."

Guy was staring into Austin's lap, and when Austin looked down, he realized he had an erection. He looked up nervously.

Time seemed to stand still.

Finally Guy spoke up. "Austin... I.... Jeez...." He looked away, took several steps, crossed his arms in front of him. "Maybe you should go home."

Austin was shocked. "What? But...." His tongue seemed to stick, stopped working. He didn't know what Guy would say, but he hadn't expected this! "G-Guy...?"

"Oh, Austin...."

"I-I don't understand...."

Guy turned back around, and the look on his face surprised Austin even more. He looked... afraid? Upset? Austin wasn't sure how to read him.

"Austin... you're drunk."

Austin sat up, his hands shaking. "I'm *not* drunk," he cried.

Guy shook his head, gave Austin a disbelieving look.

"Okay... I'm a little drunk." He held up a hand—stop! *"Tipsy.* I'm tipsy."

"And you're a virgin."

Austin sat up straighter. "Not exactly...."

Guy shook his head again, arms still crossed in front of him. "We've covered that."

Austin jumped to his feet. "No, we haven't. You've been totally confusing. All you've been is confusing, goddammit! *You* said I can't *not exactly* be a virgin. *You* said that if orgasms were involved, I've had sex."

Guy's shoulders slumped. "That's not exactly what I meant."

"Then *tell* me what you crapping meant," Austin shouted, not worried if neighbors heard him or not.

Guy took a step closer to him, uncrossed his arms, started to reach out, but then dropped them at his side.

"What I meant *then* was that sex is sex, even if it doesn't involve blowjobs or fucking." The man actually blushed. "I was saying that because I've always argued that you don't have to *fuck* to be having sex.... I mean.... Oh, goddammit."

He started to turn away, but Austin reached out, grabbed his elbow, and turned him back. "*Tell* me, Guy. Please. I don't understand."

Guy sighed. "It's lots of stuff, Austin. I've known guys who swear they aren't gay because they've never sucked cock, even though they've had their cock sucked by a hundred guys. Or that they're virgins because they've never been fucked, even if they've been sucking cock for a thousand years."

Austin took a deep breath. "Well, then, I've sucked cock. So I'm not a virgin."

Guy dropped his head back and groaned. "God, Austin! This is so frigging complicated."

"It's *not* complicated," Austin argued. "Explain."

Guy sighed again. "You're so new, Austin." Were Guy's eyes tearing up? "Still so naïve. Yeah, you've sucked cock—"

"I *swallowed*, Guy," Austin said. "And I liked it."

"But you're still so new to this world. You've never had *mutual* sex with another man. You've never gone to bed with a man. Kissed—"

"We kissed tonight," Austin proclaimed.

"—I mean made out. Rolled around on a bed and sucked face. You've never undressed another man and had him undress you—"

"You half undressed me tonight," Austin said. "And *you* were liking it a lot."

Guy shuddered. "Yes. Yes I did. I liked it a whole lot."

"So what the hell is going on? You want me. Now you're getting all virtuous or something? Chivalrous? The boy is innocent? The boy doesn't know what he wants? I *know* what I want. I want you to take me to bed. I am crapping tired of being a 'virgin.' I want sex with a man who wants me."

"And what the fuck about Todd?" Guy yelled.

Austin fell back. He clenched his jaws and clenched his fists and then took a deep breath. Letting it go, he forced his body to relax. "What about Todd? He isn't here."

"But you want him to be."

Austin shrugged. "I-I don't know. I don't even know if I'll ever find him. I don't know if he wants me, if he's even gay."

"You're confused...."

"You bet I'm confused. You've been flirting with me all night. Knocking people away. You've been crapping cockblocking me. We've danced. Slow danced. You were holding my hand. Kissing me. And now you're saying no?"

"God, you must think I'm some kind of sex fiend," Guy moaned.

"Fuck that," Austin said. "You explain it to me. You were on me. All night. Everyone thinks we're having sex at this very moment. You got me all worked up, and now you're saying no?"

"That's what I mean. You're all worked up. Don't you see? I don't want you doing something you'll regret."

"That'll be my problem, won't it?" Austin countered.

"Are you even thinking this through?" Guy asked. "Or is it your dick thinking? Austin...." He shook his head fiercely. "I know all about letting my dick do my thinking for me. It just about ruined my life. I could have gotten killed letting my dick do my thinking. I could have gotten AIDS, and through some miracle I didn't—"

"So you don't want me? It's just your dick thinking?" Austin shook. Is that what the fucker was saying?

"Oh God. No!" Guy leapt forward and put his hands on Austin's shoulders. "It's not just my dick. *I* want you. I... I...."

"You *what?*" Once again Austin was shouting, not caring who might hear.

"Oh, Austin. I'm really not a sex fiend. Shit." Guy shook his head, pressed his palm against his forehead, then scratched his fingers through his hair. "I guess I forgot I don't have to sleep with someone to be friends with them."

"You've said that before.... What the crap does that mean?" He paused, remembered back to the night of Guy's little party. Did that mean Guy had slept with all of them? Somehow he didn't like the idea. All those men. Too many. It wasn't like Guy was all that old. What had he figured? Twenty-eight? The idea of him being with that many men cheapened Guy somehow. It was something Austin didn't want to picture.

"Now-now-now," cried Guy. He sat down on the couch. "I see where you're going with that. No, I haven't slept with *all* my friends. I'll admit, some of them, but not all...."

Some. Not one. Not two. Some. That made Austin wonder which ones it had been. Had he been with that weird "throuple"? Had a little orgy? Or the gorgeous black man? Guy had hinted he wasn't straight.

"Stop, Austin. And don't ask. I don't kiss and tell." He dropped his head back and let out a long sigh. Then he turned his face toward Austin once again.

"You don't get it. *Aarrrgh.* How do I explain?" Guy jumped up again, put his hands behind his neck, looked at Austin. "Sex can be a great way to start a friendship. It's one of the things I like best about being gay. From what I've seen, it seems to be pretty unique in the gay community."

"Well, great then," Austin said. "We're friends already, aren't we?"

"Hear me out. Fuck, this *is* so confusing!" Guy began to pace. "Austin. I don't want you to be just a name on my list."

Austin sighed. List. List? What the crap was that supposed to mean? How many men had Guy slept with? He looked down at the floor. Well, with all those guys in the bathrooms, who knew. He shook his head. But that was years ago. How many men had Guy actually *slept* with? And then before he knew it, he asked Guy just that.

Guy's eyes widened. "I.... Probably more than you want to know."

Austin looked away. Jeez. What did that mean?

"It just happens, Austin. It's so easy. Men have sex. Straight men might have to work a little harder at it because women are a little harder to get into bed. But make it two horny men in the same apartment?"

"Like us?"

Guy sighed. "Just like us."

"Then why aren't you crapping taking me to bed? Do you want me or not?"

"Oh, Austin. I want you. I admit it. I want you in my bed. You are so beautiful—"

"Beautiful?" Austin shook his head. Why did Guy keep saying that word? Beautiful? Skinny, maybe. Looked like he was ten, maybe. But beautiful? Never....

"—and sweet and funny and smart, and yes, I'm attracted to you. A lot. You really are like some kind of exotic butterfly. That is what I think of when I think of you. Like those glistening blue ones. Or the kind that shimmer green."

"Butterfly?"

Guy shook his head. "You really don't know how fucking gorgeous you are, do you? You frigging take my breath away."

"Guy!" Austin looked down at the floor, deeply self-conscious.

"And you're...." Guy's words petered out. "Never mind." He looked away again.

"What? Tell me," Austin said and hated the almost whining he heard in his voice.

"Austin. I don't want to take the chance that with you, sleeping with you will fuck everything up. One of the things I like about you is the romantic in you. You're in love. You've put on your shining armor, and you've come to the big city to rescue your lover. And you know what? Losing your virginity to the man you love could be the best thing in the world for you." He reached out and cupped Austin's cheek in his hand, then to Austin's surprise, pulled him into his arms. "I'm so sorry. I'm messing up everything."

Austin hesitated a moment and then put his arms around Guy as well. It felt good. This man in his arms. This being held by another man. So different from the way Joan had felt in his arms. It felt right. Like what it was supposed to feel like. Wasn't it what he'd been longing to do forever? "I'm so confused...."

Austin felt Guy take a deep breath, felt his strong chest swell against his own.

"And that's why I'm not taking you to bed."

AUSTIN woke to the gentle sound of his uncle's phonograph. Alone. In his own bed.

Crap. What a night.

He got up, dressed, peed, and went to find his uncle drinking coffee in the kitchen.

"When did you get home?" Uncle Bodie asked, a twinkle in his eyes. "I didn't hear you come in."

"I got in about a half hour after I went to Guy's apartment last night." Austin poured a cup of coffee. "What time is it?"

"Only eleven. You're up much earlier than I expected. Are you okay, son?"

"No, I'm not crapping okay." He sat down across the small kitchen table from his uncle. Lucille whined and jumped up, her forefeet on Austin's knee.

"What happened?" Uncle Bodie asked. "If you don't mind telling me."

"He sent me home. He took me up there for sex, and then he made me leave. He said I needed to wait to find Todd. He said a lot of crap that doesn't make any crapping sense."

Uncle Bodie reached out and laid his hand on Austin's hand but didn't say a word.

"I want to scream. I want to jump up and scream my ass off. I want to cry. I want to break things."

His uncle nodded quietly. "Then do it. Not break things, of course. But do it. Scream. Cry. It's okay."

"It's not okay, Uncle Bodie."

They grew quiet again. Then his uncle said, "I think he was just trying to do the right thing. He's a good man, Austin."

"Fuck him."

Lucille whined again, and Austin absently rubbed her head. Then: "Any calls from the tenants? Anything need done?"

"Just a kitchen sink," his uncle said. "I was going to call a plumber."

Austin shook his head. "I'll do it."

"No. This is your birthday."

"It's the day *after*," Austin said.

"Indeed it is," Uncle Bodie said. "But the rule around here is when your birthday falls on a weekend, you get to call the whole three days your birthday. So no work, okay?"

"I need to do something, Uncle Bodie." It was true. The night before had been way too confusing. "Give me something to do to take my mind off of it, okay?"

"I-I.... It's Guy's sink, Austin."

Austin's shoulders slumped.

"I'll call the plumber."

"No," said Austin. "I'll do it."

Half an hour later, he was knocking on Guy's door. It opened, and Guy's eyes went wide with surprise. "Austin. Your uncle said he was calling a plumber."

Austin nodded. "I know." He held up the awkward wheel of cable that was the plumbing snake. "This will probably only take a minute. Unless you need a new disposal, that'll take longer. Let me in?"

Guy sighed and stood aside. Austin entered and headed back to the kitchen. The apartments on this side of the building were pretty much all the same layout, so he found it easily enough. He quickly set to work. The sink was indeed backed up, and luckily, it wasn't the disposal side. In fifteen minutes, the job was done. Throughout it all, neither of the two men said a word.

"That's it, then," Austin said. "I'll just clean this up and—"

"I'll do that," Guy said.

Austin nodded and headed to the door.

"So that really is it, then?" Guy asked.

Austin stopped, stood for a moment, and then turned around. "What do you mean?"

"You don't want to talk to me?"

"Not really," Austin admitted. In fact, his stomach had been in knots the whole time, and now, looking at Guy? His stomach knotted even more.

"Do you hate me?"

Guy's eyes were huge. Empty. Once again, Austin had no idea how to read the man. Did he hate Guy? A strange feeling crept over Austin. Sadness, followed quickly by something else. Something that made his heart skip a beat. No. He didn't hate this man. In fact….

God. No. Was it possible? *Crap oh crap oh crap! Have I fallen in love with him?* He trembled. "No, Guy. I don't hate you." He didn't say the rest. How could he?

"Are we speaking?"

"We are right now," Austin said.

"That's not what I mean."

Austin sighed. "I know what you mean."

"And?"

The look on Guy's face! The… anxiousness? Is that what he saw on Guy's face?

"We're talking," Austin said.

Guy's mouth turned up in a small smile. "Austin, I am so sorry. I really messed up last night. I was trying to do the right thing, and damned if I know if I did or not."

Austin shrugged.

"I want it to be right. I want you to really know what you want. Thinking clearly. No beer. No rum and Cokes. No hormones."

Austin took a deep breath. "So if I asked you to take me to bed right now, would you?"

Guy startled. "Are-are you asking?"

Was he? God. Crap. No. He had way too much to think about now. Because when just those looks in Guy's eyes made his heart start speeding up like this—and how had he not known all along how he felt?—then it was time to get away from him, for at least a little bit, and get his head on straight. "No. I guess not."

The look of relief on the man's face was palpable. And what the hell did that mean?

"I better get going. Uncle Bodie might have something else for me to do."

"Okay," Guy said. Then, as Austin turned to go: "We're friends?"

Austin turned back. Saw that face, those eyes. "Yes, Guy."

Guy took a quick step forward, then back. What had he been about to do? "Thank you, Austin. And sorry about last night. I made a lot of fucking mistakes."

"Maybe you made a good decision too," Austin said. Because in light of the feelings he was beginning to realize he might have, what if they had sex, and then Guy just wanted to be friends? It would have been too much. It would have been horrible.

"You think so?" Guy asked, hope in his voice.

I do, he thought. "I do," he then said aloud.

Guy nodded and walked him to the door. Then, just as Austin was leaving, he said, "About Christmas...."

Austin froze. Crap. He'd forgotten all about that. He looked at Guy.

"Do you still want me to go? Would it be best if I just stayed here—"

"Alone?" Austin asked before he realized he was even saying anything.

Guy shrugged. "I'm used to it."

Then, once more, before he knew what he was doing: "Yes. I still want you to come." This beautiful man shouldn't spend Christmas alone. Especially since it was apparent there had been more than a few of them spent that way. "Will you?"

"Do you mean it?" Guy asked.

Austin nodded. He did mean it.

Guy's tiny smile was back. And it grew to a larger one. "If you're sure."

Austin's heart was speeding up again. "I'm sure."

The smile grew even more. "Okay, then. I'm in."

They started to hug, but didn't. That was good. Austin did need time away from Guy. But he needed something else too. After some time alone, he needed time *with* Guy. Real, quality time.

Then maybe he could figure his life out.

INTERMISSION

THE drive to Buckman was pleasant and safe, despite the smattering of snow that had chosen to arrive that morning. That was Kansas City weather. Don't like it? Wait a day. It would change.

Guy drove; it was his car, after all—a deep-blue Ford Fiesta. Austin sat up front, and Uncle Bodie and Lucille were in the back, she in her big princess bed, posing like royalty. Every now and then she would stand up, hind legs in the bed and front feet on the windowsill, watching the turning-white world go by.

They listened to the radio and considered a novel on tape, but Uncle Bodie said he wasn't in the mood. He wanted to talk.

So they talked—mostly about inconsequential things. Pleasant time-passing talk.

Once they got out of the city, there were great stretches—half an hour at a time or more—of nothing but countryside. When they did pass a town, it was small and zipped past in minutes.

They stopped at a truck stop for lunch. Uncle Bodie insisted they served good food because there was stiff competition with the truckers for business. Sure enough, the food was good. They ate light, though; Gram had made it clear she was making dinner. So it was a Reuben for Guy, beef and gravy over bread for Uncle Bodie (he was sure to save a bit for Lucille), and a patty melt for Austin. It was a sandwich that could be awesome or terrible, depending on who cooked it. Luckily, Uncle Bodie's advice was sage and the patty melt was delicious, the fries surprisingly so.

"Normally, I would take Lucille a couple," Uncle Bodie said. "She loves french fries, but not with this seasoning. Good for us, not so much for a little woman."

Then they were back on the road. Guy insisted he do all the driving. It wasn't that long a drive after all, Austin conceded. All he needed to do was get in an accident in Guy's car!

All in all, the drive felt good to Austin. He was surprised how good. Guy had been sweet and friendly the last week, making an effort to give Austin some of his time. He'd been nervous at first, both at the prospect of them *not* talking and spending time together. But things went surprisingly well.

They'd even spent a morning driving around, up and down streets, actually searching for Todd's old VW van, but no luck. Austin didn't really expect to find it—Kansas City wasn't New York or Chicago, but it was huge. Uncle Bodie even told him the Kansas City metropolitan area was bigger than Las Vegas, Salt Lake City, and even Austin's namesake in Texas.

"It could be looking for a crapping needle in a haystack," Austin said.

"It could," Guy said. "Or we could get lucky."

The trip went well, and the time flew by, and before they knew it, they saw the sign that proclaimed the exit for Buckman was in two miles. *The* exit. Only one.

"And if you miss it," Uncle Bodie said, "You have to drive eighteen miles before you can turn around and come back."

"Believe me, it's true," Austin added. "Todd and I were coming home one night from a party, and we were high, and we almost missed the next one."

"High, huh?" Guy asked.

"And you know what they say—"

"What do they say?"

"Drunk drivers kill, stoned drivers just miss their exits!"

Guy burst into laughter. "True. So true."

"It took us almost an hour extra to get home. Todd got in big trouble."

"Oh," Guy said, and stopped laughing.

"Sorry. I wasn't trying to get glum," Austin apologized. "It was out of my mouth before I could stop it." *I've been doing that a lot lately. That's Todd's thing. I'm the one who always thinks things through.*

Guy pulled off the exit without a hitch, and then Austin was giving directions—left here and right there—and quick as could be, they had pulled up in front of a lovely butter-yellow house.

"It's beautiful," Guy said. "For some reason I was expecting it to be… smaller, maybe?"

Just then the front door opened and his grandparents came out onto the porch, Gramps as thin as ever, Austin's short and stocky grandmother at her husband's side.

"Austin!" she cried.

"Grams," he called back and rushed across the lawn (now covered with a least an inch or so of snow) and up the steps into her arms.

Lucille began to bark wildly from the back, unhappy to be left out of this sudden turn of events.

Guy and Uncle Bodie climbed out of the car. Austin and his grandmother were still hugging fiercely, she rocking him in her arms as if he were a man only half his size.

"Bodie! Good to see you," Austin's grandfather said.

"Frawley," he responded. Lucille had been leashed but still barked madly. "Lucille!" He gave a gentle yank. "This is family, girl! That's my sister and her husband."

Lucille stopped her vocal assault long enough to look up at her master.

"Don't you want to make a good impression? They haven't seen you in a long time."

She gave a single loud bark, then turned to look at Austin. He could see she was trying not to growl. He bit back a laugh. Ferocious little woman!

Austin's grandmother had finally stepped back to let her husband get in a hug, and she stepped to the edge of the porch as Uncle Bodie began his slow climb up the four steps.

"Boden," she said happily. "It is wonderful to see you."

"Wilda," he nodded, holding Lucille on a short length of her leash.

Wilda squatted. "And look at you? Aren't you lovely? So sweet. Lucille?"

Lucille answered.

"I'm Wilda. You can call me Grams. And look at what I've got for you." She reached into her apron pocket and pulled out a small dog biscuit.

Lucille shook with excitement, growls and other doggie noises on hold. She had eyes only for the red bone-shaped treat. Wilda handed it over, and Lucille very delicately took it from her and then began to madly munch it down.

This gave Wilda the chance to stand and hug her brother. "Oh, Boden. I have missed you so very much."

"And I you, dear sister," he said looking down into her round face.

They both laughed happily and hugged again.

"And who is this?" Wilda asked, giving Austin's elbow a gentle squeeze and nodding at Guy, who was tentatively approaching the steps. She gave Austin a look, eyes flashing, brows rising and dropping.

Austin's stomach gave a little flip. "Grams, this is Guy. He's a friend of mine. Guy, this is my grandmother Wilda."

"Hello, Mrs. Chandler," Guy said politely. "Very pleased to meet you."

"You just call me Grams, you hear?"

"Okay, ah, Grams."

By then he'd climbed the steps, and she gave him a hug, almost as big as Austin's.

Guy's grandfather stepped forward. "And this," Austin said with a nod, "is my grandfather, Frawley Chandler."

Frawley reached out his hand and Guy took it. "Pleased to meet you," he said to the older gentleman.

"Likewise, I'm sure. And call me Gramps, please."

"Gramps," Guy said with a nod.

"Austin, you and Guy get your luggage while I take Boden inside. We don't want to freeze out here, and you aren't gonna want to go back out in this once you're all comfortable inside. Don't forget to kick off your shoes." Then she grabbed her grandson again and hugged him once more. "So is this a friend, or a *friend?*" she whispered in his ear.

"Just a friend," Austin said and blushed to the roots.

"Too bad," she said as she let him go. She stared after Guy, who was back at the car and opening the trunk. "He is *very* good-looking."

"Grams!"

She giggled. "What? A grandmother wants her boy to be happy!" She laughed and guided her brother into the house, Lucille now much more cheerful and dancing at their feet.

Still pink, Austin joined Guy and helped him bring in the suitcases. "Whatever you do," Austin told Guy and pointed at two rubber mats on the floor, lined with about four pairs of shoes. "Don't ever forget to kick them off."

Guy stiffened. "I don't know what my feet smell like, Austin."

"Weren't you taught to wear clean socks and underwear in case you were ever in an accident?" Austin asked, chuckling.

"Yeah," Guy answered. "But we had the heat blasting on our feet, and as for the underwear...." He leaned in. "I freeball it."

Austin's eyes popped, and Guy grinned. He then joined Austin in toeing off his shoes to join those on the rubber mats. The immediate scent of man rose to meet them. Guy groaned.

Austin grinned, and before Guy could protest, dragged him through the foyer and into the house.

THEY were all sitting around the dining room table, and it was laden with food: chicken, a heaping bowl of mashed potatoes, gravy, corn, and a platter of big puffy rolls. There was plenty for everyone, and they filled their plates and stuffed themselves. Everything was delicious.

"Mrs. Chan—ah—*Grams*," said Guy. "This is the best gravy I've ever had in my life."

"Aren't you just about as sweet as syrup on pancakes?" She grinned a huge one, and gave him a wink. "Austin, you better keep an eye on this one," she said.

"Grams," he hissed. Awkward! Did she have to do this? He wasn't expecting this kind of teasing. Accepting, yes, but crap, she didn't have to embarrass them all. He spared a glance at Guy, who only shrugged and grinned back. *Oh you!* he wanted to shout.

"And what is it you do?" Frawley asked Guy while scooping out a second helping of mashed potatoes.

"Well," Guy answered. "I wear a lot of hats. I work for the Pegasus Theatre. I direct, act, help with grants—even answer phones and work the box office."

"Grants?"

"Yes." Guy nodded. "The Pegasus depends on grants, and many of them are provided by the community. We have major sponsors, some pretty impressive names by the way, as well as from individuals. Our patrons keep us going."

"Guy is writing a play himself," said Austin. He took a big bite of his third roll. Lord, he had missed Gram's rolls.

"What kind of play?" Wilda sat back. "What's it about?"

"He doesn't like to talk about it," Austin said, jumping in. "He doesn't want to jinx it."

"Oh, really, now?" Wilda asked.

"It's about people," Guy said. "Five people and how they react to a circumstance they're thrown into."

Austin raised an eyebrow.

"Well, you just keep the rest to your ownself," she replied. "Don't want to jinx it. I know all about jinxin', don't I, Frawley?"

Her husband nodded. "We both do."

"When you get it done and are ready to show your play, you let us know, okay?" She stood and picked up her empty plate. "Maybe we'll come an' see it."

Guy gave a nod, and gave Austin a big-eyed stare.

This time it was Austin's turn to shrug.

Wilda asked for empty plates, and Austin asked her to sit down. "You made dinner. It's my job to clear the table."

"Not when you're a guest," she declared. "You stay right where you are. Tomorrow I'll be needin' lots a help."

Austin stayed put while the empty plates were passed down.

"Is it okay for Lucille to have somethin' from the table?" Wilda asked.

"A little gravy over her dry food is all," Uncle Bodie said. He rose from the table, and Lucille, knowing she was being talked about, got up and walked to his side. "I'll get some. It's her dinnertime too." He left the room.

"Dessert?" Wilda asked. "I hope you left room."

"Lord, Mrs.—Grams." Guy rolled his eyes. "I'm stuffed fuller than a tick."

"Well, there is always room for Jell-O," she declared and left the room.

"Austin…," he said.

"Don't argue," Austin replied. "It won't do any good."

What she brought back wasn't what Guy had expected—Austin could see that. She placed a plate with a big piece of pie. The Jell-O, mixed with whipped cream, was only one layer. Guy gave it a big-eyed look of surprise. "What? You thought it was that crap they serve in high school cafeterias?" she asked. "Would I do that, Austin?"

"No ma'am," he replied.

"Try it," she ordered.

Austin shook his head, and took the fork she offered. He cut off a bite-sized piece, popped it in his mouth, and then sighed blissfully. "Oh wow. It tastes like a Dreamsicle," he said. "My favorite when I was a kid."

She smiled serenely and left the room. "Finish that roll, Austin! I'm gettin' you some."

He smiled contentedly. As he told Guy—there was no arguing. And as happy as he was finding himself in Kansas City, there really was no place like home.

After Lucille's meal had been taken care of and everyone was done—Guy had a second helping of pie, despite his claim that he was full—Wilda announced they should go ahead and take their luggage to their rooms. "Boden, you're in the guest bedroom upstairs."

Uncle Bodie took his small case up the stairs with him, and Austin promised to bring Lucille's bed up in a moment. Wilda asked the "boys" to "come this way," and led them into the kitchen and the door to the basement. "I put you two downstairs," she said and headed down with them following after.

"Where?" Austin asked. "I took all my furniture with me."

"You remember Miss Flora?" she asked him.

"Sure."

"Well, her granddaughter Abby got married last month, and she sold her bedroom suite. It's as pretty as can be and just perfect for you two. And not too girly." They reached the bottom of the stairs, and she took them around the corner where Austin had had his bedroom for years. Having it at that end gave him some privacy. He stopped dead in his tracks when he saw what was there. Oh, it was nice all right. White dresser, end tables, desk, and a bed.

One bed.

"Ah—Grams. Ah…."

"What?" she asked, hands on hips. "You don't really want to sleep in your sleeping bags on this cement floor, do you?" She turned to Guy. "Do you?"

Guy took a deep long breath and smiled. "This'll be fine," he said. "Thank you, mmm—Grams."

She smiled again and reached out and patted his cheek. "Of course it will be. Just as fine as paint." She swiveled her big hips around and faced her grandson. "You two get settled and I'll see you upstairs. We're gonna watch *A Christmas Story*." She glanced at Guy. "It's a tradition."

With that she left the room. "Don't forget Lucille's bed, Austin," she called as she clumped up the stairs.

Austin stared at the bed.

Full-size to be sure, but not a lot of room for two full-grown men who weren't comfortable sleeping together. He looked up at Guy. "I-I… I'm sorry. I'll sleep on the floor," he said.

Guy shook his head. "No, you won't. I will if either of us does."

"No," Austin insisted. "That floor is as hard as—"

"Cement?" Guy offered.

As hard as cement was right, throw rug or not. Crap. What the hell was Grams thinking?

"It'll be fine, Austin. Now let's get upstairs. Lucille needs her bed too."

THEY sat around the living room—with its burning fireplace and a real Christmas tree dominating one corner—and watched *A Christmas Story*, and laughed, and had a wonderful time. The line "You'll shoot your eye out, kid," never seemed to get old, nor Flick getting his tongue stuck to the flag pole, nor Ralphie getting a pink bunny suit from his aunt, nor his brother falling in the snow and not being able to get up, nor the dogs stealing the Christmas dinner and the whole family eating at a Chinese restaurant. They'd all seen the movie at least a dozen times, but it was still a delight.

Austin's grandmother had not-so-subtly made sure the only place for him and Guy to sit was next to each other on the couch. She even squeezed in next to them so they had to get close. The only way they really got comfortable was when Guy put his arm around Austin's shoulder.

Wilda was also sure to serve her hot buttered rum—another family tradition.

"Crap, Grams," cried Austin, barely suppressing a cough. "You sure made this strong enough."

"You're old enough now. I thought you should have it the way me and Frawley always has it." She gave a hoot. "You like that, Guy?" she asked.

"Yes, ma'am, I do," he said, taking a good sip.

"I make it with french vanilla ice cream and more butter than you can shake a stick at!" She howled. "Get it? Shake a *stick* at?"

Guy laughed. "I get it, Grams."

"And you're finally gettin' what to call me!"

Wilda kept the hot buttered rum coming, and after the movie, brought out more Dreamsicle pie. Then she asked "the boys" to finish decorating the tree. "Austin was always the one who could do the icicles. I can't hang 'em right and Frawley just puts 'em on in big ol' clumps."

Frawley shook his head. He didn't talk all that much. There was no point. Husband he may be, and from a different time, but Wilda ruled the Chandler homestead.

The boys didn't argue and had soon opened the box Wilda gave them and began hanging the long silver tinsel in a way they hoped would please her.

"Real tree, huh?" asked Guy. Austin thought he heard a disapproving tone to his voice.

"It's live," Austin replied.

"It is?"

"Yup," said Frawley. "We been doin' it for years. We plant them after. Got the hole dug already in case the ground froze."

Guy smiled. "That's pretty cool."

"We planted a tree every year of Austin's life," he said, stepping closer and giving Guy a long look. He then turned to the tree and finally his grandson.

"We're mighty proud of you, son," he said.

Austin pivoted around. "You are?"

His grandfather nodded and adjusted his black glasses.

"Why?" What had brought this on? Austin wondered. He looked at the man who had been there for his whole life, a man he thought of as more of a father than anything else. Was he frailer? Or was that merely a trick of the eye, having not seen the man for a few months? Was he a little balder? Had his snow-white hair receded a bit more? Was he okay?

"Because of all you're doing. Making a new life for yourself. All the work you do for Bodie. He says you're amazing."

Austin gave a shrug, blushed a little, and barely avoided saying, "Ah, shucks." Instead he said, "It's all you, Gramps. You taught it to me. Taught me everything."

"But you got a natural talent, son. You look at things and just know how to fix them."

"So do *you*. You taught me *how* to look."

"He fixed my clogged sink in no time at all," Guy added.

Frawley looked him deep in the face once more, brows closing in on each other a bit. "He's a good boy."

Guy nodded. "Yes, sir."

"You're taking good care of him?"

Austin's eyes went wide. His grandparents really thought they were together. That Guy was his boyfriend. He needed to do something about it. This was going to get embarrassing.

"Austin takes good care of himself, Mr. Chandler."

Frawley nodded. "Yes, I know. But people need to watch out for each other, don't you think?"

"Sure," Guy answered. "Of course."

"Good. Now you two finish the tree. I'm goin' to bed. Big day tomorrow."

"God," muttered Austin quietly. "They think—"

"Yeah," Guy said. "I see that. Of course that's probably why they put us downstairs together, huh? One bed. Private."

Austin nodded. "Crap."

"Austin." Guy reached out, his hand full of tinsel, and took Austin's shoulder. "You're lucky. You know that, right? I haven't seen my family in a long time. If they ever wanted to see me, you wouldn't be allowed—even though we're not... you know. Lovers. They sure wouldn't put us in the same bed. It doesn't matter that we aren't... a couple. The point is, your grandparents accept you. They accept me as if I were...."

"I need to set them straight," Austin said, going back to hanging the long silver strands. He wanted to get it just right. And not think about this subject at all.

"Do you?"

"What do you mean?"

"Why tell them? Don't confirm or deny."

Austin gave a laugh. "If I don't say something, they'll be buying us his-and-his robes and towels."

"So what if they do? I'll just let you have mine and maybe you'll give them to Todd."

Austin froze. *Todd. Crap. Todd.* He shook his head. "I'm never going to find him anyway." *And you don't want me.*

"You don't know that."

"I do."

"Maybe we could go try his parents again," Guy suggested.

Austin spun on him. "Are you crazy? His crapping stepdad might shoot us."

"I'll take my chances," Guy said, "to help you."

Austin shook his head. "Why? You want to get rid of me? Is that it?"

Guy looked as if he'd been slapped, and Austin straightaway regretted his words.

"No, Austin. I... I do not want to get rid of you. You have no idea."

"Then why...?"

"Because, Austin! If we.... If you find him after, I don't want you to regret it. I couldn't stand that."

Austin looked into Guy's eyes. Regret it? Would he? Could he? Maybe?

He was so confused. Months ago all he'd wanted to do was find Todd. He was in love with him, wasn't he?

"One more hot buttered rum before I head up?"

Austin jumped, then spun around.

Of course, it was only his grandmother. "Did I scare you, Austin?"

Austin gave a half laugh and rolled his eyes. "Startled me."

"You okay, son?" she asked, concern clear on her face.

"I'm okay."

She stepped forward, patted his cheek, and smiled big. "Then how about that rum?"

"Sure," he said. Why not? He was already pretty damned tipsy. That was probably a part of why he was acting like an idiot.

"Guy?" she asked.

"Sure, Grams. I'd love one."

"I'll be right back." She winked and turned around and headed out of the room.

Austin gave Guy a weak smile. "Sorry."

"For what?" Guy carefully pulled more icicles out of the box.

"If I'm acting weird."

"No weirder than usual," Guy quipped and threw some tinsel in Austin's direction.

"Hey," he cried, and threw some back.

When Wilda returned, there were more icicles on the laughing young men than on the tree.

AUSTIN was a little nerve-wracked when they went down to bed. He didn't know what to do, what to wear. He normally slept in nothing more than his underwear, but somehow that didn't seem to be the right thing to do tonight. But he wasn't sure what else he'd brought. Thank God a quick ruffle through his bag showed he'd packed a pair of sweatpants for getting up in the middle of the night to pee, so he supposed he'd wear those and a T-shirt and…

Guy was undressing!

Austin quickly turned his back.

"Relax, Austin. I'm not going to flash my goods."

Austin blushed. "You said you were… umm… free… ah…."

"Freeballing?" Guy laughed. "I was just changing my shirt. I actually brought sleep pants and was going to change into those around the corner, okay?"

"Okay." *God, I want to crawl under the covers and die!*

"And I promise to stay on my side of the bed."

Oh crap! Austin tried to laugh and was terribly conscious of how fake it sounded.

He listened as Guy padded away, and as soon as he was gone, Austin quickly scrambled out of his jeans and shrugged into his sweats. It was all rendered pointless when he heard Guy call out, "Is it safe for me to come back?"

"Yes," he answered, flustered. *I need to act like an adult here. Why am I acting like this?*

Guy came back looking gorgeous. Austin wasn't sure how he did it when it was just some silly Superman sleep pants and a tank top, but he did. For the first time, Guy wasn't wearing something baggy. Austin could see he had a well-developed chest with a light covering of dark-brown hair, very nice arms, and damn, even his feet were sexy. Who knew bare feet could be so sexy?

I did. I always liked how manly Todd's feet were. Broad, with a bit of hair on top and a little over each toe. Austin dared a quick look down at Guy's, and damned if they weren't a lot like Todd's. Maybe a little bit hairier. Nothing gross or Hobbit-like. Just strong, manly feet. Feet you'd never mistake for a woman's….

"Is there something wrong with my feet?" Guy asked. "Are they dirty or something?"

Austin looked up, mortified that he'd been caught staring.

"God, they don't still stink, do they? I ran down here and changed my socks. Even rinsed my feet in that sink by the washing machine, and believe me that was awkward. I almost fell—"

"No-nothing… I…."

"What?"

Austin shrugged, so embarrassed he wanted to shrink away and disappear. Then, doing a Todd again, he blurted it out before he knew what he was saying. "You have nice feet," he said. "Some people have some pretty gnarly feet."

Guy looked down, wiggled his toes (and God, even that was sexy), and said, "Oh. Thanks. Yeah, some people do have some pretty fugly feet. Let me see yours."

"Huh?" *What did he just say?*

Guy walked around the bed and Austin half ducked his feet under the bed.

"Austin!"

Now he was even more embarrassed. *What are you crapping doing?* He slowly pulled them out.

"Nice."

Nice? He didn't dare look up. "Nice?" he repeated out loud. He looked down at his feet. Were they nice? They didn't look much like men's feet. One more thing about him that wasn't manly.

"Nice." Then Guy walked back around to his side and climbed in. "I'm assuming you're on that side for a reason?"

"Closest side to the bathroom in case I need to go." He didn't tell Guy how many million times he'd peed in the utility sink.

"I'm surprised you just don't piss in the sink," Guy said. "It's not like anyone washes clothes or dishes in it. And we are the male animal."

Austin burst into laughter and looked at Guy over his shoulder.

Guy grinned and winked. "It'll be our little secret."

Austin got in under the covers, turned off the bedside lamp. Then: "Oh—you weren't going to read or anything, were you?"

"Nope. I'm exhausted."

"Good. Me too."

"Good night, Austin."

"Good night, Guy," he managed.

They were silent for a moment.

"Austin?"

His heart skipped a beat. "Y-yes?"

"Thank you."

Thank you? "For what?"

"For this. For Christmas. This will be the first time I've woken up in a house full of people in, like, nine Christmases."

Oh God! That hurt Austin's heart. "You're welcome, Guy. I'm glad you came."

Then Guy was leaning over him to give his cheek a gentle and quick kiss. An instant later, he was on his side, back turned to Austin.

Austin's heart was racing again. *He kissed me.* The stubble on his upper lip had felt so… real.

I am never going to fall asleep!

Fortunately, Austin was wrong, and the long day took him almost instantly into a deep and untroubled sleep.

AUSTIN awoke to Gram's voice calling down the steps. "Boys? This is your fifteen-minute warning! I'm making breakfast!"

He also awoke to find Guy spooned up behind him, one arm around his waist, holding him close. *Oh God….* He started to move and then was shocked when he felt the hard knot pressed up against his butt. *Oh my. That's his hard-on!*

Guy began to stir. "Was that your grandmother?" he muttered, rolling over onto his back.

"Y-yeah," Austin answered, and looked to see Guy rubbing at his eyes. "Breakfast in fifteen." He scrambled out of bed, realizing he, too, had a morning woody. He snatched up his jeans and made a run for it. "See you upstairs!"

He almost lost his footing scrambling up the steps and bursting into the kitchen, nearly bowling his grandmother over.

"Whoa, boy," she said. "I said fifteen minutes, not seconds."

"Gotta pee," he said, and dashed for the bathroom.

But not before he heard her say, "Like you ever bothered coming up here for that anyway...."

Was this whole three days going to be one embarrassing occasion after another?

He relieved himself, splashed water on his face, considered going downstairs for his toothbrush, and thought, *Oh, to hell with it. I'll brush after breakfast.*

When he came back to the kitchen, Guy was there, barefoot and in a beautifully faded and painted-on pair of jeans, along with one of his baggy sweaters. He was pouring coffee and asked Austin if he wanted any.

"Coffee," he cried. "And we brought coffee."

"We can have that later," his grandmother said, opening a waffle iron and pulling out two gorgeous waffles.

"Oh, Grams," Austin exclaimed. "It seems like forever since I've had your waffles."

"I knew they were a favorite of yours, and it is Christmas," she said.

"Oh, Christmas! Merry Christmas!" He went to her and kissed her cheek.

She gave him a quick kiss and hug and then started filling the iron with batter from a big plastic pitcher.

"Smells wonderful, Grams," Guy said.

"Sit down. Take two for now while they're hot. You boys want me to make eggs?"

"This is fine with me," said Guy.

"Me too," Austin said, pulling out a chair.

"Would you get the milk and orange juice out before you sit down, dear?"

"Sure, Grams." He did so and then sat down.

Uncle Bodie came down then, holding Lucille. "You're just being a silly little woman," he was saying. He looked up. "Waffles. How wonderful. Thank you, Wilda."

"No problem, brother mine." She was bustling about, pulling out cutting boards and a huge roasting pan before returning to open the iron and peek inside.

"Lucille here wouldn't come out from under the bed this morning. I don't know how long she slept there instead of her bed. Then she didn't want to come down the stairs."

"She's outta her environment, Boden. I am sure she'll be fine." She offered the little dog in Uncle Bodie's arms one of the doggie treats—it had magically appeared from a pocket in her almost always-present apron—but this time, after a sniff or two, it was ignored.

"Huh," Wilda said. "I'll just put it in her bowl. She can have it when she's ready."

"I'm going to take her out to potty," Uncle Bodie said.

"Want me to do that, Bodie?" Guy asked.

"Nope. You don't even have your socks on. I'm dressed. We'll be back in three shakes of a lamb's tail."

The waffles were delicious—Wilda had even provided strawberries, cut up in their own syrup, and whipped cream. An awesome way to start the day. Then it was orchestrated chaos as the matriarch of the family diced and chopped and buttered and boiled and rinsed and washed and cooked, cooked, cooked. She took advantage of Austin and Guy's youth, moving the turkey in off the back porch, getting it in the oven when it was ready, and pulling it out for basting. She used foil, said oven bags were created by the devil, but they didn't mind. There was something about her orders that made them feel more like they were doing her a favor, and of course, they were.

She made a very small lunch, just crackers and cheese and a cheese ball rolled in crumbled pecans. "A snack," she said, "to keep up your strength." Then she warned them not to eat too much. "Dinner will be around three thirty, four o'clock."

At one point Austin saw that Guy had gone out on the back porch with this grandfather. Grams didn't allow smoking in the house, not even a pipe with the pleasant smell Austin had always thought of as home. The pair were talking, and when he peeked out, it looked like a serious conversation. *Crap*, he cursed, and hoped they weren't having another tête-à-tête about how Guy needed to take care of him.

To his surprise, when Guy came back in, he asked Austin's grandmother if she minded if he went for a walk.

"Of course not, darlin'. You want Austin to go with?"

The young men locked eyes, and again, Guy had gone all unreadable.

"I'll go with you," Austin said.

"No. No, I just want a little alone time."

Austin followed him out on the back porch. "Is everything okay?"

"Sure it is." Guy gave him a smile Austin didn't quite believe. "Nothing's wrong. Remember, I'm not used to all this." He waved back to the kitchen. "I'll be back. Don't worry."

It was with great concern that Austin watched as he walked down the steps and down the alley. What was that all about? Had Gramps said something to upset him? He went looking for his grandfather and found him just rising up from his knees in front of the fireplace and putting the poker back into its stand. "Gramps?"

Frawley was staring into the flames. "Yes, son?"

"What's wrong with Guy? Did you two talk about something that upset him?"

His grandfather didn't say anything for a moment. Finally, when Austin was going to ask his question again, he spoke up. "No. There is *nothing* wrong with Guy. Nothing at all." He turned around, pulled off his glasses, and began to wipe them with his shirttail. "Do you know how lucky you are to have found that man?"

Austin gulped, fell back a step. It was certainly not what he would have expected his gramps to say. "I…. Ah…."

"I hope you know how lucky. I hope you appreciate him. Guy is a very good man." He put his glasses on, and stepped up to Austin and hugged him. "Me an' your grams is gettin' old, Austin. We worry about you. Think about you all the time. Movin' away to a big city for the first time. Living a life that may be easier than it was when Bodie was your age, but it's still tough."

It was the closest his grandfather had come to bringing up the subject. Austin felt a little strange. Almost high. And he didn't know what to say.

"I appreciate him, Gramps." He gave the man squeeze.

"'Cause he obviously loves you, son. And love don't grow on a tree. You know that, right?"

Austin barely suppressed a gasp. Love? Had Guy told Gramps he loved him?

"He didn't actually *say* that, but I could tell. Two men get an understanding when they talk like that. He was all but asking for my blessing." He stepped back, and Austin could see tears in his eyes. "He's got it." He nodded and then headed back into the kitchen, leaving Austin standing there in shock.

GUY wasn't gone quite an hour, but it worried Austin all the same. Buckman wasn't a very big town, but it had snowed a few more inches during the night, it was cold out, and Guy didn't know where he was. He could get lost. Austin didn't even think about the fact that they both had cell phones. When he returned, it was all Austin could do not to throw himself into Guy's arms. But there was something funny in his eyes, something that held him back. What was it?

Wilda called them in for dinner a little after that, and it was the best meal Austin had had in ages, even better than the Thanksgiving goose. That had been fine, but Austin was a turkey man all the way.

The dining room table all but groaned under the weight of the food. "Goodness," Guy cried over seeing it. "There's only five of us, Grams. How're we going to eat all this?"

"I'll mail what we don't eat to India. Does that make you feel better?"

Guy laughed and sat where directed, next to Austin, of course. So it was Wilda and Frawley at one side, Austin and Guy across from them, and Uncle Bodie at the end.

"Boden," Wilda asked. "Do you want to say the prayer?"

"You know that's not my thing, Wilda. And you do so much prettier a job."

She blinked at him a moment, then nodded. "Let's bow our heads."

Austin glanced at Guy, who seemed uncomfortable but did as she requested.

"Dear Heavenly Father," she said. "Bless us this Christmas day, the day that Your son was born long ago, and that He showed us the way. Thank You for His message of love, for love is the greatest of all things, without which we are nothing. Thank You for bringing Austin and Boden home safely, and thank You also for our dear guest Guy. What a blessing he is. We thank You for Your many, many gifts, and for this food which we are about to receive from Thy bounty. May it nourish us and give us strength. And may we not gain one single ounce after stuffing our faces. In Your son Jesus's holy name, Amen."

When she raised her head, her eyes were twinkling. "Pretty, did you say, Boden?"

"Prettier than me!"

And they all burst into laughter.

THEY had gathered in the living room, Wilda asking them to pull the couch to the side so that it, along with the chairs, faced the tree. It was time to exchange gifts. Several had appeared since last night, and more in the last few hours. Someone had been at work, thought Austin. Maybe because his grandparents knew that, as a child, he'd liked to shake presents and try to figure out what was in them.

She had them sit down, and she forced Frawley, as usual, to put on a Santa hat and begin passing out presents. It was silly because she wouldn't be satisfied with how he did it, Austin whispered to Guy. "She'll wind up doing it herself."

But as if she heard her grandson, she did her best not to interfere, and Frawley did his best to make sure everyone got a gift before going on to seconds.

Austin had gotten his grandmother a new apron, which she gushed over, and his grandfather a new pipe, which obviously pleased him. "This is amazing, son. Beautiful."

The pair got other things as well, of course. Most of them practical, but Frawley did get his wife a lovely brooch.

Uncle Bodie got a gorgeous new housecoat. It was much like a smoking jacket, and when he saw it was from both Austin and Guy, tears filled his eyes. "I love it," he said. "You have no idea what this means to me."

Lucille was not left out. She got a new bejeweled collar from Austin and several toys. Uncle Bodie was disappointed that she didn't tear into her gifts. Apparently, he always started them, and then she knew which ones were hers to rip open. She tried to please her master, but for some reason seemed to lack her usual enthusiasm and wound up squeezed against his side, falling asleep with her head in his lap.

Guy was obviously surprised at the number of gifts he received. Uncle Bodie had bought him a director's chair. "Oh, Bodie! I love it!" Wilda and Frawley gave him a huge purple sweater. "Austin said you liked them baggy. I didn't realize how big it would be, though...."

"It's wonderful!" He ran from the room and was back in seconds, wearing the gorgeous sweater and rubbing his hand across the sleeves. It was more than purple, with deep blues and dark lavenders woven in. "I just love it," he said and gave Wilda a kiss on the cheek.

She also gave him a big container of homemade cookies. "Oh my God, Grams. Are you trying to make me fat?"

"I'm sure you'll find a way to work it off," she grinned, eyes twinkling, and Guy actually blushed—something Austin rarely saw.

Finally, he opened Austin's present. His mouth fell open. "Dear God, Austin."

"What is it?" Uncle Bodie asked, as well as the others.

Guy carefully held up what looked like a thick sheaf of typed pages for the curious onlookers. "It-It's an autographed typescript of Edward Albee's *Who's Afraid of Virginia Woolf.*"

"A what?" asked Frawley.

"A transcript. It's a typed script. This is an autographed copy of Edward Albee's script for his play. I can't believe it!"

Austin swelled up with happiness. "You like it?"

Guy jumped up and pulled Austin into his arms, hugging him fiercely. "I love it."

"I thought you liked him."

"I adore him! He's one of my all-time favorites."

"Lot of swearing in that, isn't there?" Frawley asked.

Guy turned to Austin's grandfather. "There sure is."

"Well," Wilda said. "People friggin' swear, don't they?"

And they all burst into laughter.

Austin had gotten gifts too, of course. A quilt his grandmother made. A very big one. Yellows and oranges and pure-white squares and triangles. "Grams! It's gorgeous." He looked over at Guy. "It's a tradition of hers. Family gets her quilts. I got one when I was a kid and it's seen better days."

"Children are hell on such things," she muttered.

"And now I have this one. Oh, Grams." Like Guy, he kissed her. Both cheeks. "I can't get over how big it is. You usually make twin and full-size ones. Is this a queen?"

"A king," she said. "My first. But I thought you might wind up needing a big one. You know?"

Austin's cheeks pinked slightly, and he decided to call it a blessing he wasn't beet red again. He was tired of how much he'd been blushing lately. It needed to stop.

He took it back and showed it to Guy. "She made this."

"It's what I do, Guy. Sorry, I didn't make the sweater. That's knitting and crocheting. I don't do that. I make quilts."

"It's okay, Grams. I still love it."

Austin also got cookies, as well as a sweater—this one a shimmery blue. His favorite color.

Uncle Bodie got him a book on Stonewall, which pleased Austin very much.

Finally, there was his present from Guy.

"God, I hope you like it," he said.

It was a set of tools. Nice tools. Tools obviously not bought at Walmart.

"I figured you could use your own. And you could use them to help build sets too, if you're still interested."

"Thanks, Guy," Austin said. "They're amazing. And too much. You spent way too much."

"It's okay. I didn't really get you much of a birthday present. I was waiting to give you this. It must be a bitch to be born so close to Christmas."

"It can be," Austin said. "But not today."

"Austin," said his grandfather. "Here's another one for you. Why, it's also from Guy."

"Guy!" Austin looked at his friend curiously. "Two? The first one was already too much."

"When I saw it, I had to get it."

Frawley started to read the tag further, his eyebrows raised, and he closed it quickly and handed the box to Austin. It was about eight by eight inches and a couple thick. He raised it to his ear, and Guy gave him a quick command not to shake it. Curiosity piqued, Austin tore it open—then sat back with a small gasp.

It was a butterfly.

Mounted in a black frame, it was huge and shimmering blue, and at first Austin wasn't even sure it was real. Then he saw the small tag with the words *Blue Morpho didius*. "My God," Austin sighed. "It's—it's exquisite."

"It's you," Guy said quietly in Austin's ear. "If you tilt it from side to side...."

Austin did so and let out another quiet sigh.

"See how it changes from dark to light when you view it from different angles?"

Wilda was now leaning over Austin's shoulder. "It looks like it's made out of blue tinfoil. I've never seen one like it."

"They come from South America," Guy explained. "I found it in this shop on the Plaza."

Austin found tears threatening once more. "I-I don't know what to say."

"I hope you like it," Guy said.

"I love it," Austin replied. And had he not been in a room with his relatives, he would have kissed Guy right then. "Thank you."

"It's you," Guy said quietly in Austin's ear. "A perfect shimmering butterfly."

WHEN it was bedtime, Uncle Bodie chose to carry Lucille back up with him. Austin followed to make sure they made it upstairs okay.

"I'm a little worried about my girl. Think maybe we should take her to the vet when we get home?"

"We can do it here in town tomorrow if you want," Austin said.

"Do you think they'll be open?" Uncle Bodie asked.

"It's a Wednesday," said Austin. "I don't see why not."

"This *is* Buckman, Austin."

"True. But because of that, we know where the vet lives. I'll pound on his door if you want me to."

Lucille looked up from her master's arms and gave Austin a little kiss. "Awwww...."

Uncle Bodie smiled. "We can wait until we get home. I'm sure it's nothing. She was just fine yesterday. Probably something disagreed with her. Maybe that gravy."

"Did she eat anything for dinner tonight?"

"She had some turkey." Uncle Bodie looked down at his beloved. "Didn't you, little woman?"

Lucille gave a little yap that made Austin's uncle's smile grow. "See? She's coming back already."

They had reached his door, and Austin saw them both in before giving his uncle a hug and a "Merry Christmas" and a "Good night."

"Good night to you, son. And do me a favor?"

"What's that, Uncle Bodie."

"Please make those bedsprings squeak tonight. I promise we won't hear. No one ever heard you jerking off."

Austin's eyes popped. "Uncle Bodie!"

"I know Wilda would have said something if she had. So you're safe." He stepped close to his nephew. "I even took steps to make sure of it."

Austin shook his head, amazed. "What's that?"

"Just check the top drawer of your bedside table. You'll see."

"You're crazy, Uncle Bodie."

"As a bedbug, dear boy! As crazy as a fox."

Austin went down and got another surprise when he found his grandparents kissing. It was sweet and loving. He'd never seen them kiss for so long.

"What?" his grandmother asked him. "Just 'cause there's snow on the roof doesn't mean there ain't still a fire in the furnace!"

"I'm going to bed," his grandfather said, obviously a little shy at being caught.

"You start gettin' the bed warm," she said. "There just might be a little furnace lightin' tonight."

"Wilda!" said her husband, and then he turned and climbed the steps.

Guy came up from behind Austin. "I threw all that wrapping paper away, Grams. Hope you weren't saving it for anything."

"Nope," she said. "Throw it all out, and thank you."

He nodded.

She stood there silent then, and both Austin and Guy waited for her to say something else. She obviously wanted to. After another moment, she crossed her arms. Then she gave a nod.

They both looked at each other. Guy shook his head, and Austin knew he had no idea what she was wanted. "What?" he asked her.

She sighed with great exasperation. Then pointed above their heads. To Austin's surprise, it was a ball of mistletoe. Real, of course. He looked back at her, eyes wide.

"You didn't know why we were laying such a lip-lock on each other for?"

"What did I miss?" asked Guy.

"Me and Frawley kissin'," she answered. "And Austin here watched."

"Well, I didn't have much choice," he replied.

"You did. And if you can watch me, I can watch you."

"Grams!" Austin stepped back. Surely she didn't mean it.

He looked at Guy—who only shrugged, then raised an eyebrow. Did that mean what he thought it meant? Surely Guy wasn't suggesting…. He turned back to his grandmother.

Her arms were crossed once again over her ample bosom. "Go on. I want to see. Always was curious."

"Austin?" It was Guy. And he was close.

Austin looked at Guy. At his handsome face. Those lovely brown eyes. That broad mouth. *Oh God*, he thought as Guy stepped even closer. Then that mouth was descending toward his. Oh, God—and he closed his eyes and Guy was kissing him. Nothing like the bar and Guy's apartment that night. But it was a kiss. Sweet. Soft. Gentle.

"Well damn. I don't believe I ever seen anything quite so lovely," Grams said and walked away.

Austin opened his eyes to see Guy stepping back. "Let's go to bed," Guy said. "It'll be another long day tomorrow. And there's the drive home."

Austin nodded, heart rushing once more. "Okay," he said and followed Guy downstairs.

"GUY?"

"Yes, Austin."

He was staring up through the darkness at the dim shapes of the pipes crossing the basement ceiling. His stomach was aflutter. He couldn't stop thinking about…

Well damn. I don't believe I ever seen anything quite so lovely.

… the kiss. "That kiss was nice," he said quietly.

"Thank you. Yes, it was."

Austin suddenly remembered what his uncle had told him about the bedside table. He rolled over on his side and reached over, opened the drawer, and felt inside. There was a crinkling sound and then his fingers fell upon several flat square packages. He smiled. Condoms. Uncle Bodie had provided him with condoms. It truly seemed Austin had everyone's blessing.

All I am saying is that Guy is here, and he is obviously interested in you. And you are interested in him. You have no idea where Todd is, and you don't really know if he is even gay.

He thought about the kiss again, Guy's broad mouth on his. He thought of Guy's tongue—a week ago—how it sought entrance into Austin's mouth. How he had let Guy in. How exotic, how erotic, it had been. The feel of Guy's stubble against his own. Austin felt himself growing hard.

"Austin?"

"Y-yes?"

"I need to tell you something."

For some reason, Austin felt a sense of foreboding. *Crap. What is Guy saying? Don't. Don't say it. Don't ruin it.*

Found someone. He's found someone. I've waited too long and….

"It's about the walk I took—"

The guy followed him here? He went to him and—

"I went to Todd's house."

The words were so diametrically opposed to the completely ludicrous direction Austin had found his thoughts going that it took him a moment to register what Guy had actually said.

He went where? Todd? Todd's house? Guy knows where Todd is?
"What?"

"I went to speak to Todd's parents."

Austin shifted so he was gazing up at Guy. His eyes had grown accustomed to the dark, and he could just make out that Guy had propped himself up on one elbow and was looking down at him. "What?" he asked, trying to grasp it. "You talked to—"

"Todd's parents. His mom and dad—"

"*Step*dad," Austin corrected. Then, "You talked to them?"

"I-I asked them about Todd."

Austin stiffened. *Todd?* He'd spoken to them about Todd?

"I wanted to see if they knew something they hadn't told you."

Knew something? If Austin's mind had been a swirl before, it was numb now. He found it difficult to even form a clear thought.

"I hoped they might tell me something. It's been long enough, you know? And maybe they'd be willing to speak to someone they didn't know."

I don't believe it. I don't crapping believe it. "Did they?" was all he could say.

Guy sighed. "No. But his mother? I think she almost told me something. But then his dad—"

"Stepdad."

"—*step*dad appeared at the door, and *Jesus*. For a moment I thought he *might* shoot me."

"Guy!" *That fucking asshole.* "If he hurt you—"

"No. He didn't. I-I did something stupid. But it stopped him."

"What? What did you do?"

"I...." Guy cleared his throat. "I told him I was a cop."

"You what?" Austin sat up in the bed, astonished.

"I know. I know. Dumb. And it's not like I can even claim it wasn't premeditated."

"Guy. What the crap are you talking about?"

"Before we left, I was working one night, and I saw a prop lying around in the dressing rooms. It was the badge for The Cop in *Tearoom*

Tango. I slipped it in my pocket, and when Todd's *step*dad got in my face, I flashed the badge. I had it out of my pocket as fast as can be."

Austin couldn't speak.

"He backed off quick, I can tell you. But boy, if the two of them were closemouthed before, they really shut down then. Like a couple of clams. It was frigging weird, Austin. I mean, really weird. They told me to leave and get a search warrant. A search warrant? 'For what?' I asked. All I wanted to know was where I could find Todd Burton. But that was it—they weren't speaking. Although I got the idea that if the stepdad hadn't been there, she would've said more. I thought maybe I could go by tomorrow for a while—see if he leaves for work or something—and try her again, and maybe—"

"Why are you doing this?" Austin asked. He was stunned. How, why, was this man going to such lengths to help him? "Why are you helping me like this? I can't believe it."

"Because.... Because... *I* need you to resolve this Todd thing. It would be easy for me to let you think it's *just* because I'm such a good guy, Austin. In the beginning, I was helping you because I genuinely wanted to help you. I loved the romantic in you. I wanted to help you fulfill your Cinder-fella fairy tale. I wanted you to have what I never did.

"But now? Now there's a lot of selfishness involved. I want you to find him and either get with him or go your separate ways. I *need* it to happen as fast as possible—"

"But—but why?"

"Because...." There was a hitch in Guy's voice. Was he crying? "Because I'm falling...." Another hitch. "Oh God, Austin. Don't you know? Hasn't it been obvious from the minute I first saw you?"

What was Guy saying? Falling? Surely he didn't mean....

"Austin," Guy cried in exasperation. "I'm falling—hell—I'm there already. I love you, Austin, and I'm falling harder every day. If you find Todd and the two of you want to be together, I want it to happen soon. Because the way my feelings grow every day, it will soon *kill* me to lose you to him. I need this cut off now before I get fucking gangrene of the heart."

And remember something else, my boy. No one wants to be second choice. Would you? Would you want to be a consolation prize?

Austin kissed Guy. No preliminary delicacy involved in the kiss either. He reached out, drew Guy in by the back of his neck, and kissed him hard—plunged his tongue into the man's mouth. Because in that very instant, he knew.

Guy pulled back. "Austin! No. You've got to—"

Austin forced Guy's mouth to his again. Took possession of the man. *I love him. My God. I love him.* And…

Guy was kissing him now, pushing him back, laying his chest on Austin's—kissing hard. He wrapped his arms around Austin, slipped to his side, and pulled him close, tangling their legs together. It was overwhelming. Austin felt drunk. High. Higher than the clouds. He couldn't believe how amazing he felt to be in a *man's* arms—this man's arms, held so tight. His eyes popped open for less than a twinkling when he felt the hardness of Guy's sex pressed up against his own. The thrusting, shifting.

When they finally stopped for a moment, gasping into each other's mouths, Guy asked him, "Austin. Are you sure? What about—"

Austin pressed his fingertips against Guy's full lips. "Sssshhhh. I'm sure." Oh, he was. Beyond sure. "I love you."

Guy's eyes went wide. "But what if…?"

"It's too late," Austin explained, to himself as well as Guy. "Too late. Todd doesn't love me. He's probably not even gay. He's had months to find me. Call me. He knows my number. He knows my e-mail address. He knows my grandparents' phone numbers. He hasn't tried to contact me *once*. Not one time. If he *is* gay—if he does have feelings for me? It's too late. I love you." *And you are no consolation prize. You are* the *prize. Why couldn't I see that?*

Then they were kissing again, pulling their clothes off, crushing themselves together skin to skin. Austin could feel the rigid length of Guy's erection thrust up against his own and knew he had to see it. He kissed his way down Guy's torso, doing all the things he'd ever really wanted to do. He paused at Guy's nipples, licked them, brought them up firm, sucked gently at first—all the while marveling at the hair on

Guy's chest and how wonderful it felt on his tongue—then sucked on those nipples aggressively when Guy moaned and asked, begged, for more.

Then he was traveling down, reaching the column pushing against Guy's sleepers and popping the two buttons, releasing Guy's erection. Even in the dark, Austin could see it was beautiful, powerful, and like his own—uncircumcised. He fisted it, leaning in so he could see the hood slide back and forth over the flaring glans. Guy's scent was clean and musky, tantalizing, begging to be sucked. Austin opened his mouth, but Guy cried out, "Wait!"

Guy swiveled around so they were face to crotch and he could tug Austin's sweatpants down to release his sex.

"You're uncut!"

"Is that okay?" Austin asked.

"Hell yes," Guy said and then took Austin into his mouth.

"God!" Austin shouted, then bit down on his lips, fearful that someone may have heard. But God—oh God.

Guy's words echoed back to him from weeks before…

… that warm wet heat, a tongue, lips….

… and yes, Guy had been right. The pleasure was almost unbearable—exquisite. It was a moment before he could think clearly enough to take Guy as well.

Guy's cock was perfect. Thick, long, but not unmanageable—the taste of it a flood of delight to his palate. He played with the foreskin, running his tongue beneath, but carefully. Being uncircumcised himself, he knew how sensitive the head could be.

So they pleased each other, took pleasure from each other as well. But just as Austin knew he was approaching release, was sure Guy was as well and was thrilled with the expectation of it, Guy pulled back.

Austin groaned in frustration, but Guy shushed him. "I want you to fuck me, Austin. Let me find my jeans—I have a condom."

Fuck him? Oh my God. He wants me to fuck him. Austin trembled with anticipation and excitement. He was going to fuck Guy? "There's some in the drawer," he said, heart pounding now at the thought of being inside this man.

"There is?"

"I'll explain later...."

"Bodie or your grandmother?" Guy asked, chuckling.

"Uncle Bodie," Austin answered, and giggled.

Guy reached for the dresser, laughed in delight. "There's even little tubes of lube." He opened one of the foil packets quickly and slid the condom down Austin's erection.

Damn. Even that felt wild—Guy's warm hand fisting it down his length.

"It's been a long time," Guy said. "I'm going to climb on top, if you don't mind."

Austin laughed. "I don't mind." Hell no, he didn't mind. He moaned as Guy lubed his cock and watched, fascinated, as the man straddled him, his own erection arced out in front of him. There was a moment as Guy took Austin's length in hand, found the spot, and then settled down. Austin cried out as he entered his lover, amazed at the tightness, the heat.

"Damn," Guy moaned, wincing for a moment. "Been... God... so... uh... long. Oh." Then, "Ahhhh...." The pained expressed turned to one that could only be explained as bliss.

Thank God Guy rested for a few minutes, because Austin was afraid he would have an orgasm before Guy moved even once. The wait allowed Austin some modicum of control.

They locked eyes.

"Ready?" Guy asked.

"Yes," Austin said. "Oh yes."

Slowly, almost painfully slowly at first, Guy began to rock his body over Austin, sitting up then gradually taking Austin back inside himself. Austin thought he would die from the pleasure of it all. Bit by bit, step by step, Guy built up speed until—indeed—the bedsprings were squeaking.

"I love you so much," Guy said.

"I love you too," Austin echoed.

They both held out for as long as they could, but in fact it couldn't have been more than fifteen minutes when Austin knew the time of no return had arrived.

"Guy…. Guy… I'm gonna…."

Guy, who had been masturbating, sped up his hand. "Me too, lover. Al… most… there."

Then the wave overwhelmed Austin, building and building from deep within, exploding throughout his body and finally out of his cock and into the beautiful man over him. He shouted out, bit the palm of his hand to muffle the noise, and then Guy, too, was crying out as his warm seed splashed out onto Austin's chest and belly. For a moment, the world seemed to end—and then begin again. Guy collapsed on top of Austin, the both of them panting, purring, and declaring their love.

Later, as they lay spooned together with Guy in back, Austin heard the words: "No regrets?"

"God, no," Austin answered. "I'm the happiest man alive. This is the best Christmas ever."

"You're no longer a virgin, now."

"I don't know," said Austin. "For a gay man, it would seem to me I would need to bottom to lose my virginity."

"You suggesting something?" Guy growled.

"I sure am."

"You up for it?"

Austin grabbed Guy's hand and guided it to his rising erection.

"I guess you are."

"I guess I am."

ACT *THREE*

AUSTIN was showered and ready by six that evening and heading for the door. It had been a busy day. Peter had taken to giving him jobs at an apartment building he had recently purchased—the Oscar Wilde. There were a lot of gay people living there, and so, no big surprise, that meant he saw a lot of people he'd been meeting recently—including Jude Parks and Tommy Smith, aka Dixie Wrecked. It had been a pleasant surprise and a growing part of his new gay identity.

Gay identity, he thought with a grin. *Isn't life grand?*

Now he was on his way to the Pegasus. They were putting the finishing touches on the set, one he'd helped build. He'd enjoyed that immensely, using his carpentry skills to help Guy. It was weird to create a men's room right there on stage, but the results were incredibly rewarding. It was so real. They'd tiled it and everything, including putting in urinals. That had been crazy. They'd found some old ones in a building that was being torn down, and it was perfect that they were dingy and stained. They practically got them for free. Of course, they weren't usable, and when they needed to flush, it was a sound effect offstage—although they had managed to give them some running, recycling water for added realism simply by buying a few water fountain kits.

It was incredible to be involved with the show. Such luck. He'd stepped right into it. Right into the world of the stage.

Hang around the theater long enough, and someone will hand you a broom.

Not long ago, he'd lived in the tiny town of Buckman, pretending—when he was in a community play—that he was onstage in front of hundreds of people. When the people he knew clapped afterward, he would imagine they were strangers and he was on some big stage in New York or Chicago or even Kansas City. And now he was here. Not on stage *yet*, but somehow he *knew* it was coming. And while the Pegasus didn't really have that much more seating than the theater in Buckman—the high school auditorium—a show ran for four weeks, Tuesday through Sunday, and as many as 2,000 to 3,000 or more people saw each play. Imagine! And *he* was living the life. His fantasies were coming true.

Of course, the real joy of his life was Guy. Austin couldn't begin to count the blessings and wonders that now filled his days. Who knew love could be so wonderful? Especially when the man loved you back. It was all so new: getting to know one another, figuring out the whole couple thing. This wasn't dating; even Guy said so. Austin's boyfriend—*boyfriend!*—had dated, though Austin never had, and that's why Guy said the same thing—felt the same way. This *wasn't* dating. They were a couple even before they'd finished making love that Christmas night.

And oh, the lovin' was good!

Austin would never forget coming up for breakfast that next morning, very happy, but slightly worried about squeaking bedsprings. He needn't have been concerned. There was lots of smiling at the table as Grams buzzed around the kitchen making eggs, bacon, sausage, hash browns, grits, and naturally, her famous biscuits. Apparently some old people *did* still have a working furnace.

Even Uncle Bodie had been happy—Lucille seemed to be getting her groove back, although she'd never quite returned to the fireball Austin had first met.

Not long ago, he'd lived in the tiny town of Buckman, pretending—when he held the large body pillow he'd asked for as a birthday present—that he held Todd, his lover, in his arms.

Now he slept each night in Guy's arms. A real, live man, not a pillow, although Austin did like resting his head on Guy's chest. A man loved him. *Loved. Him.*

He'd spent every night since they got home from Buckman in Guy's bed. It was one thing to make the bedsprings squeak when they were in the basement and everyone else was two floors up. It was quite another when there was someone just on the other side of a wall and you didn't want anyone to hear the sounds of lovemaking.

Uncle Bodie said he missed Austin being there, but he didn't complain. Austin came down every morning to the smell of breakfast and fresh-brewed Shepherd's Bean coffee.

This allowed Guy time to work on his stage play—a project that had gone cold, but now, with their loving, was going fast and furious. Guy called Austin his muse. He liked the idea of being a muse. Especially for the man he loved so deeply, and whom he loved more with each passing day.

Todd came to his mind still, of course. Austin sometimes found himself looking for the old, beat-up beige VW van—the Galileo 7 Todd had called it, after some *Star Wars* or *Star Trek* thing or another. He would wonder where Todd was, if he was okay, if he was living in Kansas City at all, and if he was safe. He hoped so. Todd deserved happiness with all he'd been through.

Strange how easily he'd let go of his fantasies of Todd and them falling in love and being the first gay couple who could walk down Buckman's small-town streets, holding hands and being totally accepted by all. A role model for the hidden gay community—for after all, it was said one in ten people was homosexual, and that had to include Buckman, small-town USA. In the tales he'd spin in his head, everyone came out because he and Todd showed them the way.

But now Austin was living in Kansas City, with a man he'd never imagined and a love better than anything he'd made up. He'd exchanged a fairy tale for a reality.

"I almost feel guilty," Austin said to his uncle one night. "But I don't. As a matter of fact, the only guilt I really feel is that I don't feel guilty."

"What the hell do you have to be guilty about?" Uncle Bodie asked him.

"Well... I *loved* Todd. I guess I always will, in a way. But I just—" He snapped his fingers. "—gave him up for Guy."

"And?"

"What does that *mean* about my loving?" He paused, trying to put it all into words. "Will I just *fall* for someone else one day?"

"I suppose it's possible, Austin." But then Uncle Bodie had patted him on the knee. "What I suspect is that your feelings for Todd were more akin to an adolescent crush. Not that young people don't *love*. I'm not underplaying their feelings. Or yours. I would be a hypocrite if I said that. But it's perfectly common for a young man coming to the realization that he is gay to also fall for his best friend. I certainly did." Uncle Bodie paused—nodded—went on. "Love needs to be fed to thrive. Todd didn't feed you, not as a lover would, that is. He didn't give your love any light, any nourishment. Not in that basement. How could love grow? It couldn't. Guy, on the other hand, fell for you the minute you two met."

Austin had looked at his uncle in surprise. "He did?"

"Oh yes. You can't see it even now? In retrospect? Goodness. I saw it the instant he looked at you. Right out there." Uncle Bodie waved in the general direction of the balcony and the sidewalk below. "We walked outside and he was pulling that tarp off your truck, and he turned around and looked at you… and he was lost. I saw it happen."

Austin thought about it. Isn't that what Guy had told him? Could it be true? He thought of the moment his uncle described, remembered Guy's eyes growing wide and… yes. Austin felt warmth spread out through his chest. Wow.

"So it's okay that I just… abandoned Todd?"

"My boy? Todd abandoned *you*."

Austin sighed. *Abandoned me…. He did. No matter* what *I did. He ran. He left me all alone.* "God," he said. "Uncle Bodie—what happens if I find him and realize I still have feelings for him? What if he cares for me?"

"Then I guess you would have to make a choice, huh? Guy or Todd? Of course, you could always be—what's the word?—a 'throuple'?"

Austin laughed and rolled his eyes. "No, thanks. Guy is all I can handle."

"From the bulge in that man's jeans, I can believe it."

"Uncle Bodie!"

Interestingly enough, Austin had begun talking to Joan again. After months of barely acknowledging her, he'd called her and apologized for being distant. He told her all about Guy, and she was very happy for him, asking him all kinds of questions, from the silly—"What's his favorite color?"—to the personal, to the downright naughty. What really made Austin happy about their reunion, though, was that Joan had met someone at a community event, and this one liked everything about her. From her teddy bear collection to her barely palatable cooking to making love. A man who really wanted *her*. A man with a good job. A man who made her happy.

The memory of the conversation brought a smile to Austin's face as he looked both ways and crossed the busy street. He had no tools with him today, although he did have some markers and pens of various sizes and colors, as well as a few cans of spray paint. It was graffiti night, and after they did the first off-book run-through of the script—*on* set—everyone would get to play. Not that anyone in the audience would be able to read the scrawling on the bathroom walls, but it was important it all be as real as possible. It furthered the illusion that a genuine rest stop had somehow been transported onto the stage and they were witnessing something real.

Everyone had already agreed the stall walls should include the famous "man from Nantucket" limerick, and of course, the almost-as-crude "only farted" ditty. But Austin had been googling bathroom graffiti online and found some hilarious additions he wanted to include. His favorite was "My boyfriend is 13 inches," under which had been scrawled, "That's great! How big is his penis?"

And though he knew few people would see it, and far fewer even get it—he was going to write something over one of the urinals: "I'll Be Right Back—Wait Here ~ Godot."

And he was also determined to write "Austin + Guy" inside a big red heart.

Because he *did* love Guy. Oh yes, indeed he did.

As Austin approached the front door of the Pegasus, he marveled over how almost all the snow they'd shoveled, shoveled again, and then shoveled some more was pretty much gone. A week ago—the first day of the year—a hell of a storm had come through—at least as far as Kansas City was concerned. Eight inches, and then about six more the next day, followed by a good dusting on top of all that. Looking at the sidewalks and gutters, you'd never know it today. That was Kansas City weather. Don't like it? Wait a day. It would change.

Austin pressed the doorbell by the front door and a moment later was buzzed in.

"Hey, Austin," said the stunning black woman behind the glassed-in ticket counter.

"Hey, Iyanha! You gonna join us in the graffiti party tonight?" he asked, holding up his canvas bag.

Iyanha shuddered. "God, no." She held out her hands in front of her and shook them as if they were dirty. "Grosses me out."

He stopped in his tracks, surprised. "Iyanha! This is *theater*."

She dropped her hands. "I know that. It's not the subject matter. It's dirty public restrooms, which you all have fabricated quite realistically, *thank you*." She shuddered again. "Grosses me out. I try *never* to go potty except at home."

Austin nodded solemnly.

"Your lover boy is on Main Stage," she said and gave him a big, exaggerated wink.

"Thanks," Austin replied and then sighed contentedly.

"Oh, go on," she cried. "All this young love is just *too* sweet for *my* coffee."

Austin laughed happily and headed back through the lobby, past the Wagner Stage, back past the Donors' Wall—dozens and dozens of company names, plus individuals had theirs there as well. This included two names under the thousand-dollar sponsorship level—Wilda & Frawley Chandler.

Could life get any better? People who didn't even blink (although they winked) over the fact that he had a boyfriend—*I've got a boyfriend!*—were the grandparents who loved and supported him, literally. And of course, there was the boyfriend himself.

Austin entered the main theater, and there was Guy onstage, looking gorgeous—if not studious—in his oversized hoodie. He had one hand on his hip, a big black marker in the other hand, and was examining one of the toilet stall walls. As Austin quietly approached, not wanting to startle his lover—*my lover!*—Guy dropped to one knee and began to draw a circle around the pop-can-sized hole cut in the wood partition. Guy stopped and studied his handiwork, and then seemed to go into a trance, not moving, just kneeling there.

"I thought we were supposed to wait until the graffiti party for that," Austin said.

"Shit!" Guy fell back on his ass and looked up, eyes huge. "*Dammit*, Austin. You scared the crap out of me."

"At least you're in the right place for it," Austin replied.

Guy climbed to his feet and yanked his hoodie down in front, but not before Austin thought he'd glimpsed something. Did Guy have a hard-on? When Austin looked up, he saw—was that guilt on his face?

Austin stepped up onto the stage and went to his lover. "I'm sorry I scared you."

"It's okay," Guy said, pulling Austin into his arms and giving him a quick kiss—first to the forehead and then the lips.

"You okay, Guy?"

Guy took a deep breath, then let it out slowly. "I'm glad you're here, believe me." He turned and looked around him. "This isn't easy. I thought I could handle it. You know, I'm the director. Stand back from it all. That's my job. But…."

It hit Austin then. God. Of course this would be difficult. Guy must be having all kinds of flashbacks on this set. He didn't even like to use public restrooms, and not for the same reason as Iyanha. And this set was designed to radiate the sleazy underworld of bathroom sex.

Austin stepped in front of Guy, smiled, and gave him another long kiss. "I love you," he said.

"Me too." Guy hugged Austin tight. "I'm so glad you've been here every evening. So glad *you* helped build this fucking thing. It makes it all safer somehow."

"I'm glad. And I'll be here whenever you need me."

ONSTAGE, something unexpected was happening. Two of the characters, The Loner and The Romantic, had made a connection. They'd introduced themselves. By their real names. They'd actually kissed and had decided to leave together. "It's getting late," said The Loner. "We better get going."

Just then The Kid burst onto the stage. He was wearing The Cop's jacket—the jacket belonging to the man who had kissed him passionately moments before and taken The Kid away. It had been so sexy. And scary. Because it looked like The Cop might have an ugly ulterior motive for taking The Kid with him. Now the Kid was back, already, and he brushed by The Loner on his way to the opposite corner of the room. He was shaking, trying not to look at the two men who had been leaving. He spared them a glance. "Sorry," he said.

He's so damned good, Austin thought. *That could have been me!*

The Loner and The Romantic headed for the door, but The Loner turned back, considering The Kid for a moment as The Romantic kept going. But then he stopped, came back, gently took The Loner's arm, and they left the stage.

Alone now, The Kid looked around frantically, then rushed to the sink, pulled a bloody knife out of his jacket. Sobbing, he began to wash the blood off the knife and his hands. He returned the knife to the sheath hanging from his belt. He threw off The Cop's jacket and pulled off his shirt, the bloodstains shocking even though Austin knew it was coming. This was the first time they were going for full realism, what the audience would see. The Kid buried the shirt in the trash can, picked up the jacket, and put it back on.

There was a beat. Then he checked the pockets of the jacket, found a wallet, opened it, and discovered The Cop's badge. His eyes went wide. He'd killed a cop. He ran offstage.

Silence.

Blackout.

Austin sat in his seat, tears on his face, hardly able to breathe.

Jeez, he thought. He'd seen it dozens of times, from simple reading, to actors standing on an empty stage, through blocking. But now, with them all on set? Off-book? In costume? Something magical happened. It was transformed.

The play was amazing. Completely and totally amazing. The characters, the power of their words, the desperation of their lives.... And within, a message for all.

Finally, he gained control of himself and leapt to his feet and applauded until his hands hurt. "Bravo," he shouted. "Bravo!"

The actors, looking immensely relieved and pleased at the same time, all bowed—those who had walked back onstage and those whose scenes were done and had joined him in the seats.

I could have been in *this play. If I hadn't been so crapping chicken. So damned naïve.* It was a powerful show—but it made him sad. This had been Guy's past. This was how he had discovered sex. *I had a beautiful man hold me and make love to me, cherish me. He had countless faceless men who treated him like he was nothing but a cock.*

It was that thought that made Austin determined he would do all he could to make up for the love Guy had not been given when he was Austin's age. He knew already Guy had never really been in a serious, long-term relationship.

"I'm damaged goods," Guy had said on more than one occasion. "When I tell a guy about my past, I've been pretty much dropped like I'm diseased or something. And I'm not!"

"It's not fair for them to judge you by your past anyway," Austin had said, taking his lover in his arms.

"You don't, do you?" Guy asked, eyes wet with tears. "Judge me for what I once did?"

"Of course not. How could I expect you not to judge me for things I've done if I judge you?"

"God, I love you, Austin."

"Love you too, Guy."

How could anyone *not* love Guy? Well, their foolishness was his fortune.

"You liked it?" Guy said tonight, coming down the aisle from the back of the auditorium where he had been watching his actors—pacing—observing them from different angles.

"It is incredible, Guy. It blew me away."

"I love you, Mr. Shelbourne," said Guy. "Did you know that?"

Austin smiled. "I did know that, Mr. Campbell. Did you know that I love you too?"

"Thank God," Guy said, kissing him.

After that, the graffiti party lasted an hour or two. Beers were opened—Guy waggled his eyes and handed Austin a Double-Wide I.P.A. Someone passed a flask of good ol' Kentucky whiskey—Austin passed after the first swallow. And there was a joint. He only took a single hit of that as well. Both whiskey and pot had a tendency to make him way too uninhibited, and he didn't want to embarrass himself in front of professionals—even marijuana-smoking ones.

They had a lot of fun adding art and graffiti to the walls of the stalls. A friend of one of the actors who'd been watching the rehearsal—a young man a few years older than Austin with the unlikely moniker "Hound Dog" and amazing dark-blond dreadlocks—turned out to be most proficient with his additions to the walls. He'd soon drawn quite a few penises, breasts, vaginas, and characters performing all kinds of sexual acts. It was apparently the reason he'd been invited.

And of course, there was the graffiti itself. Such literary masterpieces as: "Why are you looking up here? The joke's in your hand." "I love your Crocs—signed Nobody EVER." "Now shake it off." "Only faggots drink here." And finally, Austin's favorite: "What would Jesus do?" followed by "He wouldn't vandalize bathroom walls."

At last, everyone began to filter out, one by one, until only Austin and Guy were left.

"Might as well lock up and go home," Guy said. He was suddenly acting a little jittery, and Austin began to suspect why—he'd been watching for it, as a matter of fact.

"You okay?" he asked.

Guy shrugged. "Getting nervous again. Especially now."

"Why now, lover?"

Guy shifted his weight back and forth a couple of times, looked around him. "It's so *real* now, Austin. If I turn my back on the theater,

I'm *there*. And the lighting the way it is now? *Just* like *that* rest stop...."

Austin didn't need to ask which rest stop. It was obvious.

"What do you do, baby? When the memories of those days come back to haunt you? When something like this brings them back?"

Guy trembled. Gritted his teeth. "I turn my back on them," he said, turning away from the set and looking out at the rows of seats. "Like that. I block them. Think of puppies and fields of daisies and my favorite Calvin and Hobbes cartoons."

Austin nodded. "How well does that work?"

Guy sighed. "Not well."

Not well at all, Austin supposed.

"For all kinds of reasons."

And how well did thinking of Calvin and Hobbes work when he was confronted daily by this set? Austin wondered.

"Sometimes it works for a little while. Maybe. Or maybe not so good. It always comes back, and then I feel ashamed. There was a while back there where I even thought about killing myself."

"Oh, baby," Austin said and stepped closer.

"Especially after my parents excommunicated me."

Excommunicated him? Guy really is a writer. He took another step into his lover's space. *Help him. Find some way to help him.*

"The worst is when I start craving it. Wanting to go back. Dammit, Austin. You don't want to hear this...."

"I do. Tell me. It's okay. No judgments, remember?" And he meant it.

Guy closed his eyes. Shuddered. "I get the shakes. I see those bathrooms in my head. I think about those blowjobs. How simple it all was. I hardly ever saw their faces, hardly ever saw the men at all. Just mouths. It was so easy after a while not even to think of them as people. Sometimes I think about those days and I get so hard and horny and I want to *scream!* And I think how easy it would be to find a cruisey john and just get off. And *maybe—finally—*be the one to suck a cock. I wouldn't even have to see his face. Just do what I love to do."

Then the idea that had been forming for days in Austin's mind finally became concrete. He knew what he wanted to do.

"*Maybe*," he said, drawing the word out. "Maybe you should try something different."

"L-Like what?" Guy asked and rubbed his hands through his short hair.

"Confront it. Go there…."

"Oh my God, no," Guy said, clearly horrified, eyes wide.

Austin gave him an encouraging smile. "Not there *specifically*."

"W-What do you mean?" Guy was shifting again.

"Do you remember what you said to me when I asked you why you were doing this play? You said it was because you wanted to confront and exorcise your demons. Maybe that's what you're supposed to be doing. Exorcising your demons instead of ignoring them. Pretending they're not there doesn't help if they're real. You need a safe place and a safe way to confront them."

"I-I don't…."

"Do you feel safe with me?" Austin asked.

"I-I…. Yes, I do."

"And this place? It's safe, Guy. It's not *really* real. And there is no one around…."

Guy's eyes widened even more. "What are you suggesting, baby?"

Austin reached up, placed his hands on Guy's chest and gently pushed, gently guided him back… and back… into a stall.

"Wha-wha…?"

"Drop your pants," Austin said.

"What?"

Austin leaned up and placed a gentle kiss on Guy's lips. "I love you so much." He touched Guy's cheeks, lowered his hands and let the back of his knuckles lightly graze his lover's nipples through his oversized hoodie.

"Austin?"

Austin did it again, and Guy moaned softly. Then Austin reached for Guy's belt while continuing to kiss him, more fully now, letting his tongue touch Guy's lips. Guy moaned again, touched Austin's hands, but didn't stop him.

"W-what are you doing…? Someone might…."

"The doors lock when people leave, right?" Austin said quietly.

"Yes."

"And there's no one here but us?" He kissed Guy again.

"Y-yes."

"Jennifer?"

"Out—out of town."

Austin unbuckled the belt, popped the upper snap of Guy's jeans, kissed him more deeply.

"Aus—" He kissed back.

Austin pulled down the zipper, and Guy's jeans slipped to his ankles. Feeling bare hips, reaching behind and touching Guy's bare ass, Austin thought, *Bingo. Freeballing.*

He gently pushed his lover down so the man was sitting on the faux toilet, bent, kissed him again, and then stepped back. *I love you*, he mouthed, and then went to the next stall, undid his own jeans and underwear, lowered them, and sat down.

"Oh God, Austin… I can't…."

"You *want* to," Austin whispered back.

"God, yes. My heart is fucking pounding."

"Stick it through for me, Guy."

"But…."

Austin got down on his knees before the hole in the pretend stall wall. He could just see Guy's lap, his growing erection. To his delight, his own cock was already rising. This was sexy. It was kinky and naughty and… safe. Perfect.

"But what if—"

"What if what?" Austin asked quietly.

"What if this triggers something…?"

"Then we have this set."

"But later…?"

"We'll take this fucking partition home with us."

"Oh, baby," said Guy.

"Stick it through, my love."

"But…."

"It's okay, Guy. It's safe. I love you. Do it."

Guy stood up quickly, and then his throbbing erection came through the hole. Austin rocked back on his heels and his eyes widened. Guy's cock looked so big this way. He moaned in lust, amazed at the sight. It was so hot, so sensual, this huge bodiless cock. He wanted to pounce on it but stopped himself. He kissed it instead, lightly at first, as he had Guy's lips moments before. Then slowly, he kissed it more, lovingly, and then with more and more passion until he took it deeply into his mouth, taking it to the root.

"God!" shouted his lover. "My God!" There was a thump against the wall—Guy collapsing against the wall?—and a slight pulling away before the erection was thrust into Austin's mouth again. Guy thrust again and Austin grabbed hold of the cock, not letting him pull back. He used his fingers to pull at the scrotum and work his lover's balls through, held them at the base so that Guy couldn't fuck his mouth. He began to tenderly, adoringly, suck on his man, making love to him even through this hole. It was erotic and loving at the same time, the best of two worlds. Did Guy see it that way? He hoped so.

It didn't take long before Guy was crying out, warning Austin, and suddenly he was cumming in great blasts, surprising Austin with the power and volume. Guy was all but screaming as his orgasm rocked him, the whole wall between them shaking. When the spurts stopped, the throbbing subsided, and the erection began to soften, Guy pulled back and collapsed on his side. He was heaving in great gasps of air and… sobbing? Was he crying?

Austin grabbed his jeans and half pulled them up, then went as quickly as he could to the other side. "Guy?"

His lover looked up, and yes, there were tears in his eyes. But more. Love. And lust. He shot to his feet and kissed Austin madly, pulling him roughly into his arms. "I fucking love you," he finally said, after a long, powerful kiss that had brought Austin's erection up fully, and apparently, Guy's as well. "I love you," he said again. "That was amazing."

"Was it?" Austin asked, still a little afraid. Had he done the right thing or not?

"I've wanted this again so much, but I knew I couldn't. I knew what it might do…. But you made it okay."

Austin smiled, relieved. It had been nice.

"You are a great exorcist," Guy said, and waggled his eyebrows.

Austin laughed.

"One more thing?"

"What?" Austin asked.

"I want to do what I never have. What I wanted to do but was too afraid."

"Yes?"

"I want to suck *you*!"

"Oh," Austin said, his cock leaping at the thought.

"Go on," Guy commanded.

So he did. He went back to the wall, let his jeans fall and started to stick it through, and—

"Wait" came Guy's voice. "Sit down. Lean back."

Curious, Austin did as asked.

A finger came through the hole. Just the tip. Only for a second. *Wha…?*

Then the finger came through again, ran about two-thirds of the circumference, then was gone. That's when Austin remembered. He saw Guy's foot. It was tapping.

"What?" he asked.

"Stick it through" came Guy's disembodied voice.

"Stick what through?" he asked, trying to sound as if he had no idea.

"Your cock."

"My what?" he asked, filling his tone with surprise.

"Come on. Do it. Please, man."

So he did. An instant later, his cock was engulfed, and it was his turn to cry out in pleasure. It had almost been a shock, even though he knew what was coming. It was the alienness of it all, standing there, his body against the rough panel of wood, his erection thrust through trustingly, the not knowing for sure. And then that warm, wet mouth—

... that warm, wet heat, a tongue, lips...

—hit him, and he had to reach up and grab the top of the partition to keep from falling.

Guy began to suck him with great enthusiasm, and they both cried out, moaning, groaning. The pleasure, found not only in Guy's expertise, but the erotic nature of it all, soon had Austin on the brink. He tried to warn his lover, but the shock of his orgasm suddenly overwhelmed him. His legs shaking, he exploded into Guy's mouth. The warmth and wetness did not go away. Guy had not pulled back but moaned all the louder, greedily swallowing Austin's orgasm. At last, Austin couldn't take it anymore and practically fell back onto his toilet. Already Guy was coming around to his side, kneeling before him, kneeling and drawing him into his arms.

They sat like that for what felt like ever. They kissed, then pulled themselves together and went home. Once there—they made love again, quietly, softly, reassuringly. All was beautifully right in the world.

But somehow, Austin knew taking home that partition would lead to nothing but many more fun and erotic, loving adventures for them for years to come.

A FEW weeks later, *Tearoom Tango* opened to... interesting reviews. All agreed the show was well to excellently acted, and there was praise for its direction as well. Obviously, this made Austin and Guy very happy.

Some conservatives were outraged, of course, which bothered no one at the Pegasus. Outrage from the conservatives started controversy, and that meant more ticket sales. Then there were those who didn't understand....

"Why write something like this? Aren't there any other stories the Pegasus could have chosen to present about gay life instead of this one? I know the Pegasus is all about showing controversial pieces, but this just seemed like it was controversial to be controversial. What the hell was it about?"

Austin ranted about that one. Balled the newspaper up and threw it across the room, and then began to pace. Guy only smiled, opened it up, and smoothed it out so he could snip it from the paper and save it.

"What's so funny?" Austin raged.

"You didn't get it either."

That stopped Austin in his tracks, and he wound up sitting in Guy's lap and hugging him tight.

In an article where theatergoers were asked their opinions, there were comments like:

"I was struck at how sad it was that some of the characters thought anonymous sex was the only way to find intimacy with anyone, especially another man. I hurt for them. There are so many more ways to find intimacy. I was deeply moved."

("Hurray," said Austin. "He *got* it.")

"I was disgusted. I don't want my Mom thinking that this is the only way gay men find sexual partners. This play needs to be banned!"

("Hurray," cried Guy—to Austin's surprise. "More tickets!")

"It was very well done. Very real. I wish there had been more hot bodies. The dudes didn't have very good bodies. Well, except for The Kid. Wow. He was hot. And he gave an excellent performance too."

("What the fuck?" asked Guy. "What do the bodies have *anything* to do with anything?"—while all Austin could tell his lover was, "I could have been up there, dammit. Next time!")

After the first few days, sales dropped off, but another week's passage sent them soaring, and they were sold out almost every night. Word gets around. And it helped that Austin went out almost every night to the bars and passed out fliers. He also gave Liddle Awful

Annie tickets to give away as prizes during her show. It didn't hurt that the actor who played The Kid, and the older muscle bear who played The Cop, got on stage shirtless half a dozen nights on her show either.

Austin saw the play almost every night. What surprised him was that sometimes the show was... different. The actors could change the whole tone of the show by changing the inflection of their words, or by how the chemistry between them played out on a particular night. There were performances that left the audience quietly stunned, while another night had them weeping in their seats, and a third had them leaping to their feet, applauding. Austin saw there was even chemistry within the audience, as well as between them and the actors. It amazed and thrilled him, and he absorbed it all like a sponge.

Uncle Bodie saw it twice. He even took a nap before seeing it the second time, because he wanted to be able to go to the little cast party at Guy's afterward.

Austin knew how much Guy hated cast parties, so both he and Uncle Bodie had spent a couple of days preparing treats for the guests. They wanted it to have a fun theme, so they were sure to include little signs to make sure no one missed the jokes. There were cocktail "wieners," meatballs, nut mix, "cream"-filled éclairs. They also made a large summer sausage flanked with two cheese balls and a fringe of parsley, and a penis-shaped cake, and even salad made with, yes, penis-shaped pasta. Uncle Bodie didn't stick around long enough, though. Lucille was acting punkie again and wouldn't come out from under the bed. It made Austin sad that his uncle didn't see what a hit their food was, and how it helped take the edge off the final-night blues now that the show was over and everyone was off for new parts and new shows.

"Tell me," Austin asked Asher, the man who had played The Cop, "Why do you do it?"

"Do what?" he asked.

"Act? I've been listening to everyone for weeks. They obviously love acting. But the hours are killing, they have to be there no matter what happens...."

Asher nodded. "Like my grandmother dying during the run? Thank God the funeral was in town...."

Austin sighed. "Exactly. And sorry, I didn't mean to...."

"No, it's okay. I assume you are thinking of giving acting a go after all?"

Austin blushed. The man had been one of the witnesses when he'd run out on his audition.

"Let me just say this," Asher said. "Don't do it unless you *must*."

"Must?" Austin asked.

"*Must*. The answer to your question is I act because I *must*. I *have* to. I can't *not* act. I tried once or twice, but it always calls me back. I'm like a lemming, I guess. I have no choice. It might sound stupid or corny, but it's in my soul."

Austin nodded, his skin tingling at the words. "I think I understand...."

Asher smiled. "If you plan on coming back, then you understand. And dammit, I get to say the words of *Shakespeare*! Or Peter Shaffer or Tom Stoppard—they have a turn of phrase better than anything I'd ever be able to come up with."

"Hey," said Jennifer Leavitt, joining them. "Great party, Austin."

"Thanks." He grinned. Austin liked the woman a lot. She was so filled with energy. So exciting. So full of love for what she did. It was contagious. It probably helped that she was "family" as well.

"Young Austin here is thinking about acting," said Asher.

She nodded. "Of course he is. Maybe he'll audition for the role of James Smith in Guy's play."

"Huh?" Austin asked. What? James Smith? Guy's play?

"Well, now that it's finally finished—"

"Guy's play is finished?" Austin asked, astonished. Finished? Surely she was mistaken. Guy would have told him.

Jennifer's eyes widened a tiny bit, and she glanced at Asher. "Um," she said.

Austin shook his head. "When did he finish?"

"I-I'm sorry, Austin," she said. "I just *assumed*...."

"No. It's not finished. And there isn't a character named James Smith. There's Perseus and Jacob and Molly and… James Smith?"

Jennifer bit her lip. "I think I may have just fucked up."

Austin got in control of his face. *I can do this. I'm an actor, right?* He laughed and gave her a hug. "You couldn't fuck up anything, Jennifer! Now it looks to me like you need a refill," he said, pointing to her near-empty glass of wine.

He decided to wait until the next day before bringing it up. He hoped Guy would. Surely Jennifer would mention her "fuck-up" to her friend and employee?

But then the party went late, and they were all pretty drunk when they went to bed. He got up to the surprise of Guy making breakfast, so he thought it might be mentioned then. But over eggs and bacon and even grits—Grams had addicted him to them instantly—the only topic of conversation was the gorgeous day and should they hit the local Sunfresh for groceries.

Finally, Austin could stand it no more. "Who's James Smith?"

A look of confusion came over Guy's face. Then a slow-dawning understanding. "Ah…."

"Jennifer happened to mention you finished *Dolly Parton Play*," he said, forcing himself to be light.

"I, ah… I've been waiting to tell you," Guy replied.

Austin put his fork down. "Why, baby?" he asked, confused. It was true. It was true.

"It's just…."

"*Who's* James Smith?" This was all so confusing.

Guy leaned on the table, pushing his mostly finished plate aside. "He's Perseus. I changed my mind. I decided a couple days ago that I wanted the gay character to have the most common name there was. I googled it. Found out the most common first and last names in the United States. I thought it was important that he be as 'normal' as possible, even though he's gay and…." He stopped. Looked away.

"Even though what?" Austin pressed.

Guy sighed. "I'll go get it," he said. He rose and left the room and was back a few minutes later with his laptop. "Are you done with that?" he asked, pointing to Austin's empty plate. "Did you want any more?"

Austin shook his head and picked up his plate and took it to the sink. Guy, meanwhile, had opened his computer and was booting it up. By the time Austin had cleared the table—Guy told him he was done eating as well—the play was up on the screen. Austin looked at Guy, and he motioned for Austin to sit.

"Now before you read this, I-I want you to know it's not the final draft."

"Has Jennifer read it?" *Please say no. Please.*

Guy nodded, and for some reason, Austin felt a sharp pang in his heart.

"She's an expert, you know? I just wanted to make sure it was good."

And you didn't think my opinion would matter? "She liked it, didn't she?"

Guy nodded again. "Yes," he said quietly. "She thinks it's good enough for In-Progress Night."

In-Progress Night? He knew he should know what that was.

"Once a year, the Pegasus does a couple of weekends where we publicly read new plays, works in progress. To get the reaction from an audience." Guy sat down next to him, his face in that weird, unreadable mode again.

What was it about that? Why did he hide his feelings?

"I can take stuff out," he said, his mask slipping, eyes going wide.

What was this about? Was that worry on his face? Did he look nervous? "You won't want to take anything out if Jennifer likes it the way it is."

"*No.* If there is *any*thing you don't like, I'll take it out."

"Why would there be something I don't like…." Then he heard an echo. What had Guy said, so long ago?

Just remember that it's dangerous being friends with a writer. You never know when something you say will end up in his next work.

Austin got a weird, foreboding feeling in the pit of his stomach.

"I love you, Austin."

Austin nodded, and began to read.

AT FIRST, Austin was stunned. From the opening words, he was drawn in. The dialogue grabbed him immediately, flowing naturally and believably despite the odd nature of the setting.

Five men and women wake up in a steel room with no idea how they got there or where they are. There is only one door, and that turns out to lead to a bathroom. There is no door out of the room. There aren't even any apparent vents, yet they are getting air, no light fixtures, but they can see. Food appears through the only opening in the wall. Five beds and five small tables and chairs are the only furnishings. Bit by bit, their memories come back. They are terrified. Alliances are formed and broken. The gay character, James Smith, reveals his sexuality and is threatened by one character and befriended by others. A woman constantly talks to him and it is revealed her husband recently left her for another man and she hopes James can help her discover why.

Isla:	That's how you knew you were gay? You had sex with your best friend?
James:	Well. *(beat)* Sorta.
Isla:	Sorta? How did you "sorta" have sex? Did you guys c… (starts to say "cum" but can't bring herself to say the word.) Did you guys have orgasms or not?
James:	Well, one of us did.
Isla:	Which one? You or him?
James:	You're pretty fuckin' nosy, you know that?
Isla:	I am? Sorry. I don't mean to be.

Austin froze. *What the crap?* He trembled, his stomach fluttered. He continued to read.

James: (long beat) Him.

Isla: Him?

James: Orgasm. He came. And then he ran out.

Isla: Oh. Wow. He ran out? That really sucks.

James: Well, I did anyway. Sucked him. His cock. And he came and then he ran off.

Isla: *(long beat)* I'm sorry.

James: *(shrugs his shoulders)*

Isla: And that's how you knew you were gay? I would think after something like that—well, sucking—ah, you know—I'd think you'd never want to do it again.

James: Oh no. That part was awesome. Isla. My God. I never felt so fucking alive in my whole life. It was about the most *(beat)* edifying, illuminating moment of my fucking life! I never felt so right.

Isla: You got this from sucking a…. *(she still can't say "cock")*

James: *(laughs)* You can't even say it. Cock. The word is "cock." *(he puts great emphasis on the word)* His cock was perfect.

Austin's stomach was cramping. He stopped, closed his eyes. *This isn't happening. It's not. Guy wouldn't do this.*

He opened his eyes, the words on the screen going in and out of focus. He squinted, concentrated. Continued….

James: I'd seen him naked before. Fuck. When we were little, my mom would make us take baths together before we went to bed. We'd stand up and shake them at each other. *(he stands and demonstrates—clothed)* But we never *did* anything. Never jerked off or played with each other. I hear straight guys do that. Jerk off together when they're teenagers or something. College maybe? Anyway, we didn't. Not until one dark and stormy night. The power went off and we were lying there on the hide-a-bed together.... *(beat—takes a deep breath)* We started talking about sex. That's what guys do, you know? And suddenly I knew I wanted him. I reached right over and put my hand on his dick, and he was as hard as steel. Then he put his hand on mine. We were only wearing our underwear, you know? And we took our dicks out and started playing with each other. Never said a word. I was trying so hard not to cum. I wanted him to get off first. Then before I even knew what I was doing, I did it. I sucked his cock and he came and I swallowed it all and I was afraid I would hate it but no, I loved it. *(beat)* And when he finished...

Isla: He ran out on you.

James: He ran out on me.

Isla: *(very long beat)* And that made you know you were gay? I still don't get it. If that happened to me, I would never want to....

James: You don't want to now, do you? Suck cock? I bet you don't suck your husband's.

Isla: My *ex*-husband!

James: You didn't, did you?

Isla: And that's why he "fucking" left me?

James: *(beat)* No, Isla. He left you because he's
          gay. He left you because he tried to be
          straight with you and he couldn't do it
          anymore. He had that affair and he knew
          that he needed to be with another man. A
          good blowjob does not a gay man make.

Isla: Oh! And you know this because you were
          married?

James: *(shakes head)* No. I know this because I
          fucked his girlfriend and hated it....

Austin leapt to his feet. He was shaking. Horrified. "My God," he
shouted. "Guy!" Tears sprang to his eyes. "My God!"

Guy jumped up as well. "Austin. I can take it out. I told you—"

"How could you? Guy! That was my life! *Private*. That happened
to me. To Todd. To Joan. But I shared it with you. I trusted you. You
can't just rip that out of my heart and their hearts and put it up on a
stage for people to see!"

Guy held up his hands. "I'll take it out!"

"But. You. Put. It. In!"

"Baby... I'll take it out. It was just...."

"Did *Jennifer* like it?" Austin cried out.

Guy paused, looked away. Looked back. "She thinks it's one of
the most powerful scenes in the play."

"Does she *crapping* know it happened to *me*?"

"God, no, Austin. I would never—"

"But you *would* put it in your play." The tears began then. Rolling
down his face like if he didn't figure out how to stop then, they might
never stop. "Guy...."

"I'll take it out," Guy said, and he was crying now.

"*Fuck you*, Guy," Austin shouted.

Guy flinched. Took a step back.

"Fuck you!"

Austin fled the apartment.

HE WAS raging inside as he ran down the stairs, two at a time. *Uncle Bodie*, he would scream. *You won't believe it! He is taking my most personal life and making it a play. Things I trusted him with! That fucker. My life, Uncle Bodie! How could he?*

But as he reached the door, he heard a sound that made the hair on his arms stand up. There was a wailing from inside the apartment, a high keening that now drew the hair up on the back of Austin's neck.

He opened the apartment door and ran inside and found his uncle on the couch.

At first he wasn't sure what he was seeing. The man was crying. No, not crying. The word didn't come close to what the man was doing. He was practically shrieking, rocking back and forth and holding what looked like a fox-fur stole.

And then Austin saw what it was.

It was the limp body of Lucille.

Uncle Bodie began heaving, ratcheting up huge deep breaths, and then began to wail once more. Austin was frozen. *No*, he thought. *It can't be. Please, God. Please. If You are real. Not Lucille.*

Uncle Bodie fell back, and Lucille's limp body almost fell out of his lap and onto the floor. Somehow Austin was there in an instant, catching her and throwing himself next to his uncle.

"No!" Uncle Bodie bawled. "No. She *can't* be." He looked at Austin, eyes wide and red, face soaked with tears. "Austin. Austin, please. *Do something!* Do something." He looked down in his lap. Picked up the lifeless body, Lucille's head falling to the side, held her up to his nephew, the desperation palatable. "Breathe on her or push on her chest or something. Austin. Do something."

"Oh, Uncle Bodie," he said, and the tears, tears that had halted when he heard his uncle crying through the apartment door, were back. He wanted to hold them back, be strong for the man in his arms, but he couldn't. "There's nothing I can do."

Uncle Bodie began to shake, he closed his eyes, pulled his little dog to his chest, then opened his eyes again. "Where were you? You always come down for breakfast. Where were you?"

Austin trembled. *I was reading a play. I was acting like a big crapping baby and getting all pissed off at my lover. I was getting all bent out of shape because he used my story in his play. That's where I was. When I should have been here.* "I am so sorry, Uncle Bodie."

His uncle collapsed into his arms, shaking his head, holding his Lucille close, sobbing against his shoulder.

A long time later, when the crying had subsided, Uncle Bodie slowly sat up. "Austin," he whispered. "Would you go down to the basement? Get one of those plastic tubs? There are a few down there, almost empty. Bring one of them up, please?"

"Are you sure you want me to leave you?"

"I'm sure. Please. Go."

Austin untangled himself and got up. "Do you need me to do something?"

"Get the tub, son," Uncle Bodie said, rocking his Lucille slowly in his lap, not taking his eyes off of her.

Austin nodded and quickly left the apartment, out into the courtyard and down into the basement. He pulled out his cell phone and called Guy.

"Austin?" came the answer on one ring.

"Come down right away. Uncle Bodie needs you."

"Bodie?"

"Lucille is dead."

"Oh my God. I'm coming right now."

"Thank you, Guy."

"It's no problem. I'm on my way."

"Thank you."

"And Austin?"

"Yes, Guy?"

"I am so sorry."

"No. I'm the one who is sorry. I'm really sorry," he said. Because it didn't matter. Not in the scheme of things. Uncle Bodie mattered. That was what was real. The rest? Why, it was just a play.

He found a tub easily, several in fact, combined their contents so that one was empty, and then brought it back to the apartment as quickly as he could. Guy was there, sitting with his uncle. When Austin entered the room, his uncle gently handed Lucille over to Guy. Uncle Bodie got up, nearly fell, then held out a hand to let them know he was okay. He left the room and came back a few minutes later with a lap quilt. It looked like one Grams had made.

"Bring that here, son," Uncle Bodie said quietly and folded the blanket and draped it in the tub. He then had Guy place Lucille in as well. He started to fold the blanket inside and then stopped. He reached under the coffee table and brought out one of Lucille's toys, a shredded rabbit, and placed it inside with his beloved dog. "Goodnight, sweet Lucille, my tiny lady. Rest now, and sweet dreams." He placed the rest of the blanket over her.

"I need to call Peter," he said.

AN HOUR later, Peter Wagner was there.

Austin opened the door, and there he was. Peter Wagner. At last. He was real.

He was a tall man, thin, with almost impossibly long arms and legs. He looked to be around sixty, but it was hard to tell. Peter's eyes were ancient—Austin saw that right away. He might have been immortal with eyes like that, crystal clear and blue gray. There were many lines on his face, some tiny, but some deep as valleys, and his brown hair was shot with silver. His bearing was regal, and he carried a cane but didn't seem to need it. And although he was dressed casually in slacks and smoking jacket, it was obvious the clothes were expensive. How did one guess the age of such a man?

He put Uncle Bodie to bed, was gone for some time, then joined Guy and Austin, who sat together on the couch.

"How are you boys?" he asked, as if they were the ones who needed help.

"Okay," Austin replied. "But Uncle Bodie?"

Peter sat down in a chair next to them and stretched his long legs out in front of him. "It is difficult to say. Lucille.... She was special. A most enchanting creature. She will be missed. But by no one more than Bodie."

"I should have been here," Austin said, and just like that began to cry again.

"No, do not do that to yourself. Bodie explained. Thou wert with thy lover and there was nothing you could have done had you been here." He pulled a handkerchief from his front pocket and handed it over. "Here, dear boy."

"I could have been here so he wouldn't have been alone when he found her." Austin wiped his eyes, sniffled, started to hand it back.

"Blow your nose, Austin. It's all right. I have many more. Keep it."

Austin did as told, then stared at it. He'd never used a real hankie before. What did you do with it? Surely you didn't throw it away?

"I am so sorry that this is the way we are meeting for the first time. You are a light in Bodie's life, and I wish we could have met under better circumstances. I let myself get too busy."

Austin didn't say anything. He didn't know what to say. He tucked the handkerchief in his shirt pocket and finally said, "*Lucille* was the light of his life. I don't know what he'll do without her."

She gives me reason to get up each day, to keep going, came an echo of Uncle Bodie's voice. *After all, what would she do without me?*

"He will need you, that is for sure," Peter said. His voice was almost musical, the accent unreadable. As if he had adopted a bit from all the cultures and countries he visited. "Lucille was his best friend, and now she is gone. We are all graced by our pets. I believe it is a dog that proves there must be a God. Why else would such perfect companions exist? I think that Anatole France once said that 'Until one has loved an animal, a part of one's soul remains unawakened.'"

Austin nodded. "What do we do now?"

"Now, I would like some of your uncle's sherry. I would like a drink and mayhap you will join me. Then I think you should both go upstairs and sleep in *your* bed tonight."

"No," said Austin. "No, I need to stay. I wasn't here when he needed me."

"But you *were*," Peter said. "You were very much here when he needed you. But Bodie will not be alone tonight, worry not, and I am too tall for yon couch. Plus it is a torture device assuredly created by the Spanish Inquisition. I cannot hope to sleep there."

Despite himself, Austin smiled. He'd never thought the couch was comfortable, but his uncle loved it. Loved all of his furniture, his kitschy things, knickknacks, and pictures.

And Lucille.

"Should we take her to the vet?" Austin asked. "To see what happened? Why she—"

"I asked him the same thing, but he said it was not necessary. Eighteen years happened, young Austin. A dog does not a human lifetime have. If only they did. If only they lived threescore years and ten and we but a decade or two. It would seem more fair. Was it not Samuel Clemens who said, 'The dog is a gentleman; I hope to go to his heaven, not man's'?"

"I hope we go to the same one," Austin said. "For Uncle Bodie's sake. It wouldn't be heaven for him without her, would it?"

"Ah, yes," Peter replied. "'No heaven will not ever Heaven be. Unless my dog is there to welcome me.'"

"Who said that?" Austin asked.

"Why, I did, Austin. And I bastardized it. As for the original author, I believe we do not know. Now. Upstairs with the both of thee. Find solace in each other's arms. Bodie and I will be here. If I need you this evening, I know where to find you. And if he calls for you, I will call you down."

"Do you promise?" Austin asked.

"I do, my lad. I do."

They stood up, and Peter rose with them. He shook their hands, then pulled Austin close, surprising him with the iron quality of his thin chest. "I do say again how sorry I am we did not meet under better circumstances. If only it had been your birthday or one of the nights of the play, which I did see, but you weren't there that night."

"You did?" Guy and Austin chorused.

"Indeed. It was amazing."

"Thank you," Guy said, and Austin felt a swell of pride at the gentleman's compliment.

And so they left Peter to watch over Bodie.

Austin was there the whole next day, never leaving his uncle's side. They did take Lucille to the vet, but to have her cremated. There was no autopsy. Uncle Bodie agreed; it was eighteen years that took her, and he couldn't bear that she and her beautiful red coat, though turning white, would be cut open.

All the neighbors came over the next few days. Most of the tenants had known Lucille almost her whole life, and grieved her passing. She had been a wonderful dog, bringing delight to many lives. Austin was surprised at all the people who came by. He saw it was Bodie they loved, and everyone wanted to help in any way they could.

Uncle Bodie did not cry after that horrible, fateful afternoon. Not once. He told stories about her, and he laughed sadly when the tale was good. He could often be found staring into some corner of the room, or more likely into some corner of his memories.

"The first time I saw her, she was just this tiny ball of red fluff," he reminisced. He held out his two hands, cupped them together. "She barely filled my hands, like this."

Austin tried to imagine her so small.

"And she got into things! Oh, she did. Where there was a will, there was a way for Lucille. She had a mind of her own."

Austin listened. To every story, every anecdote. He tried to imagine his uncle when he'd first gotten her. He'd been around Peter's age, as a matter of fact. That was hard to picture as well. He had the image of his uncle as a boy, and what he looked like today, and that was it. His uncle didn't seem to have pictures, or at least not that he'd shared. Except for that first day, the man was pretty closed about his life. He had secrets for himself only.

"I loved it when she slept with me," he said. "On my chest when she was little, breathing so lightly that sometimes I would wake her for fear she'd stopped. But no, she was fine. Maybe I would be watching

TV or reading a book, and I would look down and she would be peeking up at me from the covers, two tiny black button eyes in that fluffy red face, and I would laugh so! She was my light, Austin. My light."

Austin and Guy slept in Austin's room over the following nights and, between the two of them, tried not to leave his side during the day. And meanwhile Austin finally told his uncle where he had been that morning. Reading that play and getting outraged and causing a huge fit and God, now it seemed so foolish. Shouldn't he be happy that Guy had wanted to include him in his play? Even something painful?

"You've forgiven him, of course. Right?" Uncle Bodie asked.

"Oh yes," Austin assured him.

"And asked for forgiveness?"

"Not *exactly*. But yes."

"Then you must do it *exactly*," his uncle said. "Guy just might be the love of your life. Waste not one thing you should have done. Never ever have any should-have-dones."

"Okay," Austin said, seeing the wisdom.

"Promise me?"

"I promise," Austin said.

Two weeks later, Uncle Bodie died.

THANK God for Peter Wagner. He swept in and took care of everything, for Austin was devastated. Hopeless to even begin to know what to do.

He had woken that morning without the smell of brewing coffee. That was not the way things went when it came to Uncle Bodie.

He got up, walked out of his room, and saw the morning light peeking through the sheers of the balcony doors, but that was all. The dining room was dark, as well as the kitchen. *Did I get up early by mistake?* he wondered. A check of the kitchen clock showed he was actually up a little late. The alarm clock must not have been turned on, since it was a Saturday.

Austin knew then.

No, he said to himself. He went to his uncle's door and knocked. *Please* no. There was no answer. *He's old. He sleeps deep*, he lied to himself, for his uncle slept little and lightly. He knocked again. "Uncle Bodie?" he called—quietly at first, and then louder. "Uncle Bodie?"

Austin did then what he'd never done. He opened his uncle's door and stepped into the dark room, the only light coming in tiny cracks around the pulled blinds.

He could see the shape of the man in his big bed, but he didn't make any noise. Austin turned on the light and looked and knew. At rest, yes, but Bodie wasn't asleep, and Austin could see that. People who said dead people looked like they were sleeping were crazy. Uncle Bodie did not look like he was sleeping.

He was holding a picture, and when Austin went to his uncle, he saw it wasn't a picture of Lucille like he thought it would be, but instead it was of two men—two old men.

He called Peter, and then he went to Guy and he cried. Softly and long and long.

Peter fixed everything. Took care of legal matters, Uncle Bodie's body—he knew what Boden Spitz wanted done with his body—and the funeral as well. He asked Austin all the right questions, the ones Austin could answer. What do you think? This suit, right? And songs? Bodie loved Johnny Mathis. Surely something by him at the service? It was Peter who made all the calls, even to Austin's grandparents—Bodie's sister and brother-in-law. Austin could barely speak to them.

And now the neighbors came to Austin, for they had to come to love him and wanted to try in some way to relieve the hurt. But there was no relieving such pain. His uncle had become a center to Austin's life, and it was only Guy sleeping at his side that gave him the ability to fall asleep at all. He was all but inconsolable.

"I don't know how to go on without him," he said to Guy one night, in the dark, his lover spooned up behind him.

Guy sighed, pulled him closer. "In times like this, I remember the words of one of my heroes," he said quietly in Austin's ear.

"Any advice might help."

"Ever heard of Harvey Fierstein?"

"The Broadway guy?"

Guy squeezed him. "Yeah, the Broadway guy."

"He was in *Independence Day* too. The guy that said, 'Ah, crap,' right before he dies. I think that's why I say crap all the time." Surprisingly, he almost laughed. Almost, but not quite.

"Well, he wrote this play that changed my life. It's called *Torch Song Trilogy,* and they made it into a movie. That's how I found it. I was too young to see the play. Hell, I saw the movie on videotape. Anyway.... There is this scene near the end. The main character, Arnold Beckoff, is talking to his mother—who he fights with a lot. And he is telling her about the death of his lover and how hard it is to be without him. And she tells him he has to give himself time and that it does get better. She says, 'It becomes a part of you, like learning to wear a ring or eyeglasses. You get used to it… and that's good. It's good because it makes sure you don't forget. You don't want to forget him, do you?'"

Austin sucked in a deep breath.

"You don't, do you? Want to forget him?" He pulled Austin even closer.

"Of course not," Austin whispered back, and began once more to gently cry.

"Eighty years took Bodie Spitz," Peter told Austin a day or so later, sitting next to him and pressing some of his uncle's sweet sherry to his lips. "That and Lucille. She's what kept him alive since Jimmy's passing."

Austin jolted at those words, nearly spilling the glass. "Jimmy?"

Peter nodded solemnly. "Yes, indeed."

"Jimmy?" Austin asked again. "I don't understand."

"His husband, Austin. Did he not mention Jimmy at all? I know he didn't speak of him often. It was too painful for him, but—"

"But Jimmy got married to a woman," Austin protested. "That's why Uncle Bodie left Buckman."

"Yes. Yes, he did. When he was nineteen, I believe. Jimmy, that is. He had gotten some young woman in the family way, and I am sure you know, in Buckman you marry a woman you get pregnant."

Austin leaned in, the fog of his grief lifted by his curiosity. "So how, what…?"

"Jimmy Halliburton married that young woman, and a year later he left her and came to Kansas City and found Bodie."

"What?" *He what? He did what?*

"They were together just a year short of fifty years. And never was there a couple who loved each other more."

"But…." He sat up straight. "Oh my God! The picture."

"Picture?"

Austin jumped up, ran to his uncle's room, tried not to look at the bed, but he had to when he couldn't find the framed photograph that had been clutched in his uncle's hands.

"Austin?" said Guy, standing at the door.

"I can't find the picture!" he cried.

Then Peter was there. "Austin, are you all right?"

"When I found Uncle Bodie. He was holding a picture."

"Ah, yes," said Peter. "Sorry. It's okay." He came into the room, knelt, and pulled a flat box from under Uncle Bodie's bed. "These are the things I was going to have at the service. Things to help people remember him by. Guy? Do you mind?" Peter nodded at the box and toward the doorway.

"Sure." Guy picked it up and carried it into the other room and placed it on the dining room table.

We had Thanksgiving dinner right here, thought Austin, and remembered the goose—too greasy but good—and mashed potatoes and green bean casserole with green and yellow beans and Uncle Bodie's magic stuffing.

Peter opened the lid and pulled out the photograph. It was on top. "This one?" he asked.

"Yes," Austin said in relief and took it—looked *into* it.

He recognized his uncle, although twenty years had left a mark. And the other man? He remembered the picture of two boys his uncle had shown him that first night—*I was so surprised to find out my uncle was gay and how funny Lucille had been and the sherry had been so damned sweet and then Uncle Bodie went and got that picture*—and he tried to imagine that young man and this older man as the same person.

"Just look at them," Guy said, putting an arm around Austin.

That's Jimmy on the right, Uncle Bodie had said that night that seemed so long ago. *Hot, wasn't he?*

"My God," said Austin. "I can't believe it. They were together all that time? And he never told me?"

Peter nodded. "I'm surprised he never mentioned him at all—but like I said, he didn't like to talk about Jimmy."

"And they were in love?" Austin asked.

"*Very* much in love," Peter replied. "We met in Europe many years ago, and I was thrilled to see you could be gay and have a relationship. They were an inspiration for me."

A sudden memory hit Austin—so hard it made him gasp.

"Austin?" asked Guy.

I am thankful I had Jimmy—the love of my life. Isn't that what his uncle had said on Thanksgiving? And he had felt this hurt, because he had thought the love of his uncle's life had been nothing more than a boyhood crush and that he'd been alone all his life.

Tears welled up. Good ones.

Because somehow, everything was a little better now.

Uncle Bodie hadn't been alone after all.

"It was Lucille's passing," Peter said. "You see, Jimmy gave Lucille to Bodie for his birthday. His sixty-second, I guess? Bodie near died when Jimmy passed, and it was Lucille gave him reason to go on. He had to take care of Jimmy's precious gift. Jimmy lived on through Lucille."

Austin nodded. "I understand now," he said, and took his lover's hand.

"Bodie had a rich and long life. He was ready. If there is a heaven, I am sure he is young again, and so are Jimmy and Lucille."

"No heaven will not ever Heaven be," Austin said. "Unless my dog is there to welcome me."

"Exactly," Peter replied.

Austin settled back against Guy, feeling a weight lift off his shoulders. "You know, you helped too," he told the older man. "Uncle Bodie said you saved his life."

Peter gave a slight shrug. "I gave him some purpose, I suppose," he replied. "Gave him something to do, taking care of the people in this building. But they took care of him too. That's what makes this world work you know, my boy. Caring for others. It is what gives us hope. And love." He grew quiet. "Faith, hope, and love abide, these three; but the greatest of these is love."

And then Austin heard his uncle's voice again.

"You've forgiven him, of course. Right?" Uncle Bodie had asked him concerning his anger for Guy over the scene in the play.

"And asked for forgiveness?"

"Not exactly. But yes."

"Then you must do it exactly. *Guy just might be the love of your life. Waste not one thing you should have done. Never ever have any should-have-dones."*

He had told his uncle that he would.

"Promise me?"

"I promise," Austin said aloud.

"Promise what?" Guy asked.

Austin stood, his hand still in his lover's, and then he took him out onto the porch his uncle loved so much. He thanked Guy for his love. And he asked for forgiveness. Because he knew that Guy just might be the love of his life. And he didn't want to waste one thing he should have done or ever have a single should-have-done.

Guy forgave him. Of course.

CURTAIN CALL

IT WAS the morning of the reading of Guy's play at In-Progress Night at the Pegasus, and Austin was making a coffee run. They'd run out the day before, and not wanting to resort to anything less than perfect, he was on his way to The Shepherd's Bean, was getting ready to cross the street, in fact, when he thought he saw Todd.

Impossible, he thought. *That couldn't have been him.*

He waited impatiently for the light, would have gone against it, but it was morning rush hour and Main St. was frightfully busy. The light finally changed, and he dashed across, watching the shop the whole time—searching for the young man who *looked* like Todd Burton. Dark-haired, cream-skinned, broad-shouldered Todd. That description fit a million men, right?

Two people came out, but no, they weren't Todd and didn't even look like him. He opened the door, peered in, waited a few seconds for his eyes to adjust from the brightness of the morning, and…

There he was. Todd. Standing at the counter and talking to a huge, muscular man at his side, pointing at the chalkboard menu on the wall behind the register. For a moment, Austin was speechless. Words wanted to form. He wanted to call out, but he was just too surprised.

That's when Todd turned, and God, of course it was him. Todd's eyes went wide, and then a huge grin spread across his face. "Austin? Oh my God! Austin!"

Todd ran to him and threw his arms around him, and tears sprang to Austin's eyes. Happy tears. He hugged Todd back, amazed and stunned.

Todd pulled back. "I can't believe it! When did you get here?"

Austin shook his head, hardly able to believe it himself. "Months ago. *Months* ago."

"What made you come to Kansas City?"

Austin laughed. "*You* did, Todd. I came looking for you." And damn, Todd looked good. Healthy. Whole. Not as good as Guy, maybe, but—

"Me?" Todd gaped at him.

"I thought I was in love with you, Todd. So I came looking for you and—"

"Ah-hum," said the massive, muscular man who was stepping up behind Todd, placing his hand on his shoulder. "Who's this, Todd?"

Todd looked up at the man. "This is Austin. From Buckman. *Austin.*"

The big man thought a moment, and then his eyebrows shot up. "*Oh.* Austin. He's like your childhood buddy...."

Todd turned back. "He was my best friend. God, Austin." He moaned and closed his eyes. "I'm so sorry I didn't call you. I should have."

Austin shook his head. "No. It was my fault. I really crapped up bad and—"

Todd held up a hand. "No. There were a lot of mistakes made."

"My name is Gabe," said the big man.

"Oh shit. Sorry!" Todd laughed. "Austin, this is Gabe Richards."

The big man reached out a hand, and when Austin took it, his own seemed to vanish. There was strength in that hand too. Was that... possession? He looked up in the strikingly handsome man's face and thought: *Oh my God... is he?*

Todd cleared his throat. "Austin... Gabe is my—"

"Lover," Austin finished.

Todd nodded once, and Austin saw worry on his face. *Of course. You just told him you thought you were in love with him.*

Austin smiled. "That's great." Then suddenly, he wanted to shout, he was so happy. The tears welled up. It was too good to be true. He leapt forward and hugged Todd again. *You're gay. Hurray! And you have a lover and....* "Me too. Lover." He burst into laughter. "I have a lover. A guy." He laughed again. "His *name* is Guy."

"Really?" Todd laughed. "Oh, that's great. When did this all happen?"

Gabe had gone back to the counter and was returning with two coffees with lids. "Baby, I know you two want to talk, but we're going to be late."

Todd's shoulders slumped. "Fuck. I'm sorry, Austin. I got to get to work. My boss is amazing, but she's a task master."

"Are you cooking?" Austin asked, hoping.

"Oh yes. And Austin! At Izar's Jatetxea! My dream came true—"

"What?" Austin asked, incredulous. "But I went there. This waiter told me she threw you out for—"

"For having the audacity to walk in off the streets and ask her to be my teacher." He rolled his eyes again. "That's Goya. She thought I had a lot of nerve. But in the end she hired me, believe it or not. And under that harridan's exterior, she's a little bunny."

"I wouldn't go that far," Gabe said.

"Look, I gotta go," said Todd. "We *have* to catch up, fill each other in. I just can't believe it! I'd call in sick, but you don't do that to Izar Goya! How about tonight?"

Austin shook his head. "I can't. I'm doing a reading on stage at the Pegasus tonight."

"Shut the fuck up," Todd shouted. "Oh my God! The Pegasus. Gabe, that's the place that Peter got a stage named after him and—"

"Peter Wagner?" Austin asked.

Todd stopped. "You know him?"

"I sure do. I don't know what I would do without him. My uncle just—" He paused for a beat and went on. "—died, and he handled everything and—"

"Wait," said Todd. "His friend Boden? Was your uncle?"

Austin shook his head again. Jeez. It seemed impossible. This was all too much. "Yes," he said.

"God, Austin. I am so sorry." He looked up at Gabe. "Izar would kill me if I don't show up, wouldn't she?"

"No," Austin cried. "You go. But for God's sake, take my number. Please. We have to talk. And I want you to meet Guy. It's his play we're reading tonight. Me. Can you believe it? At In-Progress Night. They let the public get a glimpse of plays in development. Local playwrights, even national. Guy got a slot and it's tonight. Sometimes the piece even goes on to get produced. This could be his big chance...."

"And you're reading one of the parts?" Todd asked, the joy apparent on his face.

Austin nodded.

"This is fucking amazing. Me working with Izar Goya and you acting." He turned to Gabe. "He was always starring in all the high school plays. He is incredible—"

Austin blushed. "Todd...."

"No. You were. And he can sing too, Gabe. You should have heard him in *Big River*. He was awesome."

"Thanks, Todd. This is just a reading, though. Sitting around in chairs."

"But it's a beginning." Todd smiled.

"Yeah," he said, and felt that joy bubbling up again. "It is."

"Okay, then. Give me your number."

Austin did, and Todd put it in his cell phone and gave Austin his. "We need to talk. Maybe we'll come to the reading tonight."

Austin thought about the infamous scene that had at first got him so angry with Guy. The scene that was as much about Todd as it was him. "Why don't you wait? I'd rather you wait until it's a real play and—"

"Nonsense," Todd said. "I want to be able to say I saw it every step of the way."

Austin shrugged. "Well, I need to warn you. You just might see some of you in it."

"Oh, really?" asked Gabe. "Now we *have* to come."

Austin gave another shrug. "Well, don't say I didn't warn you."

Todd nodded. Paused. And then jumped forward and kissed him lightly on the mouth. It was a shock, and he froze for a moment and waved as Todd and his lover left the coffee shop.

So he finally kissed me. I waited all this time, and he finally kissed me. He thought of Guy. He thought of Guy's kisses. And knew he liked them better.

THE audience burst into applause, and Austin, stomach still in knots, felt a huge wave of relief. But as he looked out over the crowd, he knew it was all right. They had done it. They had presented Guy's play, and the people had loved it.

As the clapping began to die down, Jennifer Leavitt walked out on the stage and the applause started up again. "No. No, wait," she cried out. She laughed, turned, and looked at her cast sitting in a semicircle of chairs on the stage. She locked eyes with Austin and winked, gave him a big grin. She looked back out at the faces of the people sitting in their seats. "I want you to meet the playwright. That's who you need to praise. Guy?"

Guy stepped out from the wings, and the crowd was on its feet.

"I give you Guy Campbell, author of *Anything Could Happen.*"

Guy walked up to Jennifer, but not before stopping at Austin's side and bending and kissing him.

Austin gasped, looked out at the crowd in shock. *He did that in front of everyone.*

When Jennifer handed him the microphone, he thanked the audience, then thanked them again. Then: "But I couldn't have done this without my lover and companion, Austin Shelbourne." He turned to Austin. "Baby?" he said, and held out his hand.

Trying not to cry for about the billionth time in the last few months, Austin shyly stood and walked to Guy and took his hand.

"I love you, baby," Guy said into his ear, and kissed his cheek.

The audience continued to clap, and for just a moment he saw his uncle, right there in the front row, clapping and cheering his nephew on.

And suddenly, Austin knew it was true. It was happening. It had happened. This was only the beginning. He would be standing on this stage and others. He would be standing in front of crowds and bowing and there would be applause and he was on his way. Who knew. Maybe Broadway? Why not?

He looked at Guy. With his lover at his side.

His Jimmy.

Why not?

Anything could happen.

A Note from the Author

SEVERAL years ago, while I was attending a retreat for mostly gay men, a wonderful writer I know came to us with a play he was writing called *Tearoom Tango*. He wanted to "beta test" it by hearing the parts (which had only been in his head) read aloud by different people. It's a story about sex in public restrooms, but it is not porn. Oh, no! Believe me! At that point it was basically six long monologues—very rich and powerful. I was fortunate to be able to read the part of The Kid. We were all deeply moved, many of us to tears.

A few years later, Mr. Douglas Holtz had reworked the play so that the monologues were broken up, each character giving a section of his monologue in a revolving manner. It was the perfect alteration! It changed the dynamic in a big way, and a shock ending was added that blew us all away. Once again, fortune struck! I was able to go to Madison, WI, and see the production. There are no words to describe how amazing the show was. Especially considering I got to be a part of that first reading....

The show did well enough that it was picked as part of the prestigious Fringe Festival in New York, where, to my understanding, it got good reviews. I believe there was another production of the play—forgive me, Mr. Holtz, if this is incorrect. Sadly, there have been no further productions of the piece since then—yet.

It is my hope that it will happen. If you have read my book, you already know a lot about the show. It is a significant piece and has a lot of very important things to say. It casts light on a dark subject, and it needs to be brought forth and discussed. Maybe, just maybe, this book will help. Maybe the right person will read about *Tearoom Tango* and the ball will get rolling!

Crossing My Fingers,
B.G. Thomas

B.G. THOMAS lives in Kansas City with his husband of more than a decade and their fabulous little dog. He is lucky enough to have a lovely daughter as well as many extraordinary friends. He has a great passion for life.

B.G. loves romance, comedies, fantasy, science fiction, and even horror—as far as he is concerned, as long as the stories are character driven and entertaining, it doesn't matter the genre. He has gone to literature conventions his entire adult life where he's been lucky enough to meet many of his favorite writers. He has made up stories since he was child; it is where he finds his joy.

In the nineties, he wrote for gay magazines but stopped because the editors wanted all sex without plot. "The sex is never as important as the characters," he says. "Who cares what they are doing if we don't care about them?" Excited about the growing male/male romance market, he began writing again. Gay men are what he knows best, after all—since he grew out of being a "practicing" homosexual long ago. He submitted a story and was thrilled when it was accepted in four days.

"Leap, and the net will appear" is his personal philosophy and his message to all. "It is never too late," he states. "Pursue your dreams. They will come true!"

Visit his website at http://bgthomas.t83.net
or his blog at http://bg-thomas.livejournal.com
or contact him directly at bgthomaswriter@aol.com.

Also from B.G. THOMAS

http://www.dreamspinnerpress.com

Also from B.G. THOMAS

http://www.dreamspinnerpress.com

Also from B.G. THOMAS

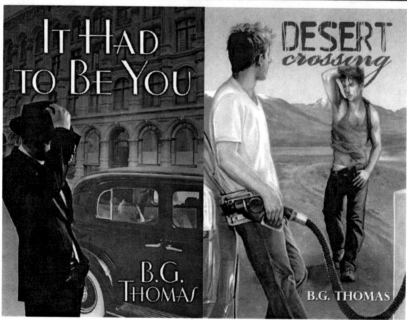

Romance from DREAMSPINNER PRESS

MOVING
ON
H.J. HOLT

http://www.dreamspinnerpress.com